TH
BLOOD
THAT
BINDS

DAVE SIVERS

ISBN: 978-1-9997397-0-6

DAVE SIVERS

Dave Sivers grew up in West London and left school aged sixteen to embark on a civil service career that took him to exotic places including Rhode Island, USA, Cyprus, Brussels, Northern Norway and Sutton Coldfield.

Along the way, he moonlighted variously as a nightclub bouncer, bookie's clerk and freelance writer. He also picked up a first-class honours degree from the Open University. Writing has always been his passion and, since giving up his day job, he has launched a second career as a novelist.

The first three books in his popular Archer and Baines crime series set in Buckinghamshire's Aylesbury Vale all made the Amazon Kindle Serial Killers chart, with *The Scars Beneath the Soul* and *Dead in Deep Water* hitting the top three. His other work includes two hybrid 'crime fantasy' novels featuring personal inquisitor Lowmar Dashiel, and a collection of coffee break short stories.

Dave lives in Buckinghamshire, England, with his wife, Chris.

For Chris

1

Monday

Judith Rawlson had always been a bit of a maverick.

Millett Wood, on the outskirts of Wendover, was popular with walkers, joggers and dog walkers, but she'd discovered a less-used part of the woods in which to ramble with George, her little Jack Russell, where they very rarely bumped into anyone else. She supposed most people preferred the main, more defined, pathways.

Judith counted herself lucky. When a shake-up at work had brought with it the opportunity for early retirement, it had been Simon who'd urged her to jump at it. And – apart from marrying Simon and producing two lovely daughters, who now had kids of their own – it was the best thing she'd ever done. A chance to live a little dream.

Simon had always resisted getting a dog while they were both working, but he'd been happy enough to agree once she'd walked out of her London office for the last time. Now she had her painting classes, her swimming, and her dog walks.

Simon still had another four or five years to go, and he left eye-poppingly early for his morning commute. So part of her new weekday regime involved dropping him off at the station and then bringing George here just as most of the world was stirring.

She loved it. Still, she couldn't help glancing up at the sky and mildly cursing the weather forecast. She had not one but two apps on her phone purporting to tell her what the weather would be like this week. Only last night, both had promised a few dry days, even some sunshine. The chirpy BBC weather girl had concurred.

So where had this drizzle come from? The sky looked like a filthy dishrag, hinting at worse to come. She hoped she and George would get home before it really started coming down, or she'd be soaked and she'd also have a soggy dog to contend with.

But maybe she'd beat the proper rain.

George was a little way off, snuffling in the undergrowth, and Judith was strolling along, occasionally kicking up some early autumn leaves, or flicking them with the walking pole she always carried. She was thinking about the week ahead. Tomorrow, her younger daughter, Sara, was coming over with her youngest. Judith made a mental note to pick up a few bits for lunch.

Her train of thought was broken by a sound from her right. As she turned her head, she was sure she saw something moving between the trees. She didn't have the place to herself, after all.

"Morning," she said, her country manners instinctively kicking in. Time was, she thought, when you passed someone else in a place like this, your hellos would be reciprocated. These days, not so often. Maybe half the people she passed might return her greeting. Others were either engrossed in their phones, or distracted by music on their headphones, or they just plain blanked her. It saddened and irritated her in equal measure.

This person hadn't responded, even though they were still nearby. She could hear them moving. What were they doing?

Were they *watching* her?

"Hello?" she said again, noting a hint of anxiety in her voice. She shifted her grip on the pole, thinking its pointed end would make a pretty good makeshift weapon if it came to it. George would probably scamper to her rescue, but he wasn't exactly an intimidating sight. He'd come off worst, possibly be killed by a well-aimed kick.

Get a grip, Judith, she thought. *No reason to suppose, whoever it is, they're up to no good.*

Still, she thought she'd let them know she wasn't alone, even if she did only have a small dog for company.

"George!" she called. "Here, boy!"

2

He completely ignored her.

My protector.

Meanwhile, she was sure the rustling sounds were slightly ahead of her now. She could stand here, frozen, with a potential attacker between her and her dog, backtrack and trust George to come after her, or shake off her funk and continue her walk.

When did I become such a scaredy cat?

Still carrying the pole like a sword, she started to move forward

And a male pheasant, its bright plumage flashing in the gloom of the damp morning, rose up in front of her, almost causing her heart to stop.

"Christ," she laughed to herself, shaking with mingled fright and relief. "You're becoming a silly old cow, Judith. George!" she called, going in search of her dog.

She found him round the next bend, his little rump sticking out of the undergrowth, scrabbling at something with his front paws. She knew Jack Russells were originally bred to hunt foxes, and had subsequently been modified for badger digging, but she didn't think it was a badger sett that had caught his attention. There was an autumnal dampness in the air, and also something sour that she couldn't identify.

"Whatever it is, come away," she scolded him. He pulled his head out, gave her a saucy look, and then returned to his endeavours.

"What is it, anyway?" Judith moved up to where the dog was delving and parted the vegetation with her pole.

She barely stifled the cry of horror that rose to her lips.

With trembling hands, she hauled George away, attached his leash to his collar, and pulled him close before pulling her phone out of her pocket and shakily tapping out a number with her thumb.

"P-p-police," she said when her call was answered. "Police, please."

2

Detective Inspector Lizzie Archer followed the young PC's yellow high-visibility jacket as he led her into Millett Wood.

It had started to rain in earnest, and she hoped the crime scene suit she wore was as water-resistant as it was cracked up to be. Apparently she'd beaten the crime scene investigators, her colleague, Detective Sergeant Dan Baines, and the pathologist. They'd better get a move on, she thought; this downpour would be compromising the scene more with every passing minute.

"Great start to the week," she grumbled to herself, knowing she was about to pay for her unusually relaxing weekend.

The only crime of significance her team was dealing with at the moment was a nasty hit-and-run in the sleepy village of Houghton, to the north of the Buckinghamshire patch that Thames Valley Police's Aylesbury Vale Division looked after. It was a case that made her blood boil, but no one was going to bust the budget by paying for the lab to prioritise what evidence had been gathered, nor to pay overtime.

There'd been a rape in Aylesbury on Friday night, but Lara Mosely, one of the other DIs at Aylesbury nick, had drawn the short straw on that one.

Archer had still slipped in to the office on Saturday morning to catch up on some paperwork, but otherwise she'd pushed work as far to the back of her mind as she could. She'd stocked up her fridge and freezer, caught up with her laundry, got a bit of sleep, and even watched a couple of schmaltzy daytime movies on TV.

She'd also gone to dinner, along with her friend and next door neighbour, Dominic Newman, at Baines's home in Little Aston.

Her batteries at least partly recharged, she set off for work on Monday hoping to ease herself into the week, but that hope had evaporated when the call had come through on the hands-free.

Local uniforms had been first on the scene, and they'd made a decent job of securing it, although it was a small mercy that it was still early in the morning and the body was located off the beaten track. At least there was no crowd of ghoulish rubberneckers to contend with.

She caught up with her escort. "So where is she?"

He led her over to some dense vegetation, where the whiff of death announced itself to her nostrils.

"We've tried not to disturb anything too much," he said. "As far as we know, the dog that found her is all that's interfered with the scene."

"Where are the dog and its owner now?"

"In the café by the car park, being given a hot drink by PC Vine, ma'am."

She hated being called ma'am, but the lad wasn't to know. She thought he might be new.

She leaned over for a better look. Shrubs and tall weeds had obscured the body from the glance of the casual passer-by, and someone had arranged a covering of fallen leaves over her for good measure. But something – the dog, presumably – had exposed a hand and most of the face. A young woman who would have been quite attractive in life, either naked or partially clothed.

"No sign of a bag or anything," he added. "Not that we could see, anyway. Me and PC Vine. We're the only ones who've been near."

"Good work," she acknowledged, remembering a case in her Met days when half the local force had traipsed all over a scene, creating a forensics nightmare.

"Insomnia, Lizzie?" a male voice with a distinctive Geordie accent enquired from behind her.

She turned to face the crime scene manager. "This is late for me, Phil. We don't all linger over breakfast in bed every morning."

In reality, she didn't often beat Phil Gordon to a scene. He simply grinned at her.

"Okay, then," she said. "I know you don't need me to tell

you what we're looking for."

"But you're going to do it anyway," he said without rancour.

"What can I say? I'm a control freak." She fiddled with the zip of her paper suit. "So I want to know whether she was killed here, or whether this was a dump, and what traces the killer might have left behind them."

"Aye." Gordon nodded. "I'll run you up an identikit picture of the killer for good measure, if you like. And his name and address."

She smiled. "If you can give me that, I'll fix you up a date with Kiera Knightley."

He gave her a look. "Don't tell me you know her?"

"Let's just say I'm as capable of delivering that date as you are of all that crap you were talking."

He shrugged. "Fair enough. The missus probably wouldn't approve, in any case."

Archer ran an eye over the ground. With luck, it wouldn't have been too churned up by human or canine traffic.

Gordon hunkered down. "She's been dead a while. Days, certainly."

Archer just nodded. The smell told her that.

"Get me some answers, Phil," she said, "preferably before this bloody weather washes all our evidence away."

He stood up, turning to face her.

"She's missing at least some of her clothes. Perhaps all, when we uncover her properly. If they're nowhere around, and no bag or other possessions…"

"She was dumped here." It sounded like a statement, and she meant it to.

Gordon gestured over her shoulder with his chin.

"Eh up. Here comes the A Team."

She followed his gaze and saw two figures, suited similarly to herself, approaching. She recognised each of them by their build and their gait.

"You two shouldn't arrive together," she said as they reached her. "People will talk."

"Our secret's out, Dan," said Dr Barbara Carlisle, deadpan.

Archer knew full well that the pathologist, who had married

6

just over a year ago, relatively late in life, was no more capable of straying than was the man with her, Dan Baines.

"So what have we got?" Carlisle asked.

Gordon gave her a quick rundown. Carlisle listened attentively, then nodded.

"You'll want to do some processing, then, before I examine her?"

"We'll be as quick as we can," he said, waving to a colleague, who began to walk over. "First thing to do is get a tent over her."

Archer motioned to the others to move away and give them room.

"Why here?" she mused. "Why not an alley, or a skip? A hedgerow, even?" She looked about her again. "We'll need to find out just how well used this part of the wood is." Not that that would get them much further forward. "Even if its remoteness is why the killer dumped her here, it's only part of the puzzle."

Carlisle spoke up. "If there really is nothing on, or with, the body, it could all be part of making identification harder."

"But hardly impossible. And why not bury her properly if you've gone to the trouble of bringing her out here?"

Baines wiped away some of the rain that was streaming down his face. "How's this for a possibility? He wants to buy time for whatever reason, wants the body away from where she died – maybe because he fears it'll lead us to him. Maybe it's in his own home. He wants rid, but he feels he hasn't got time to do anything too elaborate. So he thinks of this place."

"Maybe," Archer said. She looked up at the dark sky. "Shit. By the time Barbara gets to her, she'll be underwater, tent or no tent."

The pathologist looked grim. "I'm going to have to move her, sooner rather than later, but some things I really do need to do in situ."

* * *

Phil Gordon was true to his word. He allowed Carlisle and the detectives into the tent in less than half an hour.

"We've still a lot to do," he said, "but you know the drill by now, Barbara."

In circumstances like these, the CSIs and the pathologists all had to do the best job they could, and try their best not to compromise each other's work in the process.

The leaves covering the body had been carefully removed. The dead woman was naked and wore no jewellery. She was a white woman, perhaps in her mid-twenties, with good bone structure, long dark hair and a slim figure.

"Bruises on the shoulders," Carlisle remarked, indicating the dark smudges. "A bigger bruise around the left eye."

"She was beaten?"

"I'm not sure I'd go that far. Maybe some sort of struggle. If we're lucky, there may be DNA under her fingernails."

"And if we really hit the jackpot," Baines added, "the killer's DNA will be in the database."

"I'm going to raise the head," Carlisle said. She did so. "Okay, I think we can see what likely killed her."

Archer leaned in. Blood was matted in the hair. White bone peeped through. "That looks like quite a catastrophic blow to the back of her head."

"Blunt force trauma. I might be able to speculate on what sort of weapon was used, once we get her back to the lab."

Archer and Baines stared at her.

"You?" Baines said, acting – or, rather, over-acting – shocked.

"Speculate?" Archer continued. "Who are you—"

"...and what have I done with Dr Carlisle? Very droll." She gently lowered the head.

"Any ideas on time of death?"

"Well, rigor mortis has worn off, so more than thirty-six hours, but it's damp here and it's been chilly overnight. That must have had an effect. I'll check for hypostasis back at the mortuary, and that will help confirm she was moved after death."

She ran her gaze over the body again. "I'll take the rectal temperature in a moment, for what it's worth. But do you see how the build-up of gas has made the eyes bulge? And putrefaction has begun. The body is swelling too, and there's green staining, especially prominent on the right side of the abdomen."

Archer nodded. "Marbling of the veins, as well." She indicated the brownish-black discoloration.

"Very good, Lizzie. So, as a preliminary estimate, we're looking at between three and five days. But I need to do a lot more work before I can confirm that."

Archer sighed. Up to five days. It was entirely possible that this poor woman had met her end at around the same time that twelve-year-old Leanne Richards had been hit by a white car whose driver wasn't prepared to stop. There were times when she hated what the human race was capable of.

She forced herself to look properly at the body, not seeing her as a victim who would all too soon be dissected on Carlisle's mortuary slab, but as a person. She would have people who she'd cared about, and who had cared about her in return. She'd have had hopes, and dreams. And fears.

All of it cut short.

"I'll leave you to do your stuff, Barbara," she said, dispirited. "Let me know when the post-mortem will be."

She and Baines stepped outside the tent.

"Phone ahead," she said. "Get on to Joan." Detective Constable Joanne 'Joan' Collins was the backbone of her team. "We'll need to see if anyone matching the victim's description has been reported missing."

3

Back at the station, Baines emerged from the gents' as Archer was passing with a coffee in her hand, headed towards the briefing room. He fell into step with her.

"I'll grab a drink after the briefing," he said.

"You've got time now, if you're quick."

"No, I'll just get some water from the cooler."

"Actually," she said, halting, "I've been thinking."

He grinned. "When Karen says that, it usually means it's going to be expensive for me. Or hard work."

"Hopefully, this is neither. How would you feel about leading on the Leanne Richards case?" she asked him.

He hadn't expected that. "Me?"

"Not a good idea?"

"No, no. If that's what you want."

She searched his face, and he guessed what she was thinking. Maybe she was even having second thoughts already. She knew Baines was still seeing a grief counsellor once a month – she had persuaded him to do so – in an attempt to come to terms with the murder of his wife and the abduction of his young son more than a decade ago.

She'd also seen him take cases involving young people personally in the past. Last year, she'd discovered what a toll that really took on him. Yet now she was offering him the lead on Leanne's case.

The girl had been struck by a car in her home village of Houghton on her way home from youth club on Thursday night. She'd left her friends outside the village hall, where the club was held, her home being in the opposite direction to theirs, and been hit just around a bend in the road.

No one had seen the accident.

The experts had estimated the car that had hit her was

travelling at around 38 miles per hour.

Although the car had been exceeding the 30 mph limit, its speed hadn't been unusual for vehicles passing through the village, and neither of Leanne's friends – Jade Sheldon and Becky Day – had paid it much heed until a squeal of tyres and a scream, cut off by a thud, had got their attention. They had turned around and ran towards the sound.

Before they had even turned the corner, there had been another screech of rubber on tarmac. The car was already out of sight. The best the girls could say was that the car wasn't especially big or small, and was probably white or maybe silver.

Nearby residents who heard the impact had come outside, but Leanne was unconscious and already dying of her injuries.

"Put it this way," Archer said. "We need to catch this young woman's killer, but as for Leanne…" She shook her head. They both knew it was entirely possible that Leanne had caused the accident by a moment's inattention, maybe walking out into the road without looking. It was the driver's callousness that was sickening. "If I have anything to do with it, we'll track this heartless scumbag down and throw everything we can find in the book at him. Mowing a kid down is bad enough, but just to drive off…"

"I still think he panicked."

"I get that." They'd had this conversation a couple of times. "But if he – or she – had any conscience, they would have come to their senses and turned themselves in by now."

Baines agreed. A nice family had been destroyed. Would probably never fully recover. "More likely they need their driving licence to do their job, and are too selfish to risk losing it."

"Bastard."

"That friend of hers did well in front of the cameras."

A reporter from the local TV news had visited Leanne's school the day after the tragedy, and Jade Sheldon, who was also one of Leanne's classmates, had paid a moving tribute to her.

"Jade? Yes, she did. Although, to be honest, I'm not sure she was one of Leanne's best mates. They live in the same village, go to the same school, but…" She shrugged. "Anyway, it's irrelevant right now. Are you okay to lead on it?"

"Definitely." And he was, he knew he was.

"Only Lara Mosely's just picked up that rape case and she's in court giving evidence next week. There's Ashby, of course…"

There was no love lost between Archer and DI Steve Ashby, and Baines had little time for the man either. Archer didn't want to hand either of these cases over to him.

"No," Baines said. "I want to do it. Although it's really all down to forensics right now, unless the appeal has thrown anything up."

Some headlight glass had been recovered from the scene, and the CSIs had spotted scrapings of white paint on the zip of Leanne's jacket. These clues might help identify the make, maybe even the model, of the car involved. Various other samples and measurements were being examined as well.

"What I want," she said finally, "is for our team to manage both the cases, if we can, but we have to focus properly on each of them."

"It's fine, Lizzie," Baines assured her.

* * *

Baines sat in the briefing room, his attention on Archer and what she was about to say. All of a sudden they had a murder and a hit-and-run on their hands, and he knew she wanted to do justice to both. That wasn't going to happen without extra resources.

She briefly brought the team up to date on the body and what they knew so far. Which wasn't much.

"We're going to have to be canny with our resources," she began, as if she had read Baines's mind. "And we might need some reinforcements. Is that a problem, sir?" she added, her gaze directed DCI Paul Gillingham's way. He was in his customary place at the back of the room.

"I might be able to find you a DC or DS from somewhere else in Thames Valley," he said, "but don't hold your breath.

Otherwise, we can take a look at uniforms. There are one or two bright ones I'm sure we can both think of. No chance of a quick result on either case, I suppose?"

She tapped the pen she was holding against her palm. "I'm crossing my fingers that Phil Gordon or Dr Carlisle will come up with something on the murder that'll help us out. What we really need to know is who the dead woman was. Joan, any joy on missing persons?"

Joan Collins, young, black and razor sharp, consulted her notebook. "Just one who might fit the bill. A Carly Eustace. Age twenty-eight, from Bicester." Oxfordshire. "Told her husband she was going out with some girlfriends on Thursday night – never came home. Funny thing is this. When he started phoning round her mates to find out what had happened to her, they all denied all knowledge of any night out."

"So her car's missing too?" Archer checked.

"No, guv. Apparently she told her husband that one of her friends was meeting her from work. Local government. Husband dropped her off there in the morning. She was going to get a taxi home after the night out."

Archer opened her mouth to speak again, but Baines jumped in first. "Who's dealing with it up there, Joan?"

"A DS Amy Petrescu at Oxford. She's putting together an appeal for later today."

"I know Amy," Baines said, picturing a petite blonde whose bubbly personality concealed a gritty determination. Another image of her entered his head, but he suppressed it.

"So do we have a photograph?" Archer asked.

"She's going to email me one," said Collins, "but their system's down this morning."

"Oh, for God's sake." Archer's eyes flashed. "They must have hard copy she can snap on her camera and attach to an email." She looked Baines's way. "Can you have a word with her, Dan? See if she can try a bit harder. Find out what this Carly was last seen wearing, too."

He felt his stomach flip, but simply nodded.

"Thanks," Archer said. "Now, Jason…"

"Yes, guv." A red-haired young Scot, Jason Bell's

propensity for blushing when he was the centre of attention wasn't as bad as it used to be, but his cheeks were still tinged with pink.

"Jason, can you see if there are any CCTV cameras that will pick up people entering Millett Wood? Especially between last Thursday and Saturday?"

"On it, guv."

"And sort out a search party for her clothes and jewellery. I suspect the killer stripped her before he dumped her, but we can't be certain."

She pushed her fingers through her carefully cut hair, and Baines caught a glimpse of the crescent-shaped scar on her cheek, which was usually hidden. "We need to find a starting place for this, and fast. All right," she said, turning to the board behind her. Crime scene photographs and notes, some of them linked by lines and arrows, were already there. A young girl smiled shyly from a photograph pinned to the centre of the board. "Now, Leanne Richards. I'm going to ask DS Baines to take the lead on that one, at least until we know where the murder is going. Any news from the lab?"

"A bit, guv," Collins said, riffling through her notebook again. "A spot of luck with the headlamp glass. They managed to piece together a serial number, and it looks like the vehicle was a Ford Focus. The tyre tracks left by the vehicle that hit her are consistent with that, and they're testing the paint to see if it's the original factory finish. If it is, Ford might even be able to give us a year of manufacture."

Baines's heart sank. "A white Focus. About as common as you can get."

"It's a start, Dan," Archer said, raising an eyebrow at him.

"You're right," he admitted. "Someone'll need to contact local Ford dealers. It's just possible the driver will be stupid enough to take it in for repair."

"Jason, you're going to have to do that," Archer said. "Sorry, but we'll be multitasking until the boss can rustle up those reinforcements for us."

"Maybe it's a bit too much to expect, Lizzie," Gillingham ventured. "Juggling two big cases. Maybe Steve—"

"We're fine," Archer said, maybe too quickly. "If you can just find us those extra couple of bodies, we'll manage."

Baines fought down the urge to smile. Archer had never quite mastered the art of concealing her contempt for her colleague.

"If you're sure," the DCI said.

"What about your appeal on the local news?" Baines asked Archer. "Did we get much response?"

"Damn all, last I heard." She looked at Collins. "Anything new, Joan?"

"Nothing useful, guv. A few attention-seekers and nutters."

"We're sure that's all they were?"

"A couple of serial confessors, and a woman who said she's dowsing for the driver's name."

Archer shrugged. She knew better than to rule anything out. "And did she have a name?"

"She just wanted us to know she was working on it, guv."

"Good to know. You've got her details?"

"Yes, guv. But at the moment, it seems like Leanne's friends were the only ones who even saw the car," Collins said, "and they weren't much use, were they?"

"We're at two dead ends until we get some breaks, aren't we?" Gillingham remarked.

"We need that photograph of Carly Eustace," Archer said. "If she's really our victim, we can at least start to make some progress on that. Starting with why she lied to her husband about what she was doing on Thursday night."

"If she did lie to him," Baines said, a tiny alarm bell ringing in his head.

"Meaning?"

"Meaning it's a shaky alibi, isn't it? 'My wife was out, never came home. I thought she was with her mates, but apparently not.'"

"You think maybe the husband killed her?"

"And dumped the body a decent distance from home. Maybe he knows Millett Wood himself."

"Maybe. We'll need to talk to him."

Baines nodded his agreement. "We do. But if he's in the

clear, it leaves a woman who lied to her husband about where she was going. It doesn't take a genius to imagine what she was up to, does it?"

"No," agreed Archer, "but let's not get ahead of ourselves. First we need that photograph," she repeated. "If you can just get that out of your mate Amy for me, then after that I want you to give Leanne's hit-and-run case your full attention."

4

The briefing broke up soon afterwards, with Gillingham promising once again to find some manpower to augment the team. Archer lingered by the board, thinking that, if she and Baines were going to run both cases, it might be easier to get another board in here than to set one up in a separate room.

She was glad she'd given Baines lead responsibility for the hit-and-run. She had no doubts about his abilities as a detective and, after a shaky start to their working relationship, he'd not only become a friend, but was probably one of the few people in the world she really trusted. Trust and friendship had been in short supply for her in recent years.

She'd pretty well burned all her bridges after she left London. The incident that had left her facially scarred, together with two disastrous personal relationships, had so sapped her self-confidence that it had taken her a long time to dare to think of anyone as a friend again.

Now she had two friends in the Vale: Baines, and her neighbour, Dominic Newman. The latter had lived next door to her for weeks before she even realised the previous couple had moved out but, soon after their first chance meeting, he'd asked her round to dinner to share his brilliant homemade curry.

Since then, they'd slipped into the habit of taking it in turns to cook for them both about once a month, subject to their respective work schedules.

No, she corrected herself. *Subject to mine.* It was more often than not she who cancelled an arrangement at the last minute when a case raised its ugly head. But Dominic was always understanding. He also didn't seem to mind that most of her 'cooking' came out of an M&S packet.

They'd had a great evening with Baines and Karen, and it had been nice – and a little entertaining – to see Baines in a domestic setting, occasionally being subtly reminded by his partner to do host-type things. The get-together was a long overdue reciprocation for the housewarming dinner – if you could call it that, more than a year after she moved in – at her own house in Great Marston. It was no one's fault that it had taken so long. The return date had been set several times before, only to be cancelled when the job got in the way.

Archer had felt relaxed and comfortable in their company, even though she got the distinct feeling that her hosts had the wrong impression about her relationship with Dominic. She liked him a lot, but she wasn't about to get into bed with her next-door neighbour. At least, that was what she told herself.

Smiling, she returned her attention to her job. Two cases, no leads, two straws to clutch at. A possible ID for the dead woman in the wood, and a make and model of car in connection with Leanne's death. By the end of today, they could be full steam ahead on both fronts.

* * *

Baines had phoned DS Amy Petrescu as soon as he got out of the briefing. He got her voicemail and left a message. She returned his call about five minutes later.

"And what's this favour you reckon you're calling in, Danny Boy?" she demanded without preamble.

"More than one," he asserted.

"Such as?"

"Do you really want me to remind you?"

He and Petrescu had helped each other out professionally a couple of times, but he'd also saved her one night on a training course, after too many drinks had put her in danger of being taken advantage of by two older officers on the prowl.

"And there I was thinking you were a gallant gentleman," she said. "Not the kind to help out a lady in distress and bank it as a favour. Plus, I thought I'd made that up to you."

"Yeah, well. This is a comparatively tiny favour I need. It looks like one of your missing persons could be our murder victim, but we need to ID her."

"Oh, that? Yes, sorry, our systems are still down."

"Oh, come on, Amy. You can take a snap of the photo with your phone and text it to me. Or get someone to run a hard copy over. I'd send you one of the body, but she's not at her best."

There was a moment's silence. "Yeah, fair enough," she said. "I suppose I was being a bit lazy. Sorry. I was in here all weekend, wrapping up another case, but that's no excuse when you've got a body to ID. Tell you what. I could really do with getting out of this bloody station for a couple of hours. I'll bring a copy myself. And the file, such as it is. Just in case."

His mouth went dry. "A text would be fine. Or you could send a uniform to us."

"Nah, sod it. My mind's made up. It'd be good to see you again, Dan. I'll be about an hour."

With that, she hung up. Baines stared at his phone, wondering if this had been such a good idea after all.

Because the so-called favour on that course had only been the start. She'd thanked him the next morning while nursing the mother and father of all hangovers, and insisted on buying him dinner at a local restaurant. One thing had led to another, and they'd spent the next two nights together. It had been a while after his wife Louise's death, and long before things had become serious with Karen, so he'd been a free agent at the time. But they'd been pretty wild nights that he'd never quite been able to forget.

The relationship had continued for a few weeks after the course. Baines had let her down as gently as he could, feeling a bit guilty about dumping her instead of supporting her, but it had become pretty obvious that her drinking was a real problem. He decided he didn't need it, and couldn't cope with it, at that point in his life. He'd never thought she was a full-blown alcoholic, but she did have a problem. Maybe even a self-destructive streak.

Their relationship was purely professional now.

Except it wasn't, quite. She was always saying they ought to meet up for dinner, a drink, coffee, and he always said yes, sure, knowing he'd never follow through. But there were always things going on inside his head that shouldn't be, when he spoke to her. And that was just on the phone.

Now the prospect of actually seeing her made him nervous.

He told himself to stop being ridiculous. All the woman was doing was dropping off a photo and a file. It wasn't even as if he had to see her at all. Archer was dealing with the body in the wood. She could liaise with Petrescu.

Leaving him the hit-and-run.

He knew exactly why Archer had wanted to be sure he was happy to lead on that one, but he felt fine about it. His counselling sessions with Dr Tracey Walsh had focused on the need for him to confront his losses, especially the loss of his son, Jack.

Over a decade ago, Baines's wife, Louise, had been the last known victim of a serial killer known as the Invisible Man. Jack, then a small child, had been abducted at the same time. He had never been seen or heard of again.

Baines had never fully accepted the likelihood that his son was dead, and his dreams and waking visions of a teenage version of the boy had threatened to drive him over the edge. It was Archer who had finally forced him to seek professional help.

They say the first stage in recovery is recognising that you have a problem, and working with Tracey Walsh had certainly helped. He now understood that his dogged determination to lock his feelings in a box and get on with his job had been his way of handling a grief that was too painful to face. But that grief hadn't truly gone away. It had gnawed away at his subconscious, first in his sleep and then in the full light of day.

The last time he'd worked a case involving a young person, it had almost robbed him of his sanity.

Simply talking about things to a detached professional had seemed to help. He'd come to properly accept that his dreams and visions were not real, although that didn't mean he had to give up all hope that Jack was alive. What it did mean, however, was that he had to concentrate on the present, and not let the past define him. And things were getting better. The dreams and visions he'd been experiencing no longer dogged him.

But lately - he experienced a twinge of guilt –he'd been having a new dream, one he could never quite remember –

except that he always awoke upset, and with the smell of the sea in his nostrils.

He kept kidding himself it wasn't something he needed to mention to anyone. Not Tracey Walsh. Not even Karen.

But he knew deep down that he was deceiving himself too. He knew he shouldn't, and he didn't understand why he was doing so.

Maybe this too would pass in time.

Maybe.

* * *

An hour later, as promised, DS Amy Petrescu breezed into the office with her usual bounce, stopping to chat with Joan Collins, to whom she'd spoken on the phone, and demanding that Baines bring her coffee, just the way she liked it.

By the time he returned with the drink – not too strong, quite milky, half a spoon of sugar – she had moved on to Archer's desk, where the two were looking at the photographs she had brought with her.

"There's not much doubt, Dan," Archer said as he set the mug down. "Our victim in the wood is Carly Eustace all right. We'll need to get her formally identified."

He grimaced. "At least we know. Thanks, Amy."

She shrugged. "Your guv was just saying you're a bit short-handed at the moment and needing extra pairs of hands." She looked at Archer. "The thing is, I've already got an interest in this case. The body might have been found on your patch, but we don't know where she was killed yet."

Archer's eyes narrowed slightly. "You're trying to lay claim to my case?"

Petrescu shook her head hastily. "No, no. I don't think we need to get into that sort of tussle, although I can't guarantee that my guvnors will agree. But I have an interest in what happened to Carly, and we don't know how much the case is going to cross jurisdictions yet. I was thinking, if I can get my guys to agree, maybe I could get myself attached to your team for the duration." She looked from Archer to Baines and back again. "What do you reckon?"

Baines found himself speaking almost before he engaged his brain, pouring cold water on the idea. "I'm sure your bosses will have more than enough for you to do, Amy. I mean, they'd be a DS down..."

"I think it's a great idea," Archer said, but not before Petrescu shot Baines a sharp look, her mouth downturned. "It's worth a try, anyway."

"Not if Dan doesn't want me," Petrescu said, her expression softening into a pout.

"I wasn't saying that..."

"Of course he wasn't," Archer said. "Besides, he'll have his hands full with a nasty hit-and-run."

"I saw that on the news," said Petrescu. "You're leading on that one, Dan? I hope you find the bastard."

"So it's a great solution." Archer reached for a notepad. "I'm sure my DCI will agree. Who do I have to square it with at your end, Amy?"

While they exchanged details, Baines hovered like a spare part, wondering if he should just make his excuses and head back to his own desk. As Archer had said, it wasn't as if he'd be working on this case. So why had he been so quick to rebuff Petrescu's offer? He felt pretty stupid about it now.

As if reading his thoughts, Archer glanced across at him. "I've got this, Dan, thanks. Can I leave you to take the Leanne case forward?"

"Sure." He felt dismissed. "Good to see you, Amy."

She gave him a proper smile then, blue eyes dancing. "You too. We must have a proper catch-up. Maybe a drink after work?"

"Let's see how we go."

The smile was still there, but the eyes had stopped dancing. "Okay."

Archer looked at him quizzically, shrugged, then gave the DS her full attention. He could hear her voice as he walked back to his desk.

"What I suggest," she said, "is you see what arrangements can be made to ID Carly's body and I'll go chat to my boss about this secondment idea. If he's okay, he'll close the loop with your lot. Did you need to go back to your own office for anything today?"

Baines tuned her out, walking out of the office and heading out through reception and into the car park.

He was being ludicrous, and he knew it.

He'd never regretted ending his relationship with Amy Petrescu. Maybe even back then he'd known in his heart that he was falling in love with – was maybe already in love with – Karen. He still was, very much so, and the thing with Petrescu was all in the past anyway. So why did he care whether he worked with her or not?

"You silly sod," he told himself, squaring his shoulders and heading back inside the station. He found Petrescu just terminating a phone call at Archer's desk. Archer herself was nowhere to be seen.

"DI Archer's in with the DCI," she said. "Gillingham?"

"That's the one. Look," he said, "sorry if I made you feel unwanted just now."

She shook her head. "We're cool, Dan. You asked a fair question. So long as you weren't trying to get rid of me."

"Don't be daft." His smile felt fake, even to himself. Get a grip, he told himself. "That drink? It'd be good."

He went back to his desk, then looked over at Jason Bell, who was on the phone. Baines made 'winding up' motions to him. A couple of minutes later, the Scot put the phone down and came over.

"Jason, have you had a chance to talk to those Ford garages yet?"

"Sorry, Dan, no. I've been sorting that CCTV footage around Millett Wood. Or trying to, anyway. Someone's going to call me back."

Baines sighed. "All right. I'll start getting some phone numbers off the internet, and then maybe someone can spare me ten minutes to make some calls."

Bell was blushing again. "I'm sorry, Dan. I'm waiting for this call back, but…"

"No, you're all right. I'll talk to Lizzie when she gets back.

If she does get DS Petrescu on board, maybe I can have you or Joan dedicated to my hit-and-run, although someone else would have to do co-ord if it was Joan." He shook his head. "We really need another DC." *Not a DS. Not Amy Petrescu.*

Ten minutes later, Baines had tracked down four Ford dealers within a fifteen-mile radius, including one in Aylesbury. He printed off the list and handed it to Bell.

"Get on it as soon as you can, Jason. We need to know if anyone's made inquiries – in person or on the phone – about repairs to a Ford Focus since Thursday. Especially if they mentioned a broken headlight. Get any contact details they might have. Get them to go through any call logs or whatever to find the numbers they were called from, if that's all they have."

"What if they were asking about a mechanical repair, or a routine service? Or an MOT?"

"They go down on our list for elimination too. You don't know if someone's trying to be clever. Also, get on to DVLA and get a list of white Focuses registered in, say, a twenty-mile radius. We can cross-refer, and go and inspect the vehicles if necessary. Or we can get the local forces to do it, if they're outside our area. If nothing pans out, we can think about widening the search, but let's start there. With luck, he was driving from or to somewhere not too far from Houghton when he hit Leanne."

"And if not?"

He felt his shoulders sag. "What do you think? We'll have to check out every bloody Focus in the country."

5

"You'd better come with me to the post-mortem," Archer told Petrescu. "Meanwhile, we need to start pooling our thinking. About who might have killed her, and why, I mean."

The DS nodded. She was seated in the visitor's chair next to Archer's desk. "We half-thought she'd simply run away with whoever she'd met that night. That she didn't want to be found. Which is, obviously, her prerogative. But the fact that neither her husband, Harry, nor her mates, thought that was likely meant we had to look into it."

"Any chance any of the friends knew she was having an affair, and was simply covering up for her?"

"Can't rule it out. We'll need to re-interview everyone, I'd guess."

"You know the case. Any thoughts on what may have happened?"

"A few. I was mulling it over as I drove over here."

"Go on."

"Well, Harry – that's the husband – has a weak alibi. He could have found out she was seeing someone and lost it."

"Or there was a domestic," Archer suggested. "He loses his rag over something stupid. She dies. He didn't mean it, it's an accident – but he panics. Dumps the body and feeds her friends bullshit about her saying she was off on a girls' night out."

"Yes," Petrescu agreed. "I can see how that would work. Everyone's fixated on her being up to something, and it shifts the focus away from Harry. I'll get one of my colleagues to check with her office; make sure she really didn't arrive in her own car."

"Because if she did, the idea that the night out was a fabrication of the husband's looks shakier. Unless he was already planning to kill her." Archer leaned back in her chair.

"Other theories?"

"Well, there's the mystery lover himself – or herself, I suppose. Something went wrong. Maybe Carly said she was ending it and they saw red. Or maybe the lover had a partner who found out about the affair and asked Carly to meet them."

"A sort of 'let's be adult about this' thing?"

"Something like that."

"Whereas they were actually luring a rival to her death." She liked Petrescu's thought processes. "There's another possibility, of course."

"Yes?"

"She was just in the wrong place at the wrong time. Got picked up by some random nutjob. Never made her assignation, and the lover assumed she was just dumping him."

"Maybe he'll come forward when the news breaks. Maybe not, if he's got a wife and family." Petrescu shrugged. "There must be countless other scenarios."

"Quite," Archer agreed. "But we've got to start somewhere." She pointed to a pair of desks, empty due to cuts, but handy for the occasional hot-desker. "Grab one of those desks and settle yourself in. I'll sort out a briefing and you can introduce yourself properly then."

Petrescu was finishing a call when DI Steve Ashby put in an appearance. He'd been out somewhere most of the day, which suited Archer down to the ground.

She'd gradually come to appreciate that perhaps she and Baines had been a little unfair in their scepticism about the time he claimed to spend with his network of contacts on both sides of the law. She still thought they sometimes made a handy excuse for swanning off and doing exactly what he liked, with little or no sanction from DCI Gillingham, but she had to admit that his contacts occasionally came up trumps, supplying an invaluable piece of intelligence that helped them to unlock a case.

Did that make Archer like him just a tiny bit more? Not in a million years. He had nicotine stains on his moustache and fingers, and flecks of ash on his shiny suit, both of which evidenced a smoking habit he not-so-secretly indulged in in the tiny office he had fleetingly shared with Archer – before she'd insisted on moving out to the open office.

And then there was his smart, sarcastic mouth and his barely concealed sexism.

He could have been the template for Gene Hunt, the old-school – not in a good way – cop in TV's *Life on Mars* and *Ashes to Ashes*. All that was missing was the knocking about of suspects, and she wouldn't have put that past him if he could get them somewhere away from the cameras.

He slouched in the doorway, hands thrust in his pockets. Then, like a hunting dog that has picked up a scent, he straightened his shoulders and strode through the room, making a beeline for Petrescu. Archer winced, considered intercepting him, but decided instead to see how this turned out.

He walked up to the DS, his hand outstretched, smiling, showing his stained teeth to their worst advantage.

"Steve Ashby," he announced. "DI. I didn't know this team was expanding, but then no one tells me anything."

"DS Amy Petrescu," she said, shaking his hand, "from Oxford CID. And it's only temporary. DI Archer's murder victim is – was – my missing person, so we're going to work together for a while."

"Pity," he said, flashing what he presumably imagined was a winning smile. "We could do with some more pretty faces around here."

Archer's hackles rose.

"So there's a murder case?" He looked Archer's way. "Some people get all the luck."

"Sure, Steve," she said, pointedly turning to her computer screen.

"Well," he addressed Petrescu again. "We should have a drink after work. I can give you all the dirt on what really goes on around here."

Archer waited for Petrescu to decline.

"That'd be great," Petrescu said. "Maybe we can drag a few others along."

"Oh, they're no fun," he said. "Got a card with your mobile on?" He put his fist to his ear, cocking his thumb and little finger in imitation of a phone. "I'll give you a ring when I'm ready to go. In fact, if we go to the pub next door, they do decent food."

"Sounds good." She handed him her card and he strutted off, ego well and truly stroked.

Should Archer warn Petrescu? But what about? About Ashby not being Archer's idea of a nice guy? About him not being a good copper? About him being a Neanderthal who leered at women and wasn't above inappropriate remarks? Maybe Amy Petrescu liked all that. She was a grown woman, after all. Archer didn't know her and it wasn't her place.

She glanced at Baines, who was scowling at the DI's back. *What was that about?*

She rose from her desk and wandered over to Amy.

"You spoke to Oxford?"

The other woman's smile faltered. "Sorry, yes, I should have said before. My DI and a family liaison officer have just been to see Carly Eustace's husband. He's pretty distraught, so they're giving him some time and then they'll bring him down to the mortuary to identify the body."

"I'd better check with the pathologist then. It wouldn't do for him to pitch up just as she's halfway through the post-mortem."

"I can do that, if you like. I dare say Joan can give me contact numbers?"

"Actually, get her to make the call. And ask her to find out when the PM will be."

"Sure. I guess, once the PM's been done, we'll know if she was sexually assaulted."

"If she was, maybe that strengthens the random abduction theory. Although it doesn't rule out the husband or lover, either." Petrescu was making notes, so Archer threw her another task. "Can you talk to Jason Bell? That's him over there, with the red hair. See how it's going with the CCTV footage."

"Got it." Petrescu scribbled frantically in her notebook. As Archer walked away, she was already getting up and heading over to the two desks butted together in the middle of the room, where Collins and Bell sat.

Archer glanced at her watch and sighed. It was going to be a very long day.

* * *

Baines sat at his desk, Jason Bell standing to one side, his notebook open.

"So," he said, raising his voice above the babble and clatter of the busy office, "what you're saying is, the Ford garages you've spoken to tend to get, on average, maybe five Focuses a day in. But you've yet to find anyone who's been contacted about body repairs to a white one since Thursday?"

"That's the size of it."

"Damn. It was always a bit of a long shot, I suppose. So far there's nothing useful on CCTV, either. And how many white Focuses are there in the area?"

"DVLA are sending me a list. It'll be a lot, I think." Bell turned a page of his notebook. "There's one thing, though. A white Ford Focus was reported stolen on Thursday evening. He only realised it had gone on Friday morning. He called his insurers and got a police number late Friday afternoon. He's a primary school teacher in Aylesbury. Lives in Winslow, so he sorted it out in his break and after work."

Winslow was a market town in the Aylesbury Vale district of north Buckinghamshire, with a population of just over 4,500. The A413, linking Buckingham and Aylesbury, which ran through the centre, forming the high street, had originally been the Wendover to Buckingham turnpike, diverted to go through Winslow by an eighteenth-century Act of Parliament.

"Not a million miles from Houghton," Baines observed. "So it's possible someone took his car for a joyride and wound up killing Leanne?"

"It's got to be a possibility, hasn't it? Either that or this teacher – a Mark Briscoe – had the accident himself and has dumped the car somewhere to get himself off the hook. Either way, the car hasn't turned up yet."

Baines digested the information. "Well, we should go and talk to him." He checked his watch. "Find out where he is, and tell him to stay there. But before we go, get that registration number out to all cars. It's probably nothing, but still…"

"I'm on it."

"Good work, Jason."

Baines watched the PC striding away. He knew Amy Petrescu had been giving the Scot some tasks too, and he made a mental note to speak to her and to Archer about how he and Collins should best support the team. Overloading them would inevitably lead to mistakes. No one wanted that.

Maybe the ideal time to open the discussion was over that drink Petrescu had suggested.

Keep it business-like. That was the safest course, he reminded himself.

* * *

Harry Eustace's visit to the mortuary to identify his wife's body proved as horrific an event as Archer could remember. He'd seemed composed until he actually saw Carly's remains, and then he would have collapsed had Archer and Petrescu not been on hand to support him.

He'd howled and howled, crying out his wife's name, expressing denial, asking why. He'd hammered on the glass partition he was viewing through, although Archer wasn't sure if he was trying to break through or hoping the noise might wake her up.

He asked if he could go in there and touch her, but permission had to be denied until the post-mortem had been conducted. Barbara Carlisle was not going to run the risk of trace transfers from him that would have to be eliminated, especially as he hadn't yet been ruled out as a suspect.

When they finally had him seated in a private room with a cup of sweet tea, Archer expressed sorrow for his loss – a statement that sounded hollower to her ears every single time she uttered it – and then gently explained that she needed to ask him some questions.

He sank his head into his hands. "Can't it wait?"

He was a big man, more muscle than fat, but still bulky, with brownish hair that looked difficult to tame. He had what her father would have called a 'drinker's complexion': ruddy, with a lot of red veins on his nose. She knew he had no alibi. Was this going to prove a simple case? One too many, a flash of temper, a scuffle? A blunt object too handy? Then self-preservation? A need to get rid of the body and come up with a cover story?

"Can I call you Harry?" she coaxed.

"I s'pose."

"Harry, these questions can't wait, because we're anxious to catch whoever did this to Carly. You must want that too."

He swiped a sleeve across his reddened eyes. "Course I do."

"Good. So, how long had you and Carly been married?"

"Oh, it was… coming up for four years in November."

"And everything was good between you?"

"Yeah. Yeah, I thought so."

"But maybe not?"

She let the silence play out while he stared at her, his gaze occasionally flashing across to Petrescu.

"What's that supposed to mean?"

Petrescu picked up the ball. "Harry, the night Carly disappeared – the night we believe she was murdered – she told you a lie, didn't she?"

He looked as if he had been punched. "What?" He looked baffled. "No. No. Not a lie, I don't think. I'm sure it was a mix-up. She'd have explained it if… if…" His face crumpled again.

"Heck of a mix-up, Harry," Petrescu pressed. " Saying she's on a night out with friends and then it turns out she wasn't. I mean, even if she got the date wrong, she'd have just come home, wouldn't she?"

"Not if she couldn't," he said. Too quickly?

That thought had briefly crossed Archer's mind too. If she'd got the date wrong, she could have got chatting to someone. He could have lured her outside or to his car. Maybe he'd spiked her drink, although it was unlikely that a date-rape drug would still be detectable after all this time. Except….

"But it wasn't a case of the wrong night, was it Harry?" Archer pointed out. "According to DS Petrescu here, there never was a get-together with her friends, not in anyone's diary. Not for any date."

"She was lying to you, Harry," Petrescu said with a degree of blunt force. "You know, and I know, that the most likely reason she told you a story about meeting her mates is that she was seeing someone."

"Which leaves a few possibilities, Harry," Archer said. "Either whoever she was seeing killed her. Or you suspected her of having an affair, confronted her, and it got ugly."

He stared at her again.

"I didn't... I wouldn't..."

"I understand you told DS Petrescu you stayed in the night Carly went out and didn't come back. So no one can vouch for you."

"So? I got home from work, Carly had left me something to heat up in the microwave. I had that, then I watched some telly. You must have a lot of nights like that, when your husband's out?"

Archer had a lot of nights like that because she lived alone. She knew Petrescu was single too.

"Did she go out?" she pressed. "You're sure she didn't stay in with you? Maybe you had a row?"

He stared at her, his eyes full of tears. "You think I did it?" He swallowed hard. "I don't know where Carly went that night. I don't know if she saw anyone, and I didn't think she was cheating. She never gave me any reason to think she was. She didn't come home. I didn't hurt her."

"Can you think of anyone who might have?"

"No."

"All right." Archer made a note. "I'm really sorry we have to ask you all these questions." It was true. If she had been the one in the raw stages of grief, this was the last thing she'd want. But, much as she thought the so-called 'golden' hours, soon after a crime was discovered, were overrated, she knew it was vital to get momentum going early in an investigation. This one had got off to an especially sluggish start, not least because the body had lain undiscovered for several days.

He looked as though he was about to get belligerent, and then his shoulders slumped.

"I'm sorry too," he said. "I do understand. Let's get this done."

"Harry, Carly's body was discovered in Millett Wood, near Wendover. Does that mean anything to you?"

He looked blank. "I know of it. Can't remember going there. What was she doing there?"

"We think she was killed elsewhere and then taken there."

"Why there?"

"We don't know."

"Harry," Petrescu said, "you've already given me a list of Carly's friends and family, details of her workplace and other places she goes. Can you think of anything you may have missed?"

"I..." He pinched the ridge between his eyes. "No. I don't know. Can I have a think and get back to you? I mean, if there is anything..."

"Of course," Archer said. "Also, I'm afraid some of our guys will be searching your house. It's just routine, but you can't go back there until it's done. They'll take away any computer Carly may have had access to. We'll make it quick, I promise. And what's her mobile number?"

He found it in his phone and scribbled it on a page of Petrescu's notebook.

"One other thing," Petrescu said, flicking through her notebook. "The clothes she had on that day. An emerald-green coat, you told me. Any more thoughts about what else?"

"I'm sorry, no." He clutched his head. "I mean, she always asks me if she looks all right, and I always say yes. Because she always looks... looked... stunning. But I can't remember now. I had a look through her wardrobe to see if it was obvious what's not there, but she had so many clothes..." He spread his hands.

"Now, jewellery. You described her wedding ring – a simple, slim gold band – and her engagement ring with the three diamonds. Anything else? Earrings?"

"Earrings." He screwed up his face. "Yeah, now I think of it. She's got a pair she always wears with that coat. Like dangly? A pearl and then an emerald. Well, not a real emerald. I'll check they're not at home, make sure..."

"Thanks. That's all for now, Harry," Archer concluded. "I think you've got DS Petrescu's number but, just in case, we'll give you our cards."

They handed them over. Soon afterwards, they had shown Harry Eustace out to the car that was waiting to take him home to collect a few things under supervision. He was going to stay with his brother for the time being.

"So what do you think?" Archer asked Petrescu, back in the room with the door closed.

"Not sure, guv. But if he's Carly's killer, he's not only a consummate liar, but an awesome actor. When he saw the body and it was beyond doubt that Carly was dead..."

"I've seen some Oscar-winning performances in my time," Archer said. "And that one would be right up there with them if it was an act. Seemed pretty genuine to me, but let's not rule him out just yet."

"The clothing and jewellery. If the killer wasn't Harry, do we think he took them to try and slow identification? Or as trophies?"

Archer shuddered. "I don't like the trophy idea. If they do that, they're usually starting a collection." She shook off her dismay at the idea. "Anyhow, first things first. We need to issue her picture and appeal for any sightings on the night in question. And we're going to have to get talking to everyone Carly knew."

"I can get some of my people helping with that at the Oxfordshire end, if you like?"

"Makes sense," Archer concurred. "If she'd been dumped your side of the border, my team wouldn't even be involved, would we?" She sighed. "Lucky old us. I take it you've still got that list of her contacts handy?"

"On my tablet. And I might be able to pull in another resource."

"Yes?" Archer was interested, but hoped Petrescu didn't have in mind one of those old and bold officers with retirement in their sights who no one quite knew what to do with.

"He's good." Petrescu seemed to have read her mind. "Just coming back after an accident. He has to be office-bound at the moment."

"Really?" Archer saw an opportunity. "That could work well. It's about time I prised Joan away from her desk and got her outside, at the sharp end." Collins was DS material, Archer had no doubt, but she needed to broaden her experience. "He's done co-ordination stuff before. He's pretty sharp. And it was his body that was bust up, not his brain. Silly sod came off his motorbike. He'll be wheelchairing it for a bit..."

"I'm not worried about that. See if you can get him." She glanced at her watch. "I just want to check when the post-mortem's likely to be, and if it's worth hanging around."

6

"Okay," Barbara Carlisle said as her assistant, Bruce Davenport, closed the drawer containing the remains of Carly Eustace. "That's that, I think. Nothing more I can really tell you."

The post-mortem had thrown up no major surprises, insofar as the cause of death had been trauma to the back of the head, but there was an interesting detail that the initial examination hadn't revealed.

"I'd say the damage was caused by a sharp edge, rather than a blunt one," the pathologist had said. "A single blow, but looking at the shape of the wound…"

"Something like an axe?" suggested Petrescu.

"Well, perhaps not an actual sharp cutting edge. And the impact was horizontal. It's possible she fell and hit her head on something like the edge of a table."

"Seriously? It could have been an accident?"

The green eyes flashed behind their glasses. "I didn't quite say that. The bruising to her shoulders suggests a struggle of some sort, but then there's that more significant bruise to the side of the face. I'm not about to guess, but one possibility is that her assailant first struck her across the face, then grabbed a sharp-edged object – it would be your job to find out what – and finished her off with that. Maybe she had been knocked to the ground and was helpless."

"And the table-edge scenario?"

"There's some sort of scuffle. The killer lashes out, hits her. She goes down, striking her head on the way. Death could have occurred quite quickly."

"Either way, it's possibly manslaughter, if not murder," Archer said. "The theory that he panicked and hid the body still holds water."

Carlisle had confirmed that the body had been moved after

death. Her examination had revealed no traces of any kind of sexual assault, and little sign of the victim fighting back.

"No skin under the nails, and no sign that they were scrubbed."

"A bit of a one-sided struggle," Petrescu said.

"Or the assault took her by surprise."

Archer's stomach knotted with frustration. "So all we know is she went out, lied to her husband about where she was going, and wound up dead in woodland." She turned to Petrescu. "We need to get back to the station and have a catch-up with the team."

"My gut's telling me she knew her killer," the DS said as they walked back to the car park. "I know it's possible she was attacked at random, but on top of her lies..."

"Agreed. Maybe your guys will have some luck with the family and friends list."

Inside Petrescu's elderly Saab, Archer regarded the other woman. "I was thinking. How would you feel about booking into a hotel over this way for as long as you're with us? I mean, I know Oxford's not a world away, but you're going to be working long hours and you never know when you might have to get here quickly in the morning."

"All right," Petrescu said. "Although the only connection to your patch at the moment is where the body was dumped. She could have been killed in my area and the body dump's just an accident of geography."

"Sure. If that's what it turns out to be, you can have the case back with my blessing."

Petrescu started the car. "Thanks. I think. So have you got a hotel in mind?"

"We usually use the Holiday Inn at Aston Clinton. I stayed there when I first came up from the Met. It's fine."

"Okay. Well, if someone can get me booked in, then maybe you can spare me for a couple of hours after the team meeting, so I can pop home for a toothbrush and some clean knickers." She reversed out of her parking space.

"Done. We'll have that meeting, then I suggest you do that and get settled into your room. We can pick up the threads tomorrow."

As Petrescu drove away, Archer noted that she was smiling. The prospect of a stay at the Holiday Inn must be more exciting than she'd realised.

* * *

Baines and Bell walked into the head teacher's office, and the owner of a stolen white Ford Focus stood up. He looked awkward – as well he might. When they had set up this meeting, Bell had made it clear that their interest lay in something other than the actual theft.

The man, Mark Briscoe, was probably in his early thirties. He had close-cut hair, designer stubble, and the look of a man who cared about keeping in trim. The head had put his office at their disposal.

"So," Briscoe said when Baines had made the introductions, "I'm told this is about my car, but you've no news for me."

"No, sir," Bell stepped in, "and as you were told on the phone, this is a bit more serious than a stolen car."

The teacher sat down, arms folded across his lumberjack shirt. "In what way?"

"You'll have heard about the girl who was knocked down and killed in Houghton last Thursday night?"

He blinked. "Yes, of course. Houghton, you say? To be honest, I didn't take much notice of the where. But what's that to do with—"

"Your car matches the description of the one we're seeking in connection with the incident."

"Hang on." Briscoe was staring. "You're saying it was my car that killed that kid?"

"No, sir. I'm saying it matches the description, and we're anxious to trace it."

Briscoe showed no sign of relaxing. ""But it's what you're thinking, right? Someone steals my car, goes joyriding, knocks the girl down. Christ." He shook his head. Denial or disbelief?

"I think you said you only noticed it missing in the morning?"

"That's right. I got home maybe half past six in the evening and didn't put my nose outside the door after that. It could have gone at any time. To be honest, I've been waiting for someone to tell me it's turned up, dumped somewhere or burned out."

Baines realised he was wondering about that as well. It was unusual for joyriders to hang on to stolen vehicles, and Briscoe's Focus was a bit old to have been worth trying to sell.

"So how are you getting around at the moment?

"Hire car. Fortunately my insurance will pay, but only for three weeks."

A thought fleeted through Baines's mind. "Do you have a garage at your home, Mr Briscoe?"

"Yes."

"So why wasn't the car in the garage?"

The teacher smiled. "I never use the garage to actually put a car in. I mean, who does? It's full of junk."

"We'd like to check."

He nodded. "Yes, fair enough. I had planned to leave after talking to you guys anyway, so why don't you follow me home when you've finished with me, and you can have a look."

* * *

Archer sat alone in the briefing room, her gaze switching between the two situation boards. The meeting had got under way as soon as she and Baines returned from their respective errands, and everyone had caught up. She knew most of the team members were still beavering away in the main office. Petrescu had headed home.

They'd had no joy from the people close to Carly Eustace and no reason to suppose they'd wanted to be anything but co-operative. Of the friends Carly had told her husband she was seeing the night she disappeared, a couple of them, when pressed, had admitted Carly hadn't seemed quite herself in the last few months.

According to Amy Petrescu's colleagues, Carly's best mate, going back to her schooldays, had been one Tina Rhodes. Despite being distraught, she'd been helpful. Over the past year, she'd said, Carly had been increasingly difficult to pin down on dates to get together, whereas she'd always been one of the keenest of the group in the past. She'd also seemed a little distracted.

Other friends had wondered if Carly was trying to distance herself from the group for some reason, but Tina had put it down to pressure in Carly's local authority job. Government cuts the way they were, a lot of people in the public sector were under the cosh nowadays, she'd said. She certainly hadn't had any reason to imagine her friend was playing away. She'd thought the marriage was fine, although she thought Harry was a bit dull. The idea that Carly had invented a night out with the girls as cover for an absence from home had seemed unlikely to Tina.

"But you never know," she had said. "You think you know a person, and then they surprise you."

Archer rose from her chair and walked up to the board dedicated to Carly's murder. A picture of a smiling, attractive woman sat in the centre, replacing the more macabre one taken in the wood.

They'd released Carly's name this evening. If there was a lover, maybe he – or she – would come forward, if they had nothing to hide. Unless they were married too.

CCTV footage was still being examined around both the victim's workplace and Millett Wood. But the initial news had not been encouraging. The CCTV camera nearest to Carly's offices hadn't been working for some days, and there were no cameras where the killer would probably have parked when dumping the body. It was going to be tedious, painstaking work.

With a sense of frustration, she turned her attention to Leanne Richards' board. CCTV footage was in play here too, looking out for a white Focus, and the one belonging to Mark Briscoe in particular. Even though the police continued to check out other cars matching the description, her instincts told her Briscoe's vehicle would most likely prove to be the one they were looking for. The right car, stolen on the right night, was a powerful coincidence.

It was out there somewhere, and they needed to get their

hands on it. Because, God knew, they didn't have much else.

* * *

A couple of hours later, Amy Petrescu sat in the bar of the Holiday Inn, relaxing with a glass of wine. The remains of her bar snack had been cleared away. This wasn't how she'd expected her day to pan out when she'd dragged her arse into work this morning.

Not that she was complaining. A change of scene and an interesting murder investigation, with a victim she was already invested in. And some new people to work with.

Well, mostly new. It was good to see Dan Baines again, even if he seemed a little nervous of her. Maybe he thought, with typical male ego, that she was eager to use their sudden proximity to try and get into his boxers again.

Well, she thought, she might. He was still a good-looking guy. She'd suggested an after-work drink, and he'd been a little cagey. But he hadn't turned her down, either. Said he might. Interesting.

She knew he had a partner now, and maybe he was the faithful kind. Petrescu had always thought fidelity was overrated.

She drained her glass and dithered between getting another or heading up to bed.

"That looks like it needs refilling," said a voice she recognised. She looked up, smiled, made a show of thinking about it.

"Why not?" She held the glass out to him. "Chenin blanc, please. A large one."

* * *

Archer arrived home with a takeaway in the passenger foot well of her Skoda Octavia, not much on her mind beyond washing the meal down with a beer and crashing out in bed.

Giving Baines the lead on the hit-and-run may have reduced the amount of legwork she had to do, but the buck still stopped with her. She had little doubt that, by tomorrow lunchtime, DCI Gillingham would be facing a two-pronged attack on both cases: from his superiors and from the media. The boss was good about soaking up pressure, but he still tended to drive some of it downwards, and he would expect answers. As things stood, Archer had little to impress him with.

As she got out of the car, wrestling with her takeaway bag, she heard a familiar voice calling.

"Mon-ty! Mon-ty!"

She smiled to herself, locked the car, and walked next door, where Dominic Newman stood at the end of the drive, hands stuffed in the pockets of his fleece jacket.

"Has that moggie of yours gone walkabout again?" she asked him. A year or so ago, she wouldn't have gone out of her way to chat to a neighbour. And as for asking after a cat...

He shook his head. "I swear he's like a teenager. Comes and goes as he pleases. He'll turn up when he's hungry, I dare say." He eyed her bag. "Something smells good."

She held the bag up. "The Haldi in Pitstone. I probably got too much, if you fancied sharing?"

She knew Dominic was a curry lover, and the Haldi was one of the best Indian restaurants in the county.

"Tempting," he admitted, "but I ate earlier. I'd better not." He checked his watch. "Another late one?"

She smiled wryly. "Good to know nothing ever happens around here, right?"

"It must be my turn to cook for us. But I bet you've no idea when you might have a gap in your diary."

"Oh, my diary's nothing but gaps. But then, I don't put 'working late' in my diary."

"I heard there was a body found this morning. Millett Wood, is that right?"

"Yep, I've landed myself a new murder case. Just between you and me, I'm feeling a tad stretched."

He nodded. By now, he knew better than to press her for juicy details.

"Well," he gestured to her takeaway bag, "don't let that get cold." He called his cat's name once more, then shook his head.

"Hey ho. I'm going in. Let me know if you solve all your cases."

She went indoors with possibly her first proper smile of the day on her face. Ten minutes later, she sat in front of the TV with her meal on a tray, a bottle of beer at her side, and an American crime drama on 5USA for company. She might as well have been watching the paint on the walls for all she was able to concentrate, though.

* * *

Petrescu found herself awake, realised she was in a hotel room and not her own bedroom, and checked the time by her phone. 3.33am.

Her head ached, her mouth was dry, and she was exhausted. This was not a great start to her temporary detachment, in more ways than one.

She should know better by now than to let her drinking run away with her. It rarely ended well when she did so. Most of the time she just had a couple and stopped, knowing her point of no return: the point where the voices of reason and common sense could no longer make themselves heard above the part of her brain that thought one more glass of wine was a really good idea.

And last night, it really had been a terrible idea. A hotel bar in an unfamiliar part of the world, and someone who was likely to be her colleague for as long as the Carly Eustace case lasted, even though he wasn't directly involved in the investigation. A colleague who was likely to judge her and might even talk to others about her indiscretions.

She needed paracetamol. There were some in her bag. As she sat up, pushing the covers aside, she glanced down to her right.

"Oh, shit," she whispered, her eyes fastening on the man who lay beside her.

As if in response, Steve Ashby snored softly.

7

Tuesday

It was shaping up to be a weird morning, Archer decided.

First, Steve Ashby had arrived not long after she did – and he was never early. He'd even said good morning to her and asked how she was doing. She'd spent about ten minutes afterwards, first examining his words and body language for any sign of veiled sarcasm or hidden insult, then wondering what he was up to.

Then Petrescu and Baines had arrived, practically together, with some sort of tension between them that she couldn't quite fathom. Whatever that was about, she really hoped they could play nicely. Things were tough enough already.

There was also another new face in the office, DC Will Tyler. Collins had been first into the office, as always, and was already bringing him up to speed. She'd been at the hub of the team's investigations, doing the unglamorous but vital backroom work behind the scenes, for so long that Archer had half-feared she'd be resentful of relinquishing her familiar role. But she'd seemed delighted at the prospect of getting out and about more.

Meanwhile, Archer thought Tyler would fit right in. His motorbike accident sounded horrendous, but he'd made light of it. He handled his wheelchair like a Grand Prix car and had already shown he had a wicked sense of humour. Every so often she heard Collins laugh.

Today's priorities involved renewed efforts to trace Carly Eustace's last steps as comprehensively as possible: viewing more CCTV footage and questioning anyone who might conceivably know what her real plans had been for Thursday evening – although Petrescu's people had already been pretty thorough on that.

Archer had commandeered a couple of civilians to go through the footage, and asked Collins to go over the statements they had so far, looking for gaps or inconsistencies. Now she summoned Petrescu over. "Amy, I want us to have another go at Carly's friends. I know you spoke to them when she was just a missing person, and I know your colleagues had another word yesterday, but – I don't know. I just feel someone knows more than they're saying."

"You're the guv." Petrescu looked tired and subdued, with no trace of yesterday's bubbly good humour.

"Are you okay, Amy?"

The DS visibly shook herself. Smiled. "Yeah. Of course. You know what it's like when you sleep in a strange bed."

"Okay. Well, if you could set up interviews for us with each of the girls Carly allegedly said she was seeing last Thursday. I don't care how you do it, but it's a priority." She frowned. "Actually, no. Set the interviews up for this afternoon. Give Joan a chance to go through those statements and make sure we have all the bases covered. You and I can go to Carly's workplace this morning. I want to get to know her better."

She glanced across at Baines, who was deep in conversation with Bell. There was a lot of advice she was tempted to give him about his next steps, but letting him get on with it was all part of delegation. Besides, she reminded herself, he'd been in charge of investigations before. He'd even been an acting DI for a spell, before her time.

She looked at Collins, back at her own desk, intensity practically radiating from her as she ran through the Carly Eustace statements. Perhaps it was high time she took a step back, Archer thought, and let her little team take a bit more responsibility.

* * *

After talking through progress – or lack of it – on the hit-and-run case, Baines decided to have another chat with Becky Day and Jade Sheldon, the only two people who'd seen the car that had killed Leanne Richards.

It was five days now since the tragedy, and it wasn't always true that details were always best harvested when fresh in the mind. Just occasionally, a shocking incident could drive those details deep into the subconscious, only for them to surface again a few days later.

They'd contacted the school and the parents and established when the mid-morning break was. Baines wanted Bell to accompany him, and so had left Will Tyler to get on with the tedious task of viewing CCTV footage, focusing on the area between Winslow, where the suspect Ford Focus had been stolen from, and of compiling a list of known car thieves and joyriders in the Winslow area.

Both girls' mothers were happy to come to the school during the break to fill the 'appropriate adult' role for their children. One of the Assistant Heads let them use her office, and Baines and Bell started with Becky.

The girl looked tearful, and Baines suspected that she had been closer to Leanne than Archer thought Jade was. She was slim with blue-black hair, which contrasted with her mother's white-blonde look. Emma Day held her daughter's hand tightly and kept glancing at her anxiously, as if she half-expected her to break.

"I tried to get her to take a few days off," she said. "At least Friday and Monday. But she didn't think Leanne would want that, did you, love?"

Becky shook her head.

"Look, this won't take long," Baines said. "Becky, I don't want you to get more upset than you already are. But we do want to find whoever hurt Leanne."

"Killed her," Becky said, with a sudden passion that gave the lie to her apparent quietness. "Not just hurt. You want the person who killed her."

Baines realised how angry she was. It must have been bubbling under the surface, barely contained. There was more to her than the quiet kid he'd met the night of the accident. He'd have to tread carefully if he didn't want her anger to boil over. If that happened, much of the value of the interview could be lost, whatever objectivity she had distorted by rage.

"That's right," he said. "You're right. And we do want to catch this person. But we need your help. We need to know if there's anything at all you remember about that night that perhaps you hadn't thought of when we spoke to you before."

She glanced at her mum. "But I told you everything. I told the truth."

Emma Day looked alarmed. "She told the truth, Detective Sergeant."

"No one's doubting that," he soothed. "Becky did very well when we spoke to her before but, as you can imagine, we haven't much to go on, and people often remember things later on." He made eye contact with the girl. "It could be something really small, Becky. Something you don't think is important."

"I know it's asking a lot, Becky." Bell's neck and cheeks were flushed, but his Glasgow burr was softer than usual. "But, for Leanne, can you just take us through it one more time?"

"Is this really necessary?" the mother protested. "Making her relive it?"

"It's all right, Mum," Becky said, barely loudly enough for Baines to hear. "Mr Bell's right. It's for Leanne. But I don't think there's anything…"

She took a deep breath, then exhaled, her cheeks slightly puffing as she did so, like a runner trying to get her second wind. Then she started to speak, softly at first, but gradually increasing the volume. She spoke about her evening at the youth club with Leanne. They'd played a couple of games of table tennis, listened to some music, even had a bit of a dance. Had a couple of cokes and chatted. About nothing consequential. School. Music. TV shows they both liked. Plans for a shopping trip at the weekend.

"We had a bit of a laugh about Jade, to be honest," she said. "She's always hanging around the older boys. She thinks one of them will ask her out, but we reckon they find her hilarious."

"That's not nice, love," Emma Day said mildly.

"I know," she admitted. "But it's pretty funny. She's so *obvious*."

"So Jade wasn't with you all evening?"

"No." Slight irritation in her tone. "I keep saying, she's not our mate."

"But the three of you left together?"

"All the boys she fancies had gone, we were leaving, and she asked us to wait while she grabbed her coat. I go her way and she often likes to walk back with me. I don't know why; we hardly talk. I think she's a bit nervous after dark."

"So the three of you left," Baines prompted.

"Yeah. We said goodnight to Leanne. She went her way, we went ours."

"So when did you see the car?"

"We hadn't gone far when it came by."

"Describe it."

"I did. Before, I mean."

"Describe it again, Becky," said Bell. "Just in case."

She grimaced. "But I hardly noticed it. I think it was a hatchback. White, silver? Grey, maybe? It was dark, and I wasn't interested in it. It was just a car going by."

"Think," Bell urged. "Try and visualise it. How many people are in it?"

She looked distressed, but Baines let Bell run with the interview for now. He seemed to have made a bit of a connection with Becky, perhaps because he was closer to her age.

She closed her eyes, squeezing them shut. Then she opened them again.

"I'm sorry." The tears finally flowed. "I just didn't take much notice. I mean, there had to be a driver, but whether there were passengers…" She shook her head.

Baines gave Bell a slight nod.

"What happened next?"

She had gone pale. "We heard these tyres squeal. There was this horrible bang. A thud. I can't describe it better. And a scream."

"Which came first? The thud or the scream?"

"The scream. Definitely. It was sort of cut off when the thud happened. I knew – knew Leanne had been run over. I stopped. Jade stopped. We looked at each other. I started running and so did she. We just got to the corner and there was another screaming tyres noise. By the time we got round the corner, all we could see was the red lights at the back of the car, and then it went round the next bend. And Leanne..." She let out a sob. Her mother put an arm round her, looking daggers at Bell.

But Baines needed to check something. "I'm so sorry, Becky, but can we just go back? You both stopped when you heard the accident, and then you started running. But the car only drove off as you reached the corner?"

"Yeah."

He didn't think this had been mentioned in previous interviews. "So the driver must have stopped for a few seconds after he or she hit Leanne and then driven off?"

She stared at him, her expression horrified as what he implied sank in.

"Yeah," she said, her voice flat. "Yes, exactly. He must have stopped when he first hit her, then decided to drive off anyway. Deliberate. He didn't care."

"You say 'he'. Was it a man?"

"I suppose so. I can't remember, but I keep thinking it's a man."

After Becky and her mother had left the room, Baines and Bell took a few minutes' break before inviting Jade Sheldon to join them.

"What do you think?" Baines asked the DC.

"I don't think that added much, to be honest," Bell said. "Other than the driver was even more of a callous swine than we thought. He actually stopped, and then scarpered anyway."

"I wonder why, though. I mean, the chances are she stepped into the road without looking. The car wasn't going mad fast. The driver probably didn't stand a chance."

"Maybe he—"

"Or she."

"Or she – although Becky kept saying 'he'. Maybe somewhere in her memory she knows it's a man."

"Maybe."

"Whatever," Bell said. "I was going to say, being in a stolen car would have made it tricky to stop. Maybe he was off his face on booze, drugs or both."

"Still, I wonder how he's been sleeping."

"If it was me," Bell said bleakly, "I wouldn't sleep a wink."

* * *

Carly Eustace had worked on a youth and community project at Oxfordshire County Council's offices in Speedwell Street, Oxford, a four-storey building housing around three hundred staff.

Her boss had been Robyn Jones, a fidgety woman with purple and yellow streaks in her dark brown hair, and an annoying habit of picking up her phone and staring at it every couple of minutes. The team's office was open plan and so Jones had had to hunt around for somewhere that they could talk privately.

Archer had decided to bring both Petrescu and Collins along. Now, squeezed into a small office whose occupant was on leave, she felt as if she'd come a little mob-handed. Maybe she should have left it to Petrescu and Collins, but she enjoyed being in the thick of things. If she ever made DCI, which she still hoped she might, she couldn't imagine being as hands-off as Paul Gillingham.

"Shocked," Robyn Jones was saying, describing the team's reaction to the news of Carly Eustace's death. "Stunned. Absolutely stunned. We couldn't believe it. Could. Not. Believe. It."

"Got that," Archer said. "You were all shocked."

"Couldn't believe it."

"Look," Petrescu spoke up, "I know we've been through all this before, Robyn, but this is a murder enquiry now. So we need you to think very carefully. What time did Carly leave the office on Thursday?"

Jones nodded several times. "I'm pretty sure it was five on the dot. 'Gotta go,' she said. It was, like, an announcement? 'Girls' night out,' she said. Those were her exact words. Yes," she added. "that's exactly what she said." She looked at her phone.

"So these girls' nights out," said Archer. "Did she do that a lot?"

"Yeah, she did them, I dunno, every six weeks, maybe? I mean, I don't really keep track, you know, but—"

"Did she say where they were meeting? Where they were going?"

"Nope."

"Was that unusual?" Collins asked. "Or did she usually say?"

"Dunno. Sometimes, maybe. Yeah, actually, because she'd say she needed to get away at a certain time. But not on Thursday. She just, like, announced it." She frowned. "Yeah, actually, it *was* unusual for her not to say earlier. At least, I think it was. In fact, yeah, her and her mates would go clubbing or out for a meal, whatever, and she'd say what they were doing." Another frown. "Well, the day after, she'd say what they'd done. Maybe that was it."

She looked at her phone again. Archer thought she might have to snatch it from her and launch it out of the window.

"So," she said. "It was at least a bit unusual for Carly to just say she had a girls' night out as she was leaving. Did it occur to you that maybe it was all a bit spontaneous?"

"No. Not then. But I see what you mean. Yeah," she added.

Petrescu chipped in. "The thing is, Robyn, I don't think it's been reported in the news, but in fact there was no girls' night planned for Thursday. Or any other day."

"So why... Oh." Jones went into another nodding routine. "I see."

"So was there any indication that she was seeing someone?"

"You mean..." The nods became headshakes. "Well, not to my knowledge."

"Anyone she might confide in?"

Robyn Jones chewed her lip. "You could ask Megan. Megan Cunningham. They're quite matey, I think. And I think she's been for a drink once or twice with Chris Pateman in Education."

"Is she in this building?"

"She? Oh, no, Chris is a he," said Jones. Then her eyes

widened. "You don't think...?"

8

Baines thought Archer's assessment of Jade Sheldon had been spot-on. It was pretty obvious almost from the start of the interview that she wasn't that cut up about Leanne Richards' death, and that she was enjoying the cachet of being one of the last people to see her alive.

It was also quickly evident that she had taken a shine to Jason Bell. She addressed her answers to him, and kept fiddling with her blonde hair. Baines had soon nudged him to assume the lead role in the interview – which he was making a decent enough job of, despite resembling a beetroot.

"So, Jade," Bell was saying, "I've reread the statement you made last week—"

"I was on telly, too, did you see me?"

"Yes, I saw that. You did ever so well. Your family must be proud of you." This was shameless buttering up, but probably struck the right note with this witness.

Her response confirmed it. "Thank you. It was so, so traumatic, but I wanted to do my best, you know. To get justice for my poor friend."

"You were close, then?"

"Like sisters."

Baines bit his lip. It was the opposite of what Becky Day had said, and an obvious lie. He had spoken to more bereaved people than he cared to remember, and none had been so clichéd, so dramatic in their grief.

Bell let the silence play out. It wasn't long before she obliged by filling it.

"I've been really struggling with her loss, you know."

"So you'll want to do all you can to help us."

"Yeah, of course."

"Well, can you think back to that night again? I know it's

53

painful, but try to remember it."

"I get these flashbacks, you know."

"I'm sorry to hear that. But maybe some good will come of them."

She looked blank. "How's that?"

"Well, we're interested in anything that's come back to you that you didn't remember before, or maybe something you didn't mention because you thought it wasn't important. Like the car. Anything about the car?"

"Not really. Although, I think…" She closed her eyes. "Yeah. It might have been a Vauxhall."

Bell showed no reaction, didn't even look at Baines. "But that's great. A Vauxhall. And we know it was a white car."

"I think it was grey."

"Grey Vauxhall. Any idea what model? Corsa, Astra?"

"I don't really know cars."

Either that, or she didn't want to push her luck. This was such bullshit, and now the girl was compounding her attention-seeking by making stuff up that would waste police time if they believed it for a moment. Baines was half-inclined to terminate the interview. Either that or suspend it and give Jade a telling off.

He decided to let Bell run it a little longer.

"What about the driver, Jade? The people in the car? You said you hadn't noticed. Anything come back to you, any impressions?"

She closed her eyes tightly, as if seeking inspiration from the insides of her eyelids. "I told you there were two of them, didn't I?"

Baines felt his irritation rising.

"No," said Bell, "your statement said you barely noticed the car. Not the make or model. Not the colour, although you thought it was light. Not the number plate."

"Certainly not who was driving," Baines added. "Now you're saying there were two people in the car?"

"Are you sure, Jade?" her mother put in. "That's not what you said."

The girl's lower lip wobbled. "Isn't it?" Her moist eyes

turned on Bell again. "I was upset. Confused. What I must have meant to say was I didn't see the driver's face."

Bell nodded, looking sympathetic. "Must have been hard for you. So what did you see?"

"Two of them. In hats, I think. Yeah, baseball caps. Men, I think, although I couldn't see. It was just, whatsit, an impression."

"Well, that's great, Jade," Bell said. "Anything else? Maybe a fragment of the number plate?"

"No, nothing like that."

The remainder of the interview played out much like Becky Day's. They heard the accident, ran round the corner, but the car was already almost out of sight. Jade had no impression of it stopping, but by now Baines was so convinced her input was worthless that he hardly cared.

"Well," he said to Bell after mother and daughter had left the room, "That was a complete waste of time. At least Becky was honest. *That* manipulative little…" He shook his head. "Maybe she hopes she'll get on TV again."

"I don't know, Dan," Bell said. "I mean, obviously we should ignore what she said about a grey Vauxhall. But the two guys in caps…"

"What, you don't think it's convenient she remembers now?"

"I think, if you don't mind me saying, Dan, that you don't like her."

"You've got that right." He focused on some of the kids' artwork on the wall, willing himself to get a grip and be objective. "So you think it might have actually been two guys in baseball caps?"

"I think we shouldn't be too quick to rule it out. Maybe in amongst all that fake angst, there's a memory. Or she might just be over-eager to help."

"Well, maybe she really is traumatised, more than we think. Perhaps she so wants us to get the driver who killed Leanne that her mind is manufacturing false memories. I mean, I'm no psychiatrist…"

But Baines found himself nodding. He knew enough, from

personal experience, about the mind's ability to manufacture things. Maybe Bell was right.

"Okay," he said. "Her memory's still different from Becky's. So actually, there are three possibilities. One, Jade's desperate to help and is misremembering. I'd need to ask an expert how that works. Two, as you say, her memory of the two guys is real. Three, she's just lying for some reason."

"Or Becky's lying," Bell said. "To be fair," he added.

* * *

Carly Eustace's friend, Megan Cunningham, hadn't been much real help. She'd never for a moment suspected Carly of having any affairs, or being anything but faithful to her husband.

"Hardly surprising, of course," she added. "You've met Harry? I mean, why would any girl stray when she had that waiting at home?"

She'd fanned herself with her hands, presumably indicating she thought Harry Eustace was a hot guy.

"So, when Carly said she was off on a girls' night out, you took it at face value?" Archer checked.

"Yes, of course. Why wouldn't I?"

"Has anything been different about her lately?" Petrescu ventured.

"No. Well," Megan said after a beat, "maybe a little, that last day I saw her."

"In what way?"

"Sad. I thought she seemed a little sad."

Chris Pateman was, in Archer's opinion, the kind of man a lot of women would have been tempted by, even if they had a husband that women like Megan fancied the boxers off: tall, well-built, with dark hair and movie-star looks. And he was a man who knew how to dress. His suit fitted him like a second skin and his blue shirt, with silver and pink pinstripes, was perfectly complemented by the motif on his silk tie.

He seemed a genuinely nice guy, too.

"I can't tell you how much I'd like to help," he said, stirring his tea as they sat in the office where they had interviewed

Robyn Jones and Megan Cunningham. "But honestly? I'm not sure how much I can."

"We'll see," said Archer, leading off. "We gather you were friendly with Carly."

"I don't know about that."

"You went for drinks together?"

"True enough. Twice – no, three times, I think. When we had a work thing to discuss that was a bit involved, we might pop out for a glass or two of wine. I mean, I liked her. We got along. I'm just not sure we were what you'd call friends."

"But you must have talked about more than just work, surely?"

"I suppose. Nothing much that sticks."

"When did you last see her?"

"Oh, I don't know. Let's see... I think we shared a lift together on – when was it? – Tuesday. I'd just had an awful meeting and she must have seen I was pissed off, because she said I looked it. I told her why. Might have asked how she was."

"So you didn't see her on Thursday?"

"I wasn't in on Thursday."

"Were you not?" That was potentially interesting.

"Talk us through your day," Petrescu prompted.

"I had a dental appointment. In London. A hangover from when I worked there. She's a dentist I trust and I've never wanted to risk changing. My appointment was..." He made a face. "Ah, I'd have to double-check my diary, but say ten in the morning. I'd have left home around eight thirty."

"Are you married?"

"Twice divorced. I live in a terraced place in Elmshurst – that's all I can afford." A neighbourhood in Aylesbury, to the north of the town. He raised an eyebrow. "Are you looking for an alibi?"

"Suppose we are?"

"Really?" He looked a little concerned. "Okay. Well, my next-door neighbour saw me drive off. She waved. And the guy in the ticket office at the station – Roy, that's his name – he can vouch that I bought a ticket, and he saw me get on the train."

"I think we're more interested in the other end of the day."

Collins observed. "After Carly left work. Where were you around five?"

"I was home by then."

"You didn't go into work after your appointment?"

"No. I haven't taken much leave this year, so after the dentist I went to Oxford Street, did some shopping. Had lunch in a pub. Got home maybe half past three."

"And stayed there?"

"I did some internet surfing. Fooled around on social media. Got myself something to eat. Probably watched TV. Oh, yeah." He snapped his fingers. "I watched *Pointless*."

"You didn't pick Carly up from work?"

"What?" He fingered his collar. "Do I need a lawyer?"

It would get a little out of hand, Archer thought, if she didn't back off a little, although it was interesting how ready Pateman was to assume he was being accused of something.

"This is all unofficial, Chris," she soothed. "Unless you see a need for us to make it more formal."

"It depends."

"You're sure you knew nothing about Carly's private life?"

"No. Well, I think she was married. Yes, she was."

"Any reason to suppose she was having an affair?"

"No. And she certainly wasn't having one with me." He tried to crack a smile, but it was a nervous effort. She felt a twinge of sympathy for him.

"So no one can vouch for where you were Thursday evening?"

The corners of his mouth turned down. "No." He gave his tea another stir. He hadn't touched a drop. Then his expression changed. "Wait a sec, though. My brother phoned for a chat. About 7pm? We talked about his family, his kids, football. He'll tell you I was there to answer the phone."

"How long was he on?"

"Maybe an hour?" He was smiling now, relieved. "That puts me in the clear, right?"

"You've been helpful," she said. "If you could jot down your dentist's number and your brother's, just for confirmation, we'll pick them up before we leave."

After he left them, Archer asked her colleagues what they thought of Pateman's story.

"His brother would cover for him," Collins commented. "And, even if that phone call did take place, it doesn't mean Carly wasn't there with him."

"Dead or alive," Petrescu added. "Although if you kill someone in a terrace, you really do risk the neighbours hearing."

"Or seeing you removing the body," Collins added.

Archer tended to agree. "Let's check out those alibis anyway," she said, "and talk to his immediate neighbours. See if anyone heard a disturbance or saw anything untoward. If we have any doubts, we should search his place. Carly's clothes and jewellery must be somewhere."

"They're probably in landfill by now," Petrescu said, somewhat gloomily.

Archer glanced at Collins. "So, Joan, check when his bins are collected and, if they already have been, find out where the waste goes. There might be a dirty job in the offing for some poor devil."

9

Becky Day sat on the school bus, trying not to listen to Jade Sheldon and her mates having a laugh at the back. The effort to tune them out made her teeth ache and was ultimately unsuccessful.

To think it was – what was it? – four days since Jade's shameless TV appearance, pouting and weeping for the cameras and saying nice things about Leanne when she really couldn't give a toss about her. She hadn't even been living in the village when Becky and Leanne had bonded in primary school, and she wasn't really a friend. Knowing someone meant more than just living in the same area, going to the same youth club, and attending the same school.

Becky kept reminding herself that she wasn't actually jealous that Jade had got on the telly. It wasn't something she would have wanted to do herself – she'd have been as nervous as anything. But at the same time, she would rather have shaken and stammered all the way through it than have to watch someone else being insincere.

But Jade had been almost comical in her eagerness to grab her five minutes of fame. Becky was sure Jade had recorded the thirty-second piece, and she'd bet that she played it back over and over. Yesterday, she'd asked everyone, "Did you see me on the telly?" at least twice each. She probably imagined some talent scout would spot her and be on the phone offering her a part in a soap before the week was out. Talk about cashing in.

And now Jade was laughing and joking with her hyena friends when all Becky had wanted to do since the accident was to cry in a corner for the friend she'd lost. It made her so angry, she'd like to shake Jade. Or worse.

"Course," she heard Jade saying, "the papers will probably be on to me to buy my story. You know – tragic best friend of dead girl?"

Becky felt her anger rising. She spun round in her seat to tell Jade to shut up, but the bus pulled up at its first stop, not yet out of Aylesbury. A couple of the kids regularly got off here, but Becky was surprised to see Jade getting up too.

As the girl started making her way to the exit, Becky said, "This isn't your stop."

Jade glanced round at her, a shifty look on her face. "It is tonight."

"Where are you going?" Becky didn't care, but she was annoyed that she wouldn't be able to have a go at her.

The other girl winked. It wasn't a nice wink. "Wouldn't you like to know?"

It was the wink that did it. Becky had never picked a fight, or even a real argument, in her life, but now she was riled. As Jade sashayed down the aisle, Becky got out of her seat and followed her.

* * *

It was after 4pm when the team assembled in the briefing room. DCI Gillingham sat at the back, his expression unreadable.

It was still damp and autumnal outside, but the room felt stiflingly hot. It wouldn't be the first time whoever was responsible for the central heating had got over-enthusiastic.

Baines went first, updating everyone on the hit-and-run. He asked Will Tyler if he'd had any joy with CCTV footage, and the newcomer trundled his wheelchair forward to join him at the front of the room.

"A few glimpses of the car stolen from Mark Briscoe between his home and Houghton, a couple more further south. But it's where we draw the line at widening the search, to be honest. The direction I last saw it travelling in – well, it's evaded, or just missed, the next couple of cameras it could have passed, and then it's anyone's guess where it went."

"How many in the car?" Baines asked.

"Just the driver."

"Can you see the driver?" Archer prompted.

"That's the really maddening thing, guv. The angle's always wrong. I even got Ibrahim Iqbal to try and enhance it or whatever, but he couldn't do anything with it."

Ibrahim Iqbal was a civilian IT wizard. If he could do nothing with an image, it was a lost cause.

"Not even a shape? Male or female? What they're wearing?"

"Looks like a hoodie. Grey, guv. You really can't tell the gender. Sorry."

"A hoodie?" Baines echoed. "You're sure?"

"Certainly looks like it."

"Maybe Jade mistook hoodies for caps," Bell suggested. "Maybe he picked up a passenger who was in a hoodie. Then it would fit with Jade's recollection."

Archer could see the scepticism on Baines's face. She thought she shared it, despite her efforts to keep an open mind.

"And he was headed south?" she checked. Tyler nodded.

"Okay," Archer said. "Keep looking, and remind all cars to keep an eye out for it. I know it's not conclusive, but everything in my gut tells me that's the car we're looking for."

"How's that list of known joyriders and car thieves in the Winslow area?" Baines asked.

"I've got some names," Tyler said. "I was going to see if I could whittle it down to likely candidates we could pull in for questioning."

"Do it," Archer said. "Now, do we have anything else on Leanne?"

"Not for the moment," Baines admitted.

"Thanks, Dan."

Baines made to return to his seat.

"Hang on," Gillingham said. He stood up to address the room. "I know you've all got a lot on your plates, but I want to make it clear this case is a high priority, even though we have a murder to solve too."

Archer bristled. "We do actually know that, sir."

He smiled, and some of the tension went out of her. "I know you do. It's just that the local media are on at us about this all the time, Lizzie. They're at least as interested in what we're doing to catch this driver as they are in Carly Eustace's murder.

That TV appeal you did, with the tearful little girl, probably helped fuel that. Not that we seem to have had much useful response, though."

She couldn't decide if he was criticising her or not. "Can we discuss it later, boss?"

"All right. But I'm under pressure on two fronts here. A murder victim on our doorstep and a kid knocked down by some callous fucker who never even stopped."

"That's not strictly true, sir." Baines had stopped halfway to his seat and now he moved back to the board. "We've got witnesses who heard the accident, although they didn't see it. One is convinced the driver did stop, then sped off."

"That makes it worse." Gillingham wrinkled his nose as if at a bad smell. "As God's my witness, we're going to nail this sod, whatever it takes."

"Can we move on?" Archer asked.

Gillingham waved a dismissive hand.

"Right. Carly Eustace." She proceeded to outline the visit to Oxfordshire County Council's offices.

"So this bloke," Gillingham said, "this Chris Paxman…"

"Pateman."

"Is he a serious suspect? Or are we just going through the motions?"

"We're doing what needs to be done to eliminate him." Archer could hear the defensiveness in her tone again.

"Going through the motions." Gillingham repeated, his voice booming from the back like a heckler. "We're getting nowhere. No clues and no suspects. What about her phone? Her computer?"

"Nothing on the computer. Well, the experts are still going over it, but they say if there's any email exchange with a lover, it's well hidden. I don't think Carly was an IT boffin, was she?"

"I'll check that with Harry," Petrescu said. "You never know."

"Nothing in her phone records either," Collins added. "The phone itself has gone. But there's no trace of calls to numbers out of the ordinary in the week or so before her death."

"It's always possible, if she was having an affair, that she had a separate phone to make the calls on." Archer said. "Probably a pre-paid. Which is doubtless in the bag with her other stuff."

"Bloody pre-paids," grumbled Gillingham. "I'd ban them. Everyone who wants to hide what they're doing knows they just have to get a twenty-quid Nokia on pay-as-you-go and not register it. Then we won't have a scooby who's using it."

He sat down heavily, his seat protesting. "All right. We all know what we have to do. We've got to find out who this lover was, and rule them in or out. We also need to be sure the husband's ruled out."

"I'll talk to Harry Eustace again," Petrescu said, "but I'm as sure as I can be that he's not hiding anything."

"Me too," Archer admitted.

Gillingham sighed. "Are we done?"

Archer scanned the room. "Anything else, anyone?"

A few heads shook. No one volunteered anything.

"That's about it, then."

The DCI nodded, his expression grim. He rose and moved forward, joining Archer at the front. He dropped his voice so Archer could barely hear him over the cacophony of scraping chairs and chatter that had started as soon as the meeting broke up. "All right. But next time we're in here, I need some progress. On both fronts. Are we clear?"

"Yes, sir. Although I can't work miracles."

He scowled and strode off. Archer winced. She had the beginnings of a headache.

* * *

Cath Sheldon glanced at the kitchen clock. Jade was a bit late today. Maybe the bus had been held up, or maybe she'd decided to do something with her mates and hadn't thought to call and say she'd be late home.

It wouldn't be the first time. Cath loved her daughter dearly – was incredibly proud of her most of the time. She might not be great academic material, but she was very pretty and had the sort of personality that ensured she'd never be short of friends.

The way she had conducted herself on TV the other night showed how self-assured she was.

Yet Cath knew that Jade also had a selfish, thoughtless side. She loved her parents fiercely, Cath knew that. She'd been lovely to her dad, Andrew, since he'd lost his job. She just didn't always understand what was important to them. Like calling when she'd be late home.

Cath wondered if it was her own fault. She knew her own mother didn't approve of the dynamics of her relationship with Jade and her younger sister, Melanie.

"You can't be their best mate," she'd told Cath one time when both the girls had pissed her off. "It's about boundaries. Especially Jade – she's almost a teenager. It's a damn sight easier to instil some discipline as a parent than as a friend."

At the time, she hadn't welcomed the advice. Had thought it old-fashioned, stuffy, and – frankly – interfering. But in her heart of hearts, she had known her mother had a point. She loved her kids so much that maybe she'd crossed the invisible line between authority figure and just one of the girls.

It wouldn't get easier in the next few years, that she knew. Was it too late to redraw the line? She'd talk to Andrew about it. If she was going to instil a greater sense of responsibility in Jade, she'd need his buy-in. There had been times when she could almost believe the girl was playing her parents off against one another.

Cath smiled. Like she hadn't tried that ploy when she was a kid. Not that it had ever worked. *Have you asked your mother/father? What did they say?* It was a protocol she and Andrew had never quite mastered, and her husband was even softer than she was.

She finished chopping onions and began peeling carrots. Maybe this wasn't a good time to sit down with Andrew and talk about this sort of stuff. Being out of work had hit him really hard. His pride at being the family's main breadwinner had been shattered, and each job application that didn't even lead to an interview – half the time, he didn't even get a reply – seemed to add to the invisible weight that was crushing him. She believed in him – maybe more than he did himself right now – and she

65

was sure it was only a matter of time before he found another job.

The amazing thing was that Jade, for all her apparent self-absorption, had responded to the situation much better than Cath could have expected. Not only had she accepted, with neither argument nor sulk, that money was going to be tighter for a while, impacting on her social and shopping activities, but she had even asked what sort of job she might be able to get at her age. They'd looked into it together, but even for a paper round she'd have to wait until she was thirteen – and Andrew had rejected that option outright.

"I'm not having you out on the streets in the dark of a morning," he'd told her. "You get all sorts these days. It's sweet of you to want to help out, love, but if anything happened to you…" He'd left the thought unspoken. "No," he'd said firmly. "But maybe *I* could get a paper round instead." He'd laughed without humour.

Cath hoped he'd find something soon. Meanwhile, she stole another glance at the clock. Jade's selfishness hadn't completely evaporated. She'd have to have a serious word with her when she finally deigned to come home.

10

The late team briefing had left Archer and Gillingham visibly frustrated, Baines thought.

The trail on Leanne Richards' hit-and-run was already going cold and, for all the public outrage – and the team's commitment to tracking down the driver – the case was, Baines knew, a lower priority than the Carly Eustace murder. The worst-case scenario would be that she had been abducted and killed at random – and that her killer would strike again. If so, the clock was ticking.

Yet none of the news was helpful. Harry Eustace had confirmed that Carly's computer skills were fairly basic. She certainly hadn't possessed the know-how to hide her online activities.

Archer had wrapped up a sombre meeting.

"Let's all get an early night, unless you've got urgent tasks to complete first. I want everyone in here tomorrow morning with at least one fresh idea on either of our cases. We're going to brainstorm some new angles. Nothing's out of bounds"

Baines thought he'd struggle this evening to think of much else beyond tomorrow's session with his therapist, and he wondered what wacky ideas others might come up with that would actually help.

As he made his way back to his desk, Amy Petrescu fell into step with him.

"Hi, Dan." She said it lightly enough, but he detected a hint of tension in her voice. "We haven't had much chance to talk today."

"It's a madhouse," he conceded. "Busy, busy."

"Yeah. Well, now we're both off the hook for the evening, can we get a drink? I really need to talk to you."

His heart sank. "Really? It wouldn't be about that drink you suggested, would it?"

She coloured. "Something like that."

He sighed. "Amy, I just can't. I've got a partner at home, and she means a lot to me."

"Oh, for Christ's sake, Dan!" Her vehemence shook him. "Get over yourself. It's one drink, not a bloody marriage proposal." She took a breath. "Please?"

He sighed, thinking it was a bad idea. "All right. But not your hotel."

She rolled her eyes. "You really flatter yourself, don't you? All right. You choose somewhere."

He chose the Black Horse in Tring, for no particular reason. They found a free table and he got drinks in: a white wine spritzer for her and a pint of bitter for himself.

"Just the one," he told her as he put the glass in front of her.

"Of course," she said, a little frost in her tone. "I'm driving."

"You wanted to talk," he reminded her, cutting to the chase.

She sipped her drink, then toyed with her glass. "What do you think of Steve Ashby?"

He stared at her. "Ashby?"

"Yeah."

This was getting weird. He took a gulp of his beer. "Why do you ask?" He set the glass down. "Don't tell me the bastard's made a pass at you already?"

That pink tinge to her cheeks again. "It really wasn't like that."

The other shoe dropped. "You mean… You don't mean..? No." He shook his head. "No, no, no." He had a vague recollection of the DI speaking to Petrescu yesterday, in his smarmy, worming-his-way-in sort of way. "What happened? And why are you telling *me*?"

"Why d'you think? I'm new here, Dan. I don't know anyone else, and you're a nice guy. As for what happened…" She sighed. "I went back to the hotel last night. Had something to eat. Had a drink in the bar. I half hoped you'd show up. Not because I had – what's the word? – *designs* on you. I just fancied some company. But you didn't. Then who comes strolling into the bar, but DI Ashby? He admitted he'd made it his business to find out where I was staying, but he seemed nice enough. He suggested we get a bottle of wine."

"I bet he did," Baines commented grimly. He was pretty sure he knew where this was going. He was also pretty sure he didn't want to hear about it.

"Oh, Christ," she said. "This sounded easier to say in my head. I mean, I'd already had a glass, he turned up and got me a top-up, then we shared the bottle. I mean, it all seemed like a good idea at the time. But somehow it all got out of hand..."

"Tell me you didn't..."

"I don't know how it happened."

"Did he spike your drink? Or just get you pissed and take advantage?" He felt his outrage rising. Whether it was some sort of protectiveness towards Amy, or his loathing of Ashby, or both, he wasn't sure, but he itched to get his hands on the DI.

Petrescu's eyes widened. "What? No!" She shook her head vehemently. "Nothing like that. Definitely no spiking. No getting me drunk, either. That was my fault. And no advantage-taking. It just... happened. But this morning I felt such a fool. A colleague! I man I hardly know! Despite what happened on that course, Dan, I don't make a habit of that sort of thing."

"All right." He took another drink. A long one. "So what you're telling me is two consenting adults had a good time, right? I mean, there's no accounting for taste, but..." He sighed. "You asked me what I thought of him. It might have made more sense to ask me before."

"What I'm worried about is, is he the kind of guy to go around bragging about it? I mean, he *seemed* really nice..."

"You're asking the wrong person, if you want a character reference, or some sort of reassurance, Amy. If you're asking my honest opinion, he's an utter shit. A lazy, useless copper who gets away with it because, for some reason none of us can fathom, DCI Gillingham lets him. He's an unreconstructed scumbag – homophobic, misogynistic... He'll try and get in the knickers of anything in a skirt."

"Thanks a lot."

"And would he brag around the station? I'm surprised he hasn't already told me – not because we're mates, but just to tell me."

"So I'm busted." She pulled a face. "That's going to make life here interesting, isn't it?" She took a sip of her spritzer. "You know, I really thought he was a nice guy. Funny, attentive. A bit shy, even."

Baines, who'd just taken another mouthful of beer, almost sprayed it, then choked on it instead. When he'd finished coughing and wiped his eyes, he sat dumbfounded.

"I'm sorry. I thought we were talking about DI Stephen Ashby."

She slid her phone in her bag and wound her scarf around her neck.

"This was a rubbish idea. I had no idea you'd be jealous."

"I promise you I'm not." He wasn't so sure about that. He'd bottled the drink last night precisely to avoid any possible temptation. "But either he was putting on an act, or he's had a personality transplant, or there's some sort of Invasion of the Body Snatchers thing going on."

"I've kept you long enough," she said, a little less cold than she'd been a moment ago. "You'll want to get back to that partner of yours."

"I'm sorry," he said, feeling a bit crass. It couldn't have been easy for her to open up like that. "For my reaction, I mean. I just don't like the guy."

"You could have fooled me." But her eyes were smiling at last. "Look, if I've shot myself in the foot, it's self-inflicted. But can you do me a favour?"

"I expect so."

"Let me know if he says anything to you?"

Before Baines could reply, his phone started ringing. Petrescu's was doing likewise even before he could answer his.

* * *

Archer splashed cold water on her face, patted it dry with a paper towel, then automatically checked that her hair and make-up were disguising her scar.

As she did so, she examined her face in the mirror. The

circles under her eyes were just a little darker, and her complexion was pale – or was that just the lights in here? She'd only just arrived home, her mind set on something to eat, a glass of wine, and some much-needed sleep, when the call had come through. Everyone who could be reached was being dragged back in. A young girl missing. A briefing at 8pm sharp.

She'd been getting in her car to head back to the station when she'd spotted Dominic from next door heading her way, his hand raised in a wave.

"Can't stop," she'd said. "It's all kicking off at work." She'd closed the Skoda's door, started the engine and reversed out while he stood watching her. He hadn't looked happy, but then neither was she.

She checked her watch as she emerged from the ladies'. Too late to make a much-needed coffee. She gave in to a yawn, not even attempting to stifle it, and stopped off at the water cooler. Cardboard cup filled, she turned away and bumped into Steve Ashby, who was standing in her personal space. Some water splashed down her trousers.

"Oops," Ashby said. "Careful there."

She bit off a retort about how close he'd been standing. Instead, she assumed an astonished expression.

"Blimey, Steve. I didn't know you could find your way here after dark."

"Funny lady," he said. "And so original."

She supposed she did make a fair few cracks about how rarely he was seen in the office, especially early or late.

He took a cup and started to fill it. Archer turned away and then stopped.

"Any idea who this missing girl is?"

"I hear she's the one who appeared on the news last week. From Houghton? That hit-and-run of yours."

Archer gaped at him. "Jade Sheldon?"

"That's the one. That's all I know, other than she never made it home from school tonight."

Stunned, she headed for the briefing room, conscious that Ashby was only a few paces behind her. She pushed the door open and held it for him. Baines was seated next to Amy

Petrescu. He waved at her and indicated the vacant seat on his other side.

"I can't believe it," he whispered. "Jason and I only saw her today."

Gillingham strode to the front of the room, strain etched on his face.

"Right, I'm going to start," the DCI said. There was a whiteboard set up beside him, a photograph of Jade held in place by a magnet. He tapped it.

"Jade Sheldon. Twelve years old. Went to school as normal this morning, but was late home. According to her parents, that's not unusual. It wouldn't be the first time she's gone off and done something with her mates and hasn't phoned home."

Archer wasn't surprised. She'd already marked the girl down as a self-centred drama queen and she knew Baines was similarly unimpressed.

"When it got late enough for her parents to worry, they started phoning round," Gillingham continued. "They spoke to her best friends. Spoke to another girl in Houghton, where they live, one who gets the same school bus. They all said the same thing. Jade got on the bus as usual, but got off at the first stop – still in Aylesbury."

"Did she say why?" Archer prompted.

"No, she didn't. Just winked, so her mates said, and said 'wouldn't you like to know?' when someone asked her where she was going, then got off the bus."

"Meeting someone?" Ashby's voice, from the back of the room.

"We don't know," Gillingham admitted. "Although one of her friends mentioned that Becky Day got off with her, and they were seen arguing at the bus stop."

Archer was jolted. "Becky was the other girl who left the youth club with Leanne Richards on Thursday night. Where's she now?"

"Jade's parents called Becky's family," Gillingham said. "She's safe at home, although she was apparently ten or fifteen minutes later than usual. Jade's parents finally called in Jade's disappearance with us about an hour ago. Someone needs to find out what Jade and Becky rowed about, though."

"You think Becky had something to do with this?"

"We can't rule it out," the DCI said, "although it's hard to believe that one twelve-year-old could make another disappear in broad daylight. Still, we'll see if there's a camera at that bus stop. Meanwhile, we have a twelve-year-old girl missing, no one knows where she is, and it's getting late..." He raked his fingers through his thinning hair. "We have to mount a search. Question her contacts, have a look at her computer, pull her phone records."

Archer felt a queasy lurch in her stomach. "One possibility we have to face, sir, is that someone saw her on TV and liked what they saw."

"That's what worries me too." Gillingham looked gloomy. "It's been, what, four days since the broadcast. Plenty of time for a determined person to track her down on social media."

"But..." Ashby again. "There are age restrictions on those platforms."

Amy Petrescu snorted. "Yeah, right, Steve. The minimum age for most of the sites is thirteen, but about sixty per cent of kids under that age ignore the restriction. Parents think it's okay. Twelve? It's as near as dammit. If her parents even know she's on there."

"Or how about this?" Baines added. "That TV news programme said she was the nearest thing we have to a witness to Leanne's accident. What if the driver got scared? Thinks she can identify him? After all, we didn't say on the news that she can't. He knows what school she goes to. All he has to do is follow the bus..."

"Slow down, though," Ashby said. "Maybe she just went shopping on a whim, lost her bag with her phone and money in, and is trying to get home."

It almost sounded less plausible to Archer than the online grooming scenario.

"Maybe she was teasing her mates for the fun of it," she said. "Lost track of time. Maybe her phone ran out of battery. Now maybe she's scared to go home and face the music." It sounded lame, even to her ears.

"Doesn't explain why she's still not home," Gillingham said. "Even if she is okay, finding her going to be a nightmare. She could be anywhere between Aylesbury and Houghton, and that's if she didn't head off somewhere else entirely. Or get snatched." He scanned the faces in front of him. "We drop everything else for this evening and we find this kid. Steve," he jabbed a finger in Ashby's direction, "you lead for now."

Archer's heart sank at the idea of Ashby trying to find the girl, but she recognised that Gillingham's options were limited.

Gillingham pointed at Collins. "Joan, you're co-ordinating. Go now and ring Jade's parents. Get as comprehensive a list as you can of people she spends time with, and when we've wound up here we can start allocating people to talk to them all. I want a comprehensive picture of her. Will, you help her."

"On it, boss," Collins said, closing her notebook and rising from her chair. Tyler followed her.

"There's one other scenario," Ashby said. "Suppose she got off the bus early just to do some shopping – and she was just taking the piss by being mysterious about it – but something happened to her subsequently? She got off for one reason, but then it all went wrong."

Archer had seldom seen Steve Ashby so engaged.

"You're thinking what?" Gillingham said. "A random abduction?" He shook his head. "I can't see it. It's to do with the TV appearance. Has to be."

"We can't rule it out," Ashby persisted. "But we just don't know. So we need to get out there and talk to people who knew her. Are there any clues in her recent behaviour? And we need to do our best to trace her steps."

He rose from his seat and walked to the front of the room, joining Gillingham by Jade's picture. "She's twelve years old and she's missing. It could be just a silly thing, and we'll all be angry that she's wasted our time. Or it could be something really bad – but if it is, maybe it's not too late to save her. So let's find her. Yes?"

Just for a moment, Archer sensed she was seeing the police officer Steve Ashby could have become. Somewhere along the line, it had all gone wrong.

She looked at him standing beside Gillingham. Two old pals who went back years. One day she was going to make some time and poke around in their backgrounds. There was a story there she wanted to get to the bottom of. But for now she had more on her plate than she could comfortably handle.

11

Baines and Bell had been detailed to speak to some of Jade Sheldon's closest friends. If the girl had gone missing deliberately, there was always a chance that her mates would be in the know but were protecting her through misplaced loyalty.

Baines had been concerned about the allocation of this task when Ashby had handed it to him.

"Wouldn't a female officer be more appropriate to draw out young girls?" he suggested.

"Maybe, maybe not. Amy Petrescu's coming with me to talk to the parents, and Lizzie's going to speak to Becky Day." He shrugged. "I need you to find out more about her other mates, talk to them. If there are any clues to her disappearance, they might know." He actually reached out and clapped Baines on the shoulder. "You're good with young people, Dan, and Jason's a good-looking guy. You'll be fine."

Baines searched his face for some sign that he was being patronising, and was a little surprised to find none. It made him suspicious.

Before leaving with Bell to make the rounds of Jade's friends, he made a quick visit to the gents'. As he washed his hands, Ashby walked in.

"Ah," the DI said. "The very man."

"What?" he said as he dried his hands. "Change of plan?"

"No, no." The other man shuffled his feet. "I wanted to ask you something, actually." He ran an eye along the cubicle doors, evidently checking that none of them was occupied. "You know Amy Petrescu, don't you?"

"A bit," he agreed, cagily.

"She seems nice."

"She *is* nice," Baines said. "You should stay away from her." The words came before he had a chance to think what he was going to say.

Ashby threw up his hands. "Whoa! Where did that come from?"

Baines thought fast. Why had he blurted that out? Amy had confided in him.

"Sorry," he said. "That was out of order."

"It was. What, do you fancy her for yourself? I thought you were in a relationship?"

"I am," said Baines, although he rarely talked about it in the office and Archer remained the only colleague who had actually met Karen. Partly because he didn't want to get into the complications of Karen being his dead wife's identical twin sister. He didn't want his life to become a topic of office gossip.

Still, he supposed it was no secret that he had a partner.

"I mean, yes, I'm in a relationship," he said. "And no – I've no interest in Amy in that way. I just don't want to see her hurt."

Ashby looked amused. "What are you, her dad?" But he didn't say it in his usual snide way. "Look, I'm not going to hurt her. We… well, we had a drink last night, and—"

Here it comes, Baines thought. The boasting.

"—and I really like her." Ashby looked at Baines earnestly. "Look, I'm not stupid. I know some people around here probably think I'm interested in getting into any pair of knickers I can. But with Amy, I really think we had a connection. I just wondered if there was anything I should know. Like, is she married? Got a partner? What sort of flowers does she like?"

Baines was astonished. Ashby the lovesick puppy? Flowers? Seriously?

His performance in the briefing. The personality transplant. Was it possible that he could change?

Or was this all more of an act for Amy's benefit? The cynical side of Baines wondered if Ashby, having found what seemed to be an easy lay last night, was simply trying to secure a place in her bed for as long as possible.

Yet there seemed to be something like sincerity in Ashby's eyes.

Baines felt like some sort of go-between. Suddenly, Amy

and Ashby were treating him like an agony uncle.

"Look," he said, "I'm not exactly the world's greatest authority on Amy. I've no idea what flowers she likes. Or chocolates, perfume, or anything else you might think to buy her. But, for what it's worth, I'm pretty sure she's not in a relationship at the moment. I do know she can be her own worst enemy when she drinks, so if you're seriously interested in her you shouldn't let her get pissed. That's about it, I'm afraid."

"Okay." Ashby nodded. "That's something."

"One other thing," Baines added, remembering one of the reasons Amy had confided in him. "I hope you're not going to go bragging all over the station about last night."

"I wouldn't do that. Not about her. It wouldn't be right."

"You told *me*, though."

"I told you because you're the only one who knows her." He looked Baines in the eye. "And because I know it'll go no further."

Gillingham walked in, his hand moving towards his fly. He saw the two men facing each other, stopped, and frowned.

"What are you two falling out over now?"

Baines felt a smile tugging at the corners of his mouth. "Nothing, boss," he said. "Nothing at all."

* * *

When Leanne Richards had been killed, Becky Day had told Archer they'd been best friends. She'd seemed a quiet, slightly shy girl, devastated by seeing Leanne die in front of her eyes. And she'd been about as much use as a witness as Jade Sheldon had been. Worse, since the pair had seemed unable to agree on much..

Privately, Archer wondered how much help she'd be now with Jade's disappearance.

"So, just to be clear," she said, "you and Jade aren't particularly good friends?"

"No." A pause. "We're not enemies, either. I mean, we see each other at the youth club, and we chat a bit."

They were sitting in the Days' living room. Becky was on a

cream leather sofa, flanked by her parents, Josh and Emma. She looked tired, understandably. It was probably her bedtime.

The Days' house was an unassuming semi, well looked after, but with its furnishings somewhat regimented. Even the mugs of tea and plate of biscuits that sat in the centre of the coffee table looked carefully arranged. Archer resisted the temptation to examine the placement of the biscuits.

"So when Jade unexpectedly got off the bus at the first stop today," she said, "you went after her. You were seen rowing at the bus stop."

"Becky?" Emma threw her daughter a concerned look.

"It was nothing."

"You're sure?" Archer pushed. "I mean, you both get off ahead of your stop, you have a row, then only one of you comes home."

The girl looked alarmed. "You think I've done something to her?"

"Now, hold on," her father protested. "What are you accusing Becky of?"

"Let's not get excited," Archer soothed. "We're just trying to find out what was in Jade's mind when she was last seen. Did she seem excited? Worried? Anxious?"

"You could tell she was up to something." The girl shrugged. "She was just Jade."

For an instant, there was something about her look that reminded Archer of someone. She couldn't think who. Maybe a young actress or model she'd seen on TV?

Archer tried again. "What did you quarrel over?"

"It was a stupid thing. I don't know why I followed her." Becky's lower lip trembled. "It's just… Well, Leanne's dead, and Jade doesn't care. Doesn't care at all. She pushed her way in when they wanted someone on the telly." She was crying. And angry at the same time. "She puts on this big act, pretended she was Leanne's best friend. And now she thinks she's some sort of star. And she was going on about it, and I just wanted to tell her."

"Tell her what?"

Her hands closed into fists. "To stop. Just stop."

"And did you? Tell her?"

"Yeah, sort of." She sniffed. Pulled a tissue from a box on the coffee table and blew her nose. "Well, I sort of screamed at her. What I just told you, only screaming. And she just stood there with this grin on her face. Then she says, 'Are we done? Cos I've gotta go.' Something like that. Then she walked off."

"And you didn't go after her?"

"No. I just stood there, feeling stupid. Embarrassed." She looked from parent to parent. "I made a scene. Sorry."

Emma put an arm around her shoulders and squeezed. "Don't worry about that."

"Which direction did she go in?" Archer asked.

Becky frowned, stuck her hands out in front of her, and turned her body. "Left. I think."

If she was telling the truth, it was the right direction for the main shopping centre, Friars Square.

"And what did you do?"

"Got the next bus home."

With luck, a CCTV camera would confirm that.

"What do you know about her other friends?" Archer asked. "Does Jade have any boyfriends?"

"Not really." Becky looked at the carpet. "I mean, she talks a lot about fit boys. She likes older ones. She's been asked out a few times by boys in our year, but it's like she thinks they're beneath her. The ones she does fancy won't ask her out."

"So who does she fancy?" Collins wondered.

"There's a couple of guys who come to youth club. Sam Yardley and Ollie Field. They're fourteen. They're nice. She hangs around them, tries to flirt with them. They probably laugh about her behind her back. She's embarrassing herself, but it's none of my business."

Archer had a mouthful of biscuit. She'd hardly eaten all day and her stomach was rumbling alarmingly. She finished chewing, swallowed, washed it down with some tea.

"But is it possible that one of them did ask her out? That she was meeting one of them?"

"I so doubt it. She thinks she's got more, what is it, charisma, than she really has. They're not rude to her at the

THE BLOOD THAT BINDS

club, but you can tell they just think she's a little kid."

"Still." Archer helped herself to a bourbon cream. "I'd like their addresses, if you've got them."

"I'll find them for you," said Becky's mother. "I know both their mums from village things." She got up and heading for the kitchen. Archer thought it was time to move on to a more awkward line of questioning.

"What about adults?" she asked. "Any teachers, or anyone at the youth club – anywhere else, for that matter – she's especially friendly with?"

The girl stared at her. "You mean, she might have been meeting them after school?" She wrinkled her nose. "Eww. Not that I've ever noticed."

"Any teachers from primary school she might still see? I take it you both went to the village school?"

"No." Josh fielded that one. His fair hair was a shade lighter than his wife's. "The Sheldons only moved here a year or so ago. Cath – Jade's mum – had a hankering for village life."

"Do you know the family well?"

"No, but Cath and Emma have chatted a few times."

"So where did they live before?"

"Aylesbury."

"Do you know if the family still has contacts there?"

"You'd have to ask them." He frowned. "You're asking a lot about Jade's relationships with older boys and adults. Do you think..?"

"We don't know what to think right now, Mr Day. We're just building up a picture."

Emma Day returned with a piece of paper with two names and addresses written on it in a neat, small hand.

"That's Sam and Ollie's addresses," she said, returning to her seat. "But I can't see them having anything to do with Jade going missing. They're nice boys."

12

Baines arrived home feeling like an extra from *The Living Dead*. It had been a long, exhausting day for everyone, and a frustrating one too. Tomorrow morning he'd be seeing Tracey Walsh for a counselling session, and he'd much prefer to do it with his eyes open and feeling properly awake.

His talks to Jade's school friends had proved fruitless. The girls apparently closest to her had seemed to have a similar sense of the dramatic to the missing girl herself. Lots of "and I thought, OMG" and "I literally *died*", but he'd learned nothing meaningful. Her friends had assumed Jade was meeting someone when she so mysteriously got off the bus, but hadn't a clue who, or how she'd met the boy – or man.

Since Jade hadn't actually told anyone she had a boyfriend, Baines had his doubts. He tried to imagine these girls keeping something like that a secret, and failed.

And, if Jade wasn't meeting someone, what did that leave?

Unless, of course, she was meeting someone so wrong that she wasn't even prepared to tell her friends.

Nothing helpful had come from Ashby's and Petrescu's interview with Jade's family, who had been numb with worry. Tech staff were looking at Jade's computer. It was still early days, but the chances of finding anything sinister were looking remote. Jade had been active on several social media sites and Ibrahim Iqbal had already hacked in to her accounts. There was no sign of anything amiss, and there was nothing unusual or unexpected in her recent phone records either. Iqbal intended to dig deeper.

They had acquired CCTV footage that appeared to back up Becky Day's story about their row at the bus stop.

As he put his key in the lock, his thoughts slid back to Jack. He couldn't help but identify with the Sheldons' agony of not knowing, and he prayed for their sake that – whatever the outcome – the uncertainty didn't last as long as his own. Even if the news was bad, it was better to know than to spend a lifetime wondering.

Karen met him in the hallway and put her arms around him. He returned her embrace and kissed her hair.

"You've had a shit day, by the sound of it," she said as they broke the embrace. "Any sign of the girl?" Baines had called her earlier to explain what had happened.

He shook his head. "I'm back on my hit-and-run tomorrow. Steve Ashby will be leading the search."

"Ashby?" She puffed out her cheeks. "Mr Care and Compassion, searching for a missing kid?"

"Yeah, well, he might be turning over a temporary new leaf."

"How so?"

He looked her in the eye. "I think he might be in *lurve*."

She held his gaze, then broke it as the laugh bubbled out of her. "Love? Ashby? Does he even understand the meaning of the word?"

He told her about their conversation in the gents'.

"Sounds like he's found an easy lay and wants to get all he can while she's around," she said.

"That's what I thought at first. There was something, though – I almost felt he meant it. I mean, he didn't use the 'L' word, but still…"

"Hmm." She shrugged and moved towards the kitchen. "What about your hit-and-run? Any progress?"

"Not much. We're picking up the threads of it tomorrow, but there's so little to go on, apart from a car we're interested in. Even that seems to have vanished off the face of the earth."

"I'm not sure Houghton's ever made the news before. Now twice in a week. The community must be reeling."

Karen had poured him a glass of wine. She passed it to him and he took a gulp. "The media circus is already pitching its tents."

"And Lizzie's murder case? Another dead end?"

"Well, I wouldn't say anything's quite a dead end yet. More

like bloody hard going."

* * *

Similar thoughts were going through Archer's mind as she drew up on her driveway. Three cases, resources stretched as tight as piano wire, and no real leads.

She'd spoken to the two lads, Sam and Ollie. Ollie Field seemed to have a pretty solid alibi for last night: at home doing homework, unless his parents were covering for him. Which, she recognised, wasn't beyond the realms of possibility, but her gut told her no.

Sam Yardley, she felt less confident about. Becky Day's parents might consider him a nice boy, but that wasn't quite the impression she had got of him. He smirked throughout the interview, as if everything was a huge joke. His gaze kept switching between her breasts and the side of Archer's mouth the result of a broken bottle shoved in her face, which had scarred her for life and severed a nerve.

He was pretty vague about his movements last night.

"Y'know." He grinned. "I went to Friars Square after school." A shopping centre in Aylesbury town centre. "I just, y'know, hung out for a bit before I went home. Looked round a few shops."

"On your own?"

"Yeah. Me mates are slow with their homework. I don't need so much time, if I can get home, have me tea and get started." He looked at his watch, making a point. Archer thought it was probably just bravado, or cockiness, but she wasn't getting much from him.

"It's true," his mother said. "He's a fast worker. Gets good marks, too."

"Did you see anyone you knew there?" she probed again.

"No."

"What shops did you go in?"

"Dunno. I might have looked in Waterstones."

"You're a bookworm?" She didn't quite hide her surprise.

"Graphic novels."

"Oh, right. Buy anything?"

"No."

"Where else?"

"Phone shops, I s'pose."

"You suppose?" Archer snapped. "It was only last night."

"Look, I was just chilling, yeah?"

"So will anyone at all remember seeing you?"

"Dunno. Honestly," he added.

"You didn't happen to see Jade Sheldon? Meet her, maybe?"

He sneered. "Is that a joke? A kid like that?"

Archer was pretty sure he was hiding something, but whether it was from her or his parents, she wasn't certain. She certainly didn't have enough to justify hauling him down to the station, as much as she might have liked to. All the same, the last thing she'd done this evening before releasing the team had been to ask them to look for Sam Yardley on CCTV images from Friars Square. If the lad had been there, he should have been picked up on CCTV. She needed to tick that box.

She hated feeling powerless, feeling as though the investigation was going nowhere.

As she let herself in, she realised that her phone had been switched to silent since the first briefing about Jade, and she hadn't checked it lately. She did so now, noticing that she had three missed calls and a similar number of messages. But before she could check them out, her doorbell rang.

It was after midnight. She opened the door a crack, the chain on, not altogether happy with an unannounced caller so late at night.

It was Dominic. He looked terrible, his face pale, his hands thrust in the pockets of his fleece. She'd never seen him like it.

"Dominic? Whatever's the matter?"

"Can I come in?"

"Of course." She slipped the chain off and opened the door.

He stepped in and stood in the little hallway, shoulders slumped.

"It's Monty," he said. "He's dead."

"Oh, shit." She knew how much the slightly haughty tabby meant to him. She had a soft spot for him herself. "How?"

"He must have been hit by a car, and then he crawled into a hedge to die. It happened last night, I think, but no one found him until the postman spotted him this morning. He contacted me from the details on his collar."

"I'm so sorry, Dominic."

"I thought you might like to know. I tried to catch you earlier, but you were no sooner home than..." He shrugged. Tears were rolling down his cheeks. He looked utterly wretched.

Without thinking about it, she closed the distance between them and put her arms around him. He hugged her back for a moment, and then his mouth found hers. Startled, she placed her hands firmly but gently on his chest and stepped backwards.

"No," she said, feeling real regret. "I'm sorry. Not like this."

He looked mortified. "No, *I'm* sorry. I didn't mean to. It's just..." The corners of his mouth turned even further down. "I should go."

"Don't be daft. Stay. Have a beer, and we can drink to Monty."

"Even after—"

"Don't be daft," she said again. "I'm not about to be angry about a nice guy trying to kiss me. I just don't want something to happen simply because you're upset." Her eyes searched his face. "Is that okay?"

He flashed the nearest thing to a smile since his arrival. "I'm okay if you are."

"Then we're fine. Beer?"

"It's late. I should go."

She was determined he didn't leave with any awkwardness hanging in the air. "No, you shouldn't. Go on," she urged. "Stay a while. Have a beer. I think we could both do with the company."

He gave another half-smile, and then shrugged. "Why not?"

13

Wednesday morning

It had been well after 1am when Dominic had left Archer's. Any lingering awkwardness over his kiss had soon passed, and they'd spent the time talking – mostly Dominic talking about Monty – drinking beer, and eating cheese and crackers. By the time he'd gone home, Archer barely had the energy to undress for bed, but she somehow managed it.

She'd awoken with a slightly sore head and the sense of having had some pretty X-certificate dreams. They could have been about her neighbour. She thought they might have had more to do with eating cheese late at night. Whatever the cause, whatever the dreams had been about, they'd faded like smoke when she woke. She was sorry.

By contrast, today was going to be a nightmare, she could feel it in her bones. She'd be under pressure to make headway with Carly Eustace's death, but she knew there would also be pressure to release resources to help with the search for Jade Sheldon. It wasn't unreasonable. The bottom line was that Carly was dead, whereas Jade might still be found alive. It didn't make it any easier, though.

As she came off the A41 and headed into Aylesbury, trying not to let the morning traffic get to her, she wondered how Dominic was coping. Once, she had to admit, she'd have seen the death of a pet a little differently. There had been no cats or dogs in her childhood, apart from her brother's gerbil, which he'd allowed to escape when he opened the cage in the garden. It had never been seen again. Adam had been distraught for a day, but had then been consoled by a trip to the cinema and a new toy. Lizzie hadn't been that bothered. It hadn't been *her* gerbil.

Monty had been a bit different. She'd got to know him, as much as anyone really gets to know a cat, had found him an amusing and – yes – lovable character. She was going to miss him, and she could imagine how much more her neighbour would miss him. She thought he'd be lonely without Monty's company.

Two lonely people, a wall apart. But she knew she'd been right to keep him off-limits. Still, she couldn't help wondering what that attempted snog had been about. A desperate quest for a bit of comfort from someone who just happened to be there? Or an expression of feelings he had for her that he'd kept in check?

She smiled to herself as she turned into the car park. If it was the latter, she didn't mind. It was nice to think someone fancied her.

Will Tyler was beside her desk before she'd even got her coat off.

"I've got the CCTV footage from the shopping centre sorted, guv. Managed to get an out-of-hours number for their security guys and they promised to get someone on it at eight o'clock latest. So hopefully we'll have something soon."

She smiled, impressed by his eagerness and resourcefulness. "That's great, Will. Does DI Ashby know?"

"He's not in yet." Not a complete personality transplant, then.

"Well, make sure you update him when he is. Jade Sheldon's his case."

"Okay. But he did ring in to say he and DS Petrescu were going to Jade's school to talk to staff and pupils."

Archer felt a flare of irritation. "Did he now? Well, thanks for letting me know."

She stalked down the corridor to Gillingham's office. Counted to ten. Then counted from eleven to twenty, just to make sure she was under control. Then she knocked twice, let herself in without waiting for an answer, and closed the door smartly behind her.

Gillingham looked up from his desk, blinked, and gave her a lukewarm smile.

"Morning, Lizzie."

"Did you know Steve Ashby has whisked Amy Petrescu away to Jade Sheldon's school this morning?"

"Of course." He stared at his desk. "He called me about twenty minutes ago."

She sat down hard in one of his visitor chairs. "Well, that's just fantastic news, Paul. I thought we were keeping her on here precisely to give *me* help with my murder case."

He sighed heavily. "Yes, but that was before I had a missing girl. What am I supposed to do? Tell the parents – and the Chief Constable – and the bloody media – that we're a bit short-handed around here? That we'll get around to finding her once we've solved a few other cases?"

"Of course not."

"Of course not," he echoed. "I'm sorry, Lizzie, but we've already got all the extra pairs of hands I can rustle up for now. We're going to have to manage. We've got that guy Tyler on co-ord. You've got Joan Collins, who's bloody good. Get civvies and uniforms to support you..."

"They're all at full stretch on the search for Jade already."

He slammed his palms down on the desk, causing his fancy pen stand-cum-calendar to jump. "So what do you want me to do?"

The worst of it was, she knew he was right. It might have got under her skin that Ashby had simply taken Petrescu, a member of *her* team, and no one had thought to check with her first. And surely it was no coincidence that he'd chosen to take the attractive new woman on the team. But she had to face the fact that the missing girl was the number one priority. And she knew she would have been even more miffed if Ashby had taken one of her regular team members.

She looked at Gillingham, stress etched into every crag of his face, and reached for calm again.

"Fair enough, Paul. I guess we need to make the best of a bad situation."

"We do. We leave no stone unturned to find Jade. Meanwhile, you and Dan are on the murder and the hit-and-run. Any new leads on either?"

"Bugger all. We're spinning our wheels, anyway. We need a break, boss. Unless and until we get it…"

"I hate this job sometimes," Gillingham remarked gloomily.

Tyler waved at Archer as she plodded back into the main office. She made a detour to his desk.

"Guv, I've got some clips that might be your Sam Yardley in Friars Square."

"Any help?"

"Well, he's the only lad in what looks like the right uniform." He opened a CCTV clip on his computer. "Does that look like him?"

Archer bent over for a better look. "Yes, it does. Fast work, Sam. Can we see if he meets someone?"

A smile played around his lips. "Oh, yes. It's not Jade, but I think I know why you thought he was evasive."

"So show me."

Tyler opened another clip. Waterstones bookshop. The school-uniformed figure, again recognisable as Sam Yardley, came into view and then hung around, his back to the store.

"Who's he waiting for?" Archer demanded, half irritated that Tyler was creating suspense.

"Well, let's see." He fast-forwarded. A lad of around Yardley's age, in a different uniform, entered the frame and walked up to the other boy. He punched him lightly on the shoulder, and then the pair exchanged a man-hug.

"So he was meeting a mate?" Archer was a little deflated, not that she'd got her hopes up too high.

"Watch."

They didn't break the embrace. Archer watched as Yardley took a furtive look around, and then the two boys kissed briefly. They broke away and entered the store, perhaps walking a little closer together than was strictly necessary.

"Well, I'm damned," she said. She sighed. "I'd guess Sam's not ready to come out yet."

"I'd say so. Sorry, guv. I think it's a dead end. Unless Jade saw them and they wanted to silence her. But there's no sign of Jade on the footage."

"I'm not surprised. If she got off the bus to meet someone, it can't have been Sam, can it? All right." Her shoulders slumped. "At least we know."

* * *

Baines, however, had something to work with. Just before the news had broken about Jade's disappearance, Will Tyler had compiled a list of people with form for car theft in the area. He'd taken it home and, armed with a map and what details there were about their crimes, colour-coded the list – as unlikely, worth looking at, and definite possibles. He'd also called in some favours back at Oxford and had colleagues there double-checking on other white Focuses registered within twenty-five miles of Houghton.

Baines thought the latter exercise was going to prove quite an undertaking, and probably fruitless, but you never knew – something could fall out that would be the opening he was looking for.

Meanwhile, he and Bell had two individuals with form for car theft to follow up. Robert Verney lived in Leighton Buzzard, Bedfordshire – not far from Winslow, where Mark Briscoe had last seen his car – and had taken vehicles at least three times. At least, that was the number of times he'd been caught.

Baines had called an old mate in Bedfordshire Police to smooth the way, and they managed to catch Verney as he was leaving for work. He claimed to have spent Thursday evening at the cinema in Milton Keynes with his girlfriend. He made a lot of fuss about police harassment, pointed to a rusting heap outside his door which, he claimed, would make it unnecessary for him to "go round stealing cars", and insisted his girlfriend would back him up. His mother was similarly vociferous about the police "hounding him for mistakes he made when he was just a kid".

The other name on the list was Marlon Frost, a resident of Wingrave who, coincidentally, used to live in Houghton. He'd only been convicted of one count of car theft, when he was fifteen, and he hadn't been the driver. According to the reports, he was a decent enough kid who'd got into the wrong company on the evening in question and foolishly bowed to peer pressure. He'd been in no trouble since, and declared himself eager to help. He vaguely knew of the Richards family.

Baines found himself wondering if the guy was sounding a little *too* co-operative. But finding out would have to wait. A call came in from the station as they drove into Aylesbury, demanding they return to base immediately.

Another girl from Houghton had gone missing.

14

The atmosphere in the office bordered on pandemonium. Gillingham had decreed that absolutely everything be dropped for an 'all hands on deck' meeting. The details Collins had were sketchy, but they were enough to send a shudder of alarm through Archer. By 10am, everyone was crammed into the briefing room, with Gillingham and Ashby standing at the front.

There was a new picture on the whiteboard behind them.

"Becky Day," Gillingham said. "Twelve years old, from Houghton. Same village as Jade Sheldon, goes to the same school in Aylesbury. Set out for school this morning and never arrived. As you know, she was the last person to speak to Jade before she disappeared last night. She was also with Jade and Leanne Richards on Thursday night, coming out of the local youth club just before Leanne was knocked down and killed."

"Amy and I were at the school when it all kicked off," said Ashby. "Becky wasn't there when the register was called, so the school checked with her parents, as they hadn't rung in saying she was absent."

Gillingham looked as agitated as Archer had seen him. He let his gaze roam the room. "So what the fuck is going on? These three things – Leanne's death, Jade and Becky disappearing – these can't all be coincidences. Can they?"

"One of our theories was that the driver who killed Leanne was scared Jade might identify him, sir," Collins pointed out. "Maybe he's silencing all potential witnesses."

Gillingham nodded gloomily. "Maybe we should have warned the Days. It's going to look bad."

"Hang on, though," Archer said. "I can see that maybe with Jade – just maybe – the hit-and-run driver thought she was a threat. She was on TV. Perhaps that was a mistake on our part. But we've never said publicly that Becky was a witness. And she was never on TV."

"What if it was a local?" Bell suggested. "For whatever reason, they didn't recognise *him*, but he happened to recognise *them*. The TV item's irrelevant. At first, he expects the knock at his door but, even when it never comes, he worries away, decides just maybe their memories will be jogged, and makes a pre-emptive strike."

"It makes a crazy sort of sense," Collins added. "A local guy, steals a car from Wingrave to get home to Houghton, knocks a girl down, knows of two girls who could identify him..."

Baines spoke up. "Trouble is, where's that car now? If it *is* the one stolen from Mark Briscoe, it's either vanished into the ether or driving around with false plates. If it's not even that car, we could be looking at any white Focus."

"We're checking them out," Tyler pointed out.

"But it all takes time," said Gillingham, his face grim. "Time we might not have. Where are these girls? Are they still alive?"

Archer glanced at Baines, knowing it was a question that had always haunted him about his own son. If Jack was alive, was that necessarily a good thing? Or had he spent all these years in some living hell of captivity and torture?

There had been other cases, of course, of people disappearing without a trace. One of the victims of Ian Brady and Myra Hindley, the so-called Moors Murderers, remained undiscovered despite repeated searches; the remains of London estate agent Suzy Lamplugh had never been found, and nor had the body of Jessica Winter, a victim of West London's 'Angel' killers, Kieran Bardsley and Eddie Maxwell. There must be dozens, if not hundreds, of others that hadn't been so high profile.

Archer stole another glance at Baines. If these disappearances were striking a chord with him, he showed no sign. She remembered he had an appointment with his counsellor later today.

"Just a thought," piped up Petrescu, jerking Archer's attention back to the matters in hand. "We're thinking this might be to do with Jade being on TV, and saying Becky wasn't. But what if she was? There was a bit of footage of the school broadcast, and who knows who else might have been in shot?"

"Good point, Amy," Gillingham said, and Archer found herself agreeing. "Get someone to check our recording of the broadcast. See if Becky pops up. Best see if any other girls are in the picture, too."

"Do we know *where* she disappeared?" Petrescu asked.

"Well, she should have caught the school bus. Again, just like Jade normally did. But she never made it. So between her house and the bus stop, presumably."

"So she was snatched from the village? *If* she was snatched," Petrescu added. "Just keeping an open mind."

"Quite right, Amy, although I can't fathom why she'd bunk off school of her own accord."

"It doesn't sound like the girl Jason and I have met," Baines commented.

"One thing we do know," said Gillingham. "There's a footpath near Becky's home. It runs between fields and comes out just a short walk from the bus stop. Apparently it's not that well used, and where it emerges is quite secluded."

"Sounds exactly the place for a flasher – or worse – to hang out," Archer remarked. "No pun intended."

"Apparently she uses it. She's argued with her parents about it – her mum doesn't think it's safe – but it's quicker and she's always running late. Like most kids, she does everything last minute. Ironically she was even later this morning because her parents gave her a safety lecture because of Jade's disappearance."

He shoved his hands into his trouser pockets. "Here's what's going to happen. Dan, you keep leading on Leanne's hit-and-run, and Steve, you treat both these missing girls as connected for now. As you know, we've got uniforms out asking if anyone saw anything. Will, you're co-ordinating. Keep an eye out for anything that reads across for both the girls."

"So we're not connecting Jade and Becky to Leanne's death?" Baines checked.

The DCI scowled. "Do let me finish, DS Baines. The answer's no – we're not treating them as connected yet. But we're going to keep an open mind for now. So every scrap of information you've got, or new information you pick up, you make sure Jason shares it with Will. And vice versa."

"And Carly Eustace?" Archer threw in. "Where's she in our priorities?"

"We still don't know how or why she's dead, so that's still your number one, Lizzie. We can't rule out some sort of sexual predator. If that's what we're dealing with, we need to catch him, before he gets the itch again."

Archer nodded.

"Right, then." Gillingham rubbed his eyes. "There's already been media interest in Houghton. Expect that to ramp up when this gets out. We've seen it before. People with microphones and cameras all over the shop, getting in our way and stirring up panic and paranoia."

"I doubt they'll need much stirring," Archer commented.

"True enough. But calls are already coming in from the media asking if we're connecting all three girls. Even asking if we think Leanne was deliberately run down."

"Do we?" Baines ventured. He thought it highly unlikely, but the question needed asking.

"He'd have had to know her movements," said Ashby. "Wait for her to leave youth club and know exactly when she'd cross the road. I guess we can't rule it out, but…"

"Besides," Archer added, "why run Leanne down but abduct the other two? It doesn't add up."

"Nothing does," Gillingham said gloomily. "Anything else?" There was a general shaking of heads. "Then let's get on with it."

People got up. Archer was about to catch up with Collins when she felt a hand on her elbow.

"Can I have a quick word, Lizzie?" Baines asked.

"Sure."

They waited until they had the room to themselves, then Baines closed the door.

"It's just that I've got a session with my counsellor scheduled for…" He glanced at his watch. "… just over an hour's time. But I was thinking, with all that's going on…"

"You're going," she said. "End of. You told me the sessions

were helping, didn't you?"

"They are. I'm a lot better."

"Good. So it's important you stick with it. Make sure Jason knows what to do while you're away, but it's only a couple of hours."

"If you're sure…"

"I am."

As they headed back to the office, she reflected on just how far their relationship had come. Not so very long ago, he'd have taken her concern as a hint that he wasn't up to his job and got defensive. Not so long ago, he might even have been right to take it that way.

"How are *you*, by the way?" he asked.

She shrugged. "I've been better. I had a bit of bad news last night. Dominic's cat's been killed."

"Killed?"

She told him how Monty had been run over, how cut up Dominic was, and how she'd been surprised how much it had upset her too.

"I wouldn't have put myself down as a cat person, especially," she admitted, "although I did toy with getting one a year or so ago. You know," she picked at non-existent fluff on her jacket, "for company. But when Monty came on the scene, he often turned up in my garden, or on my drive, and I didn't want any moggie turf wars. He was quite a character. I'll miss him, and poor Dominic's devastated."

"It's a bastard," he agreed. "I don't suppose you know who killed him."

"No. And I don't plan on adding Monty to your hit-and-run caseload."

"Probably just as well."

* * *

It was like being in a steel coffin. The ties securing the girl's wrists and ankles impeded her ability to move in what little space there was, and she was terrified that, at any moment, the air would run out.

Terrified she might die even before that happened.

She wanted to scream behind the tape covering her mouth, but she thought that might just use up her air supply sooner. She wanted to weep and howl, but she was trying desperately not to give in to that. If she cried, her nose would probably get snotty. Blocked, even. And, with her mouth already sealed, she couldn't afford a blocked nose.

She wanted her mum. She wanted her dad. So badly. Just to be held by them and tell them she was sorry, so sorry, for the one stupid mistake that had led to this.

It was so hot. Was the air already getting stale? She thought it was. How long since she'd had a drink? She had no sense of time. It could be day or night. She had no idea how long she'd been here.

One thing she knew. The person who'd put her here hadn't returned. She didn't think they were coming back for her.

She might as well be buried alive.

* * *

Baines sat in Dr Tracey Walsh's unthreatening office. They were, as usual, in matching easy chairs in a corner with a coffee table in front of them. The table did not present a barrier, but provided somewhere to set down their glasses of water, and to accommodate the obligatory box of tissues.

Walsh was oval-faced with shortish hair and a fringe, her clothes casual but business-like. Baines had liked her from their first meeting, and was convinced that she was genuinely pleasant and empathetic; that it wasn't just part of her professional act.

"So," she said, "how have you been?" It was her usual first question.

"Good," he said. "I've been good."

"Any mood swings?"

"Not really. No more than normal ups and downs, I'd say." He thought about it. "Well, I got a bit anxious a couple of days ago."

"Do you want to tell me about it?"

So he told her about Amy Petrescu's arrival on the team: first his concern that she might have tried to instigate something between them, then his anger when he thought Ashby had plied her with drink to get her into bed, and finally his weird conversation with the DI, who'd confessed to having feelings for Amy that didn't sound like mere lust.

"And how do you feel now?" Walsh sipped her water.

"Okay, I guess. I mean, not jealous or anything like that." Was that entirely true? "I like Amy, but I've no interest in being unfaithful to Karen with her, if you know what I mean."

"So does that mean you'd be interested in her if it wasn't for Karen?"

He examined the question. "We're sort of friends, and I don't want anyone hurting her." It sounded evasive, even to his own ears. "But, for some reason, I think I trust Ashby not to. Mind you," he said with a smile, "I might paper the wall with him if he proves me wrong."

She nodded, but whether she was satisfied with his answers, he could never tell.

"And what about Jack? Any dreams? Visions?"

"No. And you'd think I might. Right now we've got one twelve-year-old who was killed in a hit-and-run and two more who've gone missing. A year ago, before I started seeing you, that would have been enough to trigger something. So you must be doing something right."

"That's down to you," she told him. "Not me."

Not for the first time, he realised how completely this woman had gained his trust. He was relaxed with her and felt he could tell her just about anything. Yet at the same time, he also knew he was still capable of holding things back from her.

"I mean, I still care," he said. "Those sort of cases just don't wind me up like they did. Now I can take a step back and see it as part of the job."

She nodded again and made a note. "And how do you feel about not having any more visions? Not seeing Jack any more?"

He reached for his glass, took a sip, took a swallow, took another. "Sad," he said. "It makes me feel sad. Don't get me wrong. I know it wasn't healthy. And I couldn't carry on like that. I was losing control. But, crazy though they were, those visions felt like I still had a connection with him." He swallowed. "They gave me hope." He tapped his chest. "In here. That he was still alive."

"So what do you think now, Dan? Do you still think Jack might be alive?"

"Honestly?" He sighed. "I know I ought to be saying no. All logic says he can't be. But I can't let him go, not like that. Not when I don't know for sure. Does that mean I'm still nuts?"

She laughed. "I don't think you were ever *nuts*, Dan. We've talked about this before. All I can do is help you look at what's happening and get it into some sort of perspective. So do you think the visions were in any way real now?"

"No," he told her. "How could they be?"

After their session, Walsh said, "I think you're really making progress. How would you feel about leaving our next appointment for, say, three months?"

He hadn't expected that. The sessions had become such a part of his life that he felt a twinge of anxiety at the prospect of having them less regularly. "Do you think I'm ready?"

"I think we should try it. We can always increase the frequency again if need be."

He left with an appointment for the week before Christmas. The sessions really had helped, he knew, and he really did trust Tracey Walsh.

So why was he keeping the new dreams back from her? He supposed, since he never remembered anything of them, that there was little to tell.

Except he knew that wasn't it. Something he didn't understand was holding him back. And, deep down inside, he knew that should worry him.

15

Josh and Emma Day sat at either end of the sofa in silence. The TV was on, but neither of them was watching it. The two police detectives had left an hour ago. Going through their stories over and again had left them wrung out.

"I still reckon they think we've done something to her," Josh said, not looking at his wife. "They think *I've* done something to her."

"And I still say we don't know that."

"No? Wake up, Em. It's so often the parents. The father. That Inspector Ashby—"

"Detective Inspector."

"Whatever. I don't like him. I don't know. There's something about him. Did you see the way he kept looking at that woman sergeant? I think he's more interested in her than in finding Becky."

"I don't suppose so." Josh was irritating her as only he could. She loved him fiercely, completely, but there was a whiney side to him that could grate on her. She'd always been the strong one. Now, when she could do with a bit of strength back, he was being weak and whiney.

"Something bad's happened," he persisted, "and they don't see the need to look for her, because Ashby's already made up his mind that the answer's right here."

A desperate anger surged through her. She wanted to fall apart but, as usual, she had to do the thinking for both of them. "You're giving up on her, just like that?" He opened his mouth, but she cut him off. "Of course they're having a good hard look at all the possibilities. But they must be thinking that whoever took Jade has Becky too. That's not going to be you, is it?"

"Maybe." He didn't look convinced. "Did you see his face when we mentioned that row we had with her?"

"It wasn't a row. It was an argument. You were worried after Jade disappearing. She didn't want us being over-protective and treating her like a child. And we thought she was right. We were actually proud of her."

His face softened then. "Yeah." His voice was husky with emotion. Then it dropped to just above a whisper. "We didn't tell them all the truth, though, did we? About, you know…"

She looked at him, mixed emotions on her face. "They don't need to know. It's got nothing to do with this."

"We can't be sure."

"How could it have?"

"Maybe. I don't know."

"Look," she said, "this isn't the right time to have all that come out. It won't do Becky any good, and it won't bring her back any quicker."

"I suppose. If she comes back. Oh, Christ." He shook his head, tears spilling. "Something bad's happened. Someone could be hurting her right now."

"Stop it."

His lower lip quivered. "Where is she, Em? Where's our girl?"

She slid along the sofa and took his hands in hers. "I don't know, love. But we've got to think positive thoughts for her. And pray."

"Pray?" He spat the word out. "You know I don't believe in that stuff."

She raised his hands to her lips and kissed one, then the other. "Maybe it's time you tried."

* * *

Joan Collins, one of nature's great multitaskers, had volunteered to help review the footage of Friday night's broadcast about the Leanne Richards hit-and-run, while making phone calls. As the short broadcast ran, she spoke on the phone to DC Annabel Harding, who worked in the lead team in head office with responsibility for the sex offenders register.

Collins was to partner Archer on the murder enquiry for the

time being, and she knew she should be pleased and excited that, for once, she wasn't just stuck in the office while others got out interviewing and following up on leads. She was ambitious, and knew that being a great backroom girl ran the risk of remaining there and not advancing in her career. But, she had to admit, she revelled in being at the heart of things, and slightly envied Will Tyler the role.

"Thanks, Annabel," she said to Harding. "If you wouldn't mind doing some checking and getting back to me, I'd be really grateful."

She put the phone down, satisfied that red flags recently raised about any known sex offenders in Thames Valley would be checked out. She needed to make similar calls to neighbouring forces, but first she wanted to examine something on her monitor that had caught her eye.

She reversed the broadcast, Jade Sheldon standing in the foreground, lips moving, making eye contact with the camera, her hand regularly sneaking up to fiddle with her hair. All the comments about her self-awareness and her grabbing at a schoolmate's death as an opportunity for five minutes of fame and limelight were, for Collins, borne out by those gestures. But that wasn't what she wanted to see again.

There! On the right-hand side of the frame, moving quickly into the picture, pausing, then moving out again, backwards and more slowly. She stopped the recording and played it forward at normal speed. A girl about Jade's age strayed into shot, stopped, looked straight at the camera, then hastily backed away.

Collins ran it one more time, freezing the frame where the girl was looking full-on at the camera. She captured the image, opened it in another program, and enlarged it.

There was no doubt. Becky Day, as well as Jade Sheldon, had appeared on the BBC Oxford news on Friday night.

* * *

Archer felt as though she'd wasted her morning. Forty-eight hours into the Carly Eustace murder case, they still had no evidence, no leads, no witnesses. With the two missing girls the team's main priority, Collins was pitching in to help with that, diluting Archer's support still further, even if she had made a useful spot on the footage from the BBC broadcast.

Normally a major incident would involve a large team of detectives, uniformed officers and civilian specialists. But Aylesbury Vale had never been so stretched. The worry was that, if Carly had been killed by a stranger who might kill again, then the clock wasn't only ticking for two schoolgirls. It was ticking for the killer's next victim, too.

She wondered if Ashby and Petrescu were making any better headway. Despite care being taken not to confirm that Jade and Becky were being treated as possibly linked, the social media world had already decided they were. The hashtag #findJadeandBecky was trending on Twitter, and was a mixed blessing. It meant that people were aware of the missing girls and keeping their eyes open. It also meant that a number of sightings were being reported. All had to be checked out. Most, if not all, would prove to be garbage.

Garbage. Joan Collins had been going to find out when Chris Pateman's bins were collected, so that they could check his rubbish for Carly's clothes and jewellery. There was always the possibility that the killer had kept the rings and earrings, but Collins thought it unlikely that the killer would keep her clothes. He might keep the underwear, possibly, if that appealed to him.

She asked Collins where they were with that line of enquiry, and a look of horror crossed her face.

"Oh, shit, guv, I'm so sorry. With all the panic over Becky, I haven't checked my list today. I'll do it now." The corners of her mouth turned down. "Shit, shit, shit."

Archer's irritation was minor compared to how sorry she felt for her colleague.

"Don't beat yourself up, Joan. It was you who spotted Becky on that broadcast, and we all drop a ball sometimes. Just pick it up again. It's not as if Pateman's that much of a suspect. We're just ticking a box. Still, if his bins haven't been collected yet…"

"… it would be easier than sifting through an entire recycling centre," Collins finished for her. "Okay. I'm a bit stymied on these sex offenders until Annabel Harding gets back to me, so I'll check the council website now."

"As I say, it's probably nothing, but let's get it done."

Instead of returning to her desk, Archer walked out of the office and headed for the briefing room. She stood in front of Carly's board, saddened once again that the woman in the photograph would smile no more.

She had a bad feeling about this. Unless they got a lucky break, Carly's file would eventually become just another cold case. Despite the rise of DNA analysis and other forensic advances, there were about 1,600 unsolved murders across the UK. She hated them –investigations scaled down, cases not officially closed, but not exactly live, either.

That was why they did the grunt work, ticked all the boxes. Because, somewhere out there, the person who'd dumped Carly's body in Millett Wood was sweating and hoping they'd got away with it. If they'd slipped up, then sooner or later the police would check something that would catch their mistake, and the pieces would start to fall into place.

She held that thought as her gaze roamed the board one more time. Was the answer staring her right in the face?

* * *

Collins had conducted a quick check of the Aylesbury Vale District Council website and established that bin day was Friday – bad news if Pateman actually was the killer and had put Carly Eustace's effects in the bin on the Thursday night, perhaps after disposing of her body. If that was the case, some luckless uniforms would have to go and sift through the rubbish at the recycling centre, just on the off-chance.

But what if he hadn't put his bin out? He would have been tired, stressed, still in a state of panic. Just because he'd stripped the body before dumping it, it didn't follow that he'd have had the presence of mind to bin the clothes and other evidence there and then.

Of course, he might have burned everything that would burn, chucked it in a skip somewhere, maybe miles away, or weighted the lot and dumped it in the canal or a river. But there was only one way to find out.

Collins looked around the room. Only she, Will Tyler, and a couple of civilians were present. She should find Archer and tell her what she'd learned, but she was stung by her failure to check this out before. She prided herself on being on top of her work, and now she had messed up at the very time the DI had given her a bit more chance to shine.

She picked up her bag, grabbed her coat from the back of her chair, and sauntered over to Tyler's desk.

"Will," she said, "I just need to pop out and check something. If the guv comes looking for me, tell her I'm checking out Chris Pateman's bins. She'll understand."

Tyler jotted down a note. "Sounds glamorous."

"Oh, yeah. Next stop, the catwalk."

As Collins started her car, she felt a twinge of unease. She was the consummate team player, not the sort to go off solo on a hunch. But this was her chance to show some initiative and maybe make up for her earlier gaffe. Besides, it wasn't going to take long. She could be there and back in less than a quarter of an hour, and how long did it take to rummage through a bin?

16

Baines returned to the station to find that he and Tyler were the only members of the team in the office. The others were out pursuing leads or talking to other departments. Tyler said he wasn't sure where Archer was.

"So," he said to the DC, "how are you getting on?"

"Frustrating, Sarge. It's a bit like we're banging our heads against a brick wall, isn't it?"

He laughed without humour. "You're not wrong."

Tyler's own smile had vanished. "I like doing the co-ord, but I'll be glad when I'm up and about, feeling collars."

"Any idea how long that'll be?"

"I wish. The docs need to decide when I'm ready for physio, and that'll take a while. We're talking the best part of two months, I reckon, but who knows?"

Before Baines could respond, Joan Collins' desk phone began to ring. Baines moved to pick it up, but Tyler whizzed round to pick up on the fifth ring.

As he spoke to whoever was on the phone, Baines mulled over the conversation he had with Bell just before he'd left for his appointment with Tracey Walsh.

They'd been discussing whether the time had come to widen their search for the vehicle that had killed Leanne Richards. Bell had pointed out, not unreasonably, that the theft of Briscoe's car the night of Leanne's death wasn't such a remarkable coincidence.

"It might be the same make and model, but then we know it's a very common car. I wonder how many Fords are stolen up and down the country on any given day – and how many are involved in accidents."

Baines had accepted the point, but it had filled him with gloom, because it would mean there could potentially be dozens, if not hundreds, of candidate vehicles.

"That was Jade Sheldon's school," Tyler said as he replaced Collins' phone.

"Yes?"

"They said they didn't think it was important, but they thought we ought to know. Apparently one of the school secretaries got back from lunch yesterday just in time to see Jade coming out of their office."

He shrugged. "So? Kids probably go in there all the time."

"Not over lunch. Not when it's unoccupied and locked. Except they have this rubbish security arrangement that everyone knows about, where the key gets left on top of the doorframe. It seems there's a lip—"

Baines was feeling irritable. "Is there a point to this?"

Tyler blinked. "Maybe I should just pass it on to DI Ashby."

Baines ran his hands over his face. "Sorry, Will. Don't mind me. Why did they think it was worth telling us?"

"It seems Jade tried to make out the door had been unlocked and the key left on one of the desks. Gave them a cock-and-bull story about wanting to check a timetable, but the woman who caught her said she thought it was a bit suspicious."

Baines's interest perked up. "Why are they only telling us now?"

"The woman in question only works a couple of half days. This afternoon's the first time she's been in since Jade went missing."

"And do they have any idea what she was doing in there?"

"They think she was maybe using the phone."

"Instead of her mobile?" A light bulb flashed in Baines's head. What if she was up to something, making some arrangement for later, and she didn't want to use her own phone for some reason?

"Track down DI Ashby," he said. "If we can find out who she rang, at least someone in this bloody station might finally be getting somewhere."

While Tyler called Ashby, Baines called Archer to let her know there might be a development in the Jade Sheldon case. He also wanted to update her on his latest counselling session, but that could wait.

"I'm only in the briefing room," she said. "I'll come down."

She appeared moments later, and Baines told her about the call Jade might have made.

"Fingers crossed," she said. "We could do with a stroke of luck."

Tyler came off the phone. "DI Ashby and DS Petrescu are on their way to the school now. He'd like someone who knows about phones to meet them there. Any suggestions?"

"Send Ibrahim Iqbal," Archer said promptly. "He's not strictly a telephone expert, but what he doesn't know about technology probably isn't worth knowing."

She went to her desk, pulled out her chair, and then glanced around the room.

"Where's Joan?" she asked.

* * *

Collins knew the Elmhurst neighbourhood in north Aylesbury reasonably well – her aunt had lived there when she was growing up. It occupied the area to the north and south of Elmhurst Road, a section of the town's ring road, and she remembered family visits and being sent on errands to the small shopping area on Dunsham Lane.

She was in luck. Chris Pateman's house was an end-of-terrace with a three-foot-wide path down the side – and she could see his bins halfway along the path. There was no car in the drive, so she thought she was safe to assume that Pateman was still out at work and unlikely to return any time soon. The bins were readily accessible, and she would also be relatively unobserved in her rummaging.

She slid out of her car and strode down the path as if she owned the place, snapping on gloves on the way. Aylesbury Vale operated a three-bin system: green bins for general household waste; green bins with blue lids for all recyclable material; and a smaller food waste bin. The larger bins were collected on alternate weeks and the food waste weekly. She hoped Pateman was a responsible recycler, and that anything nasty would be stowed in the food bin. She tried not to think about used condoms.

She lifted the lid on the green bin first. General waste would be the obvious place for what she was looking for. Even a panicking killer would surely have more sense than to put items like clothing in with the recycling and have some tree-hugger in waste management investigate it too closely.

She groaned when she looked inside. The bin was almost full. No prizes for guessing what was due to be collected on Friday.

In her uniformed days, she'd had to do this sort of thing more often than she was willing to remember. What people put out in their rubbish, and in what form, never ceased to amaze her. Some people, if they used bin liners at all, evidently emptied them into the bin for reuse. Some couldn't be bothered to recycle, or didn't get the concept, and just bunged things in the bins willy-nilly.

And then there were the weird things. One of her old colleagues swore he'd once found an inflatable sex doll in a bin. Collins herself had found a remote control helicopter and, on another occasion, a signed framed photograph of the New Seekers, a band her mum had been keen on in the 1970s.

Pateman, on the other hand, seemed positively anal, compared to some. The contents of this bin were contained in white, tied-up bin liners. It appealed to her sense of the methodical. There was still a lot to go through, but at least it meant she could check each bag, re-tie it, place it on the path beside her, and then put everything back – assuming she found nothing of interest.

She was on the fourth bag, having found nothing more interesting than a broken pepper mill, when she spotted a flash of emerald green. Whatever it was promptly slid further down in the bag, but Carly's earrings immediately sprang to mind. Her heart pumping, she began to remove the contents of the bag.

"What the hell do you think you're doing?"

The male voice came from her right, and sounded angry. She turned towards it, the rubbish bag still in her hands, feeling like a child caught with her fingers in the biscuit barrel.

Chris Pateman wasn't so handsome when his face was red and twisted with anger, but it wasn't just his expression that alarmed her.

He gripped a baseball bat in his right hand. And he looked ready to use it.

17

Ashby's Audi swung into the school car park. He selected a space and babied his pride and joy into it.

He and Petrescu had been having a quick sandwich lunch at a small café not far from the station when Ashby's mobile rang. Two minutes later, lunch abandoned, they were back in his Audi, speeding towards the school that the two missing girls attended.

Petrescu stole glances at the man beside her as he drove just a little too fast through the town. Baines had been pretty damning in his assessment of Ashby, and she had thought Baines was a man whose opinions she could trust. But so far, the man who had been sharing her bed since he arrived had been nothing but attentive and affectionate towards her, and had seemed both good at and committed to his job.

And he had contacts. In the communities, on the fringes of the criminal fraternity. Not paid informants, but people who might have heard things of interest and might be willing to share. She wasn't sure what the deal was, and wasn't ready to ask, but the chameleon-like way he got alongside them and spoke their language was impressive.

It didn't matter that nothing had so far come of those enquiries. What mattered to Petrescu was that he knew the right people to ask, and that what they said had a ring of authenticity about it. She didn't think Steve Ashby was the bullshitter Dan Baines seemed to take him for, nor anything like as idle as he'd been painted.

Ibrahim Iqbal was waiting for them in the car park and waved at them as they got out. The three walked into reception, where the head teacher was hovering with a worried-looking grey-haired woman. The head practically pounced on them.

"I'm so sorry we didn't tell you about this before, but Sandy here…"

She indicated the other woman.

"I know, she hasn't been in," Ashby said with a shrug.

"Well, it can't be helped. At least we know now. Could you show us the phone?"

They were led into a room that was in dire need of redecoration. It was so untidy it looked as if it had been ransacked. The head pointed to a desk phone. "That one."

"Has anyone used it since Jade was in here?"

"Only Sandy. Each of the girls has their own phone."

"We'll have to take your fingerprints," Petrescu said to the grey-haired woman. "For elimination. But if Jade did use the phone, her prints will be on it."

"At least some partials," Ashby said. "But we can worry about that later. For now, we'll assume she *did* use it." He looked over at Sandy. "Exactly when did you find Jade in here?"

She frowned. "It was the end of the mid-morning break. Say around 10.45."

Ashby turned to Iqbal. "What do you reckon, Ibrahim? Can we find out who she rang?"

"Let's see." He took a pair of latex gloves out of his pocket and slipped them on. Then he picked up the phone and pressed a few buttons. Information appeared on the phone's display screen, and the techie grinned.

"Piece of cake."

* * *

"Damn," Archer said, after dialling Collins' number for the third time. "It just keeps going to voicemail."

"Probably just no signal where she is," Baines offered.

"Jesus Christ. This is the twenty-first century, and there are still flat spots in this hick town." She shook her head in frustration. "Someone had better get round to Pateman's gaff and make sure she's okay."

She pushed her fingers through her hair, not caring if she exposed her scar. "Where the fuck is everyone?"

Tyler opened his mouth.

"Never mind. It'll be you and me, Dan. Christ, Joan had his address. I think I can remember the street name, but not the house number."

She turned to Tyler, whose fingers were already flying over the keyboard. "Chris Pateman."

"Yeah, Joan gave me the details. Just a sec. Yeah, here it is." He reeled off the address.

"Right," Archer said, "you're in charge, Will. Don't even think about going anywhere." She was already heading for the door. "You're driving, Dan."

Not that she needed to tell him.

"Oh, hell," she moaned as they emerged into the car park. "I know what this is about." She told him about the DC's failure to check Pateman's bin collection day. "She thinks she stuffed up, and now she's trying to get back in my good books." They got in the car. "I mean, I didn't exactly tell her off about it. Am I such a monster?"

"Well…"

She punched his arm. "Just drive."

"I'm sure she's fine," he said as he drove out of the car park. "The guy's probably at work anyway."

"She shouldn't go off confronting murder suspects on her own." She could think of at least one case in her past where a similar set of circumstances hadn't ended too well.

"Calm down," he said. "As I say, Pateman's probably not even at home. And she's not confronting him. She's gone to sift through his bin."

"It's so unlike her. She should know better."

"We should have been giving her experience away from the office ages ago," he said. "If you want to blame anyone, blame me. I'm her line manager."

If he expected Archer to deny any fault on his part, she wasn't in the mood for it. But she thought she might as well change the subject.

"Counselling go all right?"

"Yes, thanks. She doesn't want to see me for three months now."

"That's great! Isn't it? Progress?"

"I suppose so. Feels a bit scary not having that monthly session, though."

"If you get withdrawal symptoms, you can always talk to me," she said, then laughed. "Although you might end up worse than you started."

He smiled. "I might just take that chance. Thanks, Lizzie. I'll bear it in mind."

They drove the rest of the way in silence. Archer knew Baines was probably right in his assessment: Collins would be fine. But she'd seen a colleague die in front of her only a couple of years ago when an arrest had gone horribly wrong. She'd give Collins a bollocking – once she knew she was safe.

"There's her car," Baines said as they cruised down Pateman's road, and he pulled in behind it.

She looked at the house, and up the path to the side, where the bins were clearly visible. "So where is she?"

"Maybe—" Baines began, but Archer was already out of the car and headed for the bins.

"Oh, Christ." She pointed to a mark near the top of one of them, her heart pounding. "Does that look like blood?"

"Could be." The tremor in his voice belied the impression of calm he was trying to present. "Should I call for backup?"

"For all we know, she's in his car boot, and he's taken her to dump her somewhere. His car isn't here." She moved to the door. "Sod backup."

"All right. Let me." He pounded on the door then bent down to yell through the letterbox. "Mr Pateman? Police! Open up, please."

"Kick it down," Archer said.

"Give him a chance."

Seconds later, the door opened. Chris Pateman saw Archer's face.

"Haven't our local cops got any real work to do? You'd better come in."

"Where's DC Collins?"

"In the kitchen."

"Is she all right? I saw blood…"

"I'm fine, guv," Collins said, appearing in a doorway at the end of the hall. She held up her right hand. There was a large sticking plaster across her palm. "I cut my hand on a piece of glass in Mr Pateman's bin. He kindly cleaned the wound and put a plaster on for me. He insisted on making me tea."

"Would you like one?" Pateman suggested.

But relief had already given way to anger. "No, thank you, Mr Pateman. I'm sorry you've been troubled. Come on, DC Collins."

"She hasn't finished her tea."

"Like you say, our local cops have things to do. We can't sit around drinking tea and wasting council taxpayers' money."

Pateman watched them walk back to the cars. Collins headed for her own vehicle.

"I'm coming with you, Joan," Archer said.

"See you back at base," Baines said. He gave Collins a sympathetic smile.

She and Collins got into Collins' VW. The DC inserted the key into the ignition.

"Drive round the corner and stop," Archer instructed.

She did as she was told. As she cut the ignition, Baines's Mondeo sped past them.

"Now," Archer said. "Suppose you tell me what on earth you thought you were doing?"

* * *

By the time Archer, Baines and Collins returned from Chris Pateman's home, Ashby had called and asked for an emergency team meeting. Bell was back from Houghton, where he'd been asking a few more fruitless questions, and had helped Will Tyler to round everyone up.

Archer was still a little angry with Collins for giving her a scare – and, if she was honest, with herself too, for overreacting. It was unlike her DC to act in such a cavalier manner, or ignore the protocols that were there for her own good, but she had to learn. Archer seriously doubted she'd do such a thing again, and no harm had been done.

Pateman had taken the afternoon off to take his car in for repair. His garage had given him a lift home and promised to pick him up again when it was ready. When he had seen her rummaging in his bin, he'd been hostile because there had been a couple of burglaries in the neighbourhood recently. Once he knew what she was doing, he'd even offered to help. Collins had declined, mainly because she didn't want him contaminating any evidence she found.

The green thing that had flashed in one of the bags, just before he emerged from his front door, had turned out to be a mint wrapper, rather than one of Carly Eustace's earrings.

The broken glass was in the last bag she opened. He'd made her some tea and dressed the wound by the time Archer and Baines came on the scene.

Thoroughly chastened, she'd still been apologising as they walked from her car to the station entrance.

"Let's drop it for now, Joan," Archer said, pausing on the steps. "I'm more interested in what that escapade hasn't told us."

"What do you mean, guv?"

"Pateman sounds very co-operative. Too co-operative?"

Collins thought for a moment, then waggled her hand. "Actually, I suppose he was maybe a bit too smooth."

"Chances are, he's clean. But if he knew you'd find nothing incriminating in his bins, he could afford to be helpful, even look after you when you cut yourself. Don't be taken in by his pretty face or flattered by his attentions." She saw the other woman's eyes widen and grinned. "Just kidding."

"So he's not off the hook?"

"I don't think we should write him off as a suspect yet."

"I guess it's too late to have his house searched? I mean, if he ever had the stuff, he'd have got rid of it somewhere."

"And if not, he will now. But we've no evidence to justify a warrant. We might do a bit more digging on him, though."

"Come on, ladies," Ashby's voice said from behind them, making Archer jump. "No time to chat."

She swung round, a retort springing to her lips, but saw none of the usual smarm and sarcasm.

"Be right there," she said, as he and Petrescu swept past them.

Inside the briefing room, Archer could feel a palpable lift in the atmosphere. A couple of hours ago, the place had felt as flat as a squashed tomato. Now there was a buzz about the room. Word of a breakthrough had made a huge difference.

Ashby stood at the front of the room, waiting to start, as Archer and Collins found seats. He waited a few more moments, eyes on the door for any more stragglers, then began.

"Okay," he said. "So we had a call this afternoon from Jade Sheldon's school – the one Becky Day also attends. We found out that she sneaked into the secretaries' office yesterday and made a phone call. We know this because there was a call out recorded around the time she was caught there, and the secretaries were definitely away from their desks. We can only assume she had her reasons for not making the call from her own phone."

"So who did she call?" Gillingham pressed.

"She called a primary school, also in Aylesbury. According to school records, it's the one she attended before moving up to secondary school. Becky didn't go there, by the way. She went to Houghton Village School."

"Steve," Gillingham said from the back row, "I might die of old age before you come to the point. Who did she speak to?"

Ashby coloured, and Archer could have sworn he glanced Petrescu's way. He looked irritated, a flash of the more familiar Ashby. But he nodded, apologised stiffly, and continued.

"The secretary at *that* school remembered the call. She thought it sounded like a young woman, or a girl, and she wanted to speak to one of the teachers – a Mr Briscoe."

"*Mark* Briscoe?" The astonishment in Baines's voice was plain.

"Yes." Ashby looked a question at Baines.

"He's the owner of the car we've been looking for in connection with Leanne Richards' death. He's been claiming it was stolen, but it's vanished off the face of the earth."

"I knew the name rang a bell."

"Go on, Steve," Gillingham prompted.

"Yes, boss. Well, they fetched him, let him have some privacy when he took the call. He seemed agitated when he came out, but apparently he'd been on edge for a couple of days."

"So," Gillingham said, "whatever that call was about, it seems fair at least to speculate that Jade arranged to meet this Briscoe."

"Some romantic thing?" Bell suggested. "She wouldn't be the first kid to run off with a teacher. Maybe they kept in touch after she changed schools. Maybe it started off innocently…"

"Maybe," Baines said, "but my money's on a connection between Leanne's death and Jade's disappearance. Has to be."

"She saw him," Collins piped up. "He was driving, and Jade saw his face before he went round the corner and the accident happened. She saw him, recognised him from her old school."

"But why would she not just come forward?" Gillingham puzzled.

"Maybe Jason's romance notion isn't so wide of the mark," Baines offered. "Her sudden recollection of the wrong colour of car and two people in baseball caps, when Briscoe's car contained one person in a hoodie that night… What if she was covering for him? Putting us off the trail?"

"You think they actually had something going on?" Gillingham shook his head. "Then why wouldn't she just keep shtum? Why has she gone missing now? Why the phone call?"

"We can ask her all that if we find her alive," Ashby said.

"All right. It's a theory," the DCI acknowledged, "but what about Becky? She didn't know him, wouldn't have recognised him. Why take her too?"

"He knew there were two girls," Archer pointed out. "Maybe he was scared she'd be able to identify him or, in Becky's case, describe him."

"So he's got Jade." Baines latched on to her narrative, brainstorming with her the way they often did. "Either she went with him willingly or she said something stupid in that phone call and he took her. He decides he wants to take the other girl out of the picture for good measure, so he gets Jade – one way or another – to give up her name and address. Maybe her route to school, too."

"But why?" Bell wanted to know. "I mean, the hit-and-run must have been an accident. Why compound it by kidnapping two schoolgirls, much less killing them?"

"Fatal hit-and-run?" Petrescu said. "Six months in prison, most likely. The end of his career. Then there's the stigma. I can imagine him driving away in a panic after hitting Leanne and then everything spiralling out of control."

"These are all interesting points," Gillingham rumbled, "but Steve's right. Right now, our priority is to find out if this Briscoe character has the girls. Steve, do we know where he is now?"

"There's the thing," Ashby said. "He called in sick. He's not in school."

"Then let's get round to his house." Gillingham made a face. "Maybe we should round up a trained hostage negotiator, just in case."

"I'll see if Kim Frank's around, sir," Collins said. "She's done the training." Frank was a female DS on Lara Moseley's team.

"I'll get a warrant organised," Ashby said. "I have a tame JP we can get to quickly."

Archer found herself smiling. At Ashby. "Why am I not surprised?" she said.

18

She had been drifting in and out of sleep. Once she had awoken imagining herself to be in her own bed at home, only to remember she was in this coffin full of foul air, made worse by her own stink. That was when the final spark of hope had left her.

She'd spent a lot of time praying to a god she wasn't sure she believed in. Nothing eloquent; just increasingly incoherent mental pleadings to get her out of this, to help her, help her, please help her. She offered bargains that grew increasingly crazy. Things she'd never do again. Things she'd never done, but never would. Things she should have done and would start to do every single day, if only, please, please, if only He'd save her, make someone come and let her out.

And, when nothing happened, curses, rants, peppered with every swear word she knew, followed by contrition, vows not to do *that* again, and then more begging.

If God was there, He wasn't listening. Or, if He was listening, He wasn't saving her. Perhaps she'd just been too bad a person. Perhaps, when she died in here, she would go to hell.

Perhaps she was even there already.

Every muscle in her body seemed to ache. Her head hurt as though someone was sawing into it. Her stomach was cramped with hunger, and her raging thirst would have been unimaginable to her before this. She kept trying to stop herself from thinking about water and food, but her mind returned obsessively to images of a glass of water, an apple, chips.

She was feeling drowsy yet again. Maybe this would be the time she'd fall asleep. Maybe she wouldn't wake up. She should fight it.

But that was her last thought before sleep washed over her again, dragging her down into an inky pit of blackness.

* * *

Ashby had been true to his word. In less than half an hour, he had roused a magistrate who could sign a warrant to search Mark Briscoe's home.

Gillingham decided he would lead the raid himself. He, Ashby, Archer and Petrescu were in Ashby's Audi. Baines, the trained hostage negotiator Kim Frank, and two uniforms were in a squad car. Phil Gordon and a team of CSIs were in a van a little further down the street, ready to search the premises.

All wore stab vests. They had no idea how desperate Briscoe might be, or what they might be facing. He might give them no trouble. Or there could be an almost immediate threat to the girls' safety. Or he might try to fight his way out.

You never knew.

Baines doubted someone like Briscoe had a firearm – or, at least, he hoped so. His last brush with a gun had almost got him killed.

As the cars drew up opposite Briscoe's home, Baines's blood began to pump a little faster. He looked across at the semi, which he reckoned dated back to at least the 1920s. Solid. Far more capable of keeping secrets than some of the flimsier modern constructions.

They started getting out of the vehicles and Baines took in the quiet cul-de-sac. He'd been here before, of course, but then he'd only been looking for a car. Now he saw everything in a different light.

No one stirred. It was as good a place as any for dark deeds to go undetected. If their theory was right – and Baines feared it may be a little too neat – if it *was* right, then getting an abducted schoolgirl from the car to the house without being noticed could be relatively simple. Depending on how scared she was, how little she might resist, it was possible that any nosey neighbour might not even find her arrival at the house especially remarkable – or even memorable.

He glanced at Kim Frank, round-faced and bespectacled. "You ready for this?"

Her smile was warm. He'd always liked Frank, one of the most unflappable people he knew.

"Ready as I'll ever be," she said. "I don't get to practise these so-called skills that often." She frowned. "Actually, the last one was a domestic, and that didn't end so well." The smile returned. "Oh, well. Let's hope this works out better."

Baines was turning her words over in his mind, trying to find something reassuring in them, when Gillingham barked his name.

"This isn't a social club," the DCI told him. "Just because we're probably way too mob-handed for one man, we still need to be professional."

Baines mumbled an apology. Everyone had wanted in on this, and Gillingham had acquiesced rather than stand around arguing.

Gillingham turned to Ashby. "The missing girls are your show, Steve. You lead."

The DI simply nodded and jabbed a finger in the direction of one of the uniforms. "Hugh, nip round the back, just in case." The uniform nodded and jogged off down the street, disappearing down a little alleyway that led to the rear of the property.

"Right," Ashby said, apparently satisfied. "Let's do this."

He strode up to the door, leaning on the bell and rapping with his knuckles. "Police! Open up!"

He waited a short while, then turned to one of the waiting uniforms. "Put the door in."

The uniform in question had 'the Big Key' at the ready. The hand-held battering ram could smash in a door in no time. But Archer held up a forestalling hand.

"Christ, Steve, give the poor man a chance," she said mildly. "He's allegedly off sick. He could be in bed. Or on the toilet."

"Or killing those girls," retorted Ashby. "Or legging it." He glared at the hesitant uniform. "Put the bloody door in."

But as the words left his lips, the door swung inwards and a bemused-looking Mark Briscoe stood blinking at them, taking in the number of visitors and the stab vests they wore.

"Can I help you?"

Ashby moved towards him. "Police, Mr Briscoe. We've got a warrant to search your house."

"Search? Why?"

"In connection with the disappearance of Jade Sheldon and Becky Day, and the death of Leanne Richards."

Baines watched Briscoe's reaction closely. He hadn't seemed to be lying when he'd spoken about his stolen car, even if the story had felt – Baines was now certain – somehow wrong. Fishy. Maybe he was a good liar.

The teacher scratched his head. "I don't understand. I mean, what does any of that have to do with me?"

"It's not a matter for debate, Mr Briscoe," Ashby told him. "We'll search your house in your presence, if you're prepared to co-operate, and then you can accompany us to Aylesbury Police Station to answer some questions. Or we can do it the hard way and arrest you."

Briscoe's eyes widened. "Whoa, whoa, whoa! Arrest? Look, there's no need for that. I'll co-operate with your search, of course I will, and I'll answer your questions. But you're making a mistake."

"We'll see," Ashby said. "You need to wait with me in the car while these nice officers have a look around. Or, if you know where your car is, and where the girls are, now would be a good time to tell us."

"But," babbled Briscoe, "I don't get it. All I did was report my car stolen. Now you're trying to fit me up with half your caseload."

Ashby ignored his bleats and nodded to Phil Gordon. "Take the place apart. If the girls aren't here, look for any sign that they've been here." His gaze swivelled back to Briscoe. "I want your garage open."

"But... it's stuffed full of junk." He looked at Baines. "You know that. You followed me home and checked it for yourself."

"That was then," Baines said. "This is now."

"I'll get the key."

"No," Ashby said. "You stay put. Tell me where it is."

"On the ring with my car keys. On the kitchen work surface."

Ashby called through to the CSIs, who passed out the keys. Baines opened the up and over door and surveyed the jumble of cardboard boxes, garden tools, and general overspill from the house. Broken chairs were stacked up and thick with dust and cobwebs.

"It all looks the same as before," Baines admitted.

"There's a smell of bleach," he heard Phil Gordon say from inside the house. "Someone's been cleaning. And there's a locked door off the kitchen that might lead to a cellar."

The house was certainly old enough to have one. And a cellar would be a good place to hold a captive.

"It's just more junk," Briscoe said as Baines emerged from the garage.

For the first time since the door had opened, Gillingham spoke, bristling with irritation. "Sir, you don't seem to grasp the difference between us doing a search and you simply telling us there's nothing to find. Tell us where the key is, and tell us now, or I'll kick the door down myself."

"I haven't got those girls," the teacher protested.

"You had your chance," snapped Gillingham. "Where's this door, Phil?"

"Wait!" Briscoe said. "The key's in the top drawer in the kitchen, next to the cooker."

They waited while the crime scene manager went back inside. To Baines, the time seemed to pass slowly. Then Gordon re-emerged, a grim look on his face.

"What?" Gillingham prompted. "Have you found the girls?"

"Not yet. But he's got one of those chest freezers," Gordon said. "An old one. And it's padlocked shut."

19

Archer, Petrescu and Gillingham sat huddled around the monitor, watching Mark Briscoe's interview unfold. Ashby and Baines had been elected to question the suspect, and the most claustrophobic interview room in the station had been chosen for the process.

The CSIs would be processing Briscoe's house for some time to come, but that freezer had already yielded an interesting piece of evidence. Even over the video link, Archer could see the sheen of sweat on Briscoe's brow. It was as if he'd never quite expected to find himself in this situation, not even when he'd been cautioned. He kept wringing his hands, as if he was trying to squeeze moisture out of them. Or was he, like Lady Macbeth, washing away imaginary blood?

Names had been said for the record, and other formalities completed. Adina Walker, black, posh and uncompromising, was the duty solicitor, which was not the best of news. She'd look out for her client's rights like a hawk.

"Mark," Ashby said, "I want to start with your living-room carpet. Our crime scenes people tell me it's been cleaned recently. With bleach. Can you explain that?"

Briscoe blinked. "Oh, yes. I managed to spill a bottle of red wine."

"Bleach? Not carpet cleaner?"

"It was all I had to hand. Ruined the damn carpet. I had to buy a rug to cover it."

"You couldn't cover up the smell, though, could you?" Archer remarked.

Ashby leaned back in his chair. "And what if I told you they found traces of blood? But no wine?"

Without missing a beat, Briscoe said, "Oh, yes. The bottle

broke and I cut myself."

"So you completely eradicated the wine, but not the blood?"

He shrugged. "Must have."

"So they'll find your DNA? No one else's?"

"I suppose." On the monitor, Archer could see something crafty in Briscoe's look. Something squirmed inside her. "Unless the bleach has degraded any DNA, of course."

Ashby was nodding. His casual attitude hadn't changed. "That phrase rolled easily off your tongue, Mark. 'Degraded'. Very scientific. But DNA's harder to destroy than you might think."

It was time to throw some new information from Phil Gordon at the suspect. "There was a coffee table on top of that rug you used to hide the stain, and our CSIs found indentations in the carpet, right where you bleached it, suggesting that the table stood there previously."

Was that a flash of panic that passed across Briscoe's face?

"Admittedly," Ashby continued, "the table itself *appears* free of any blood evidence. That's obviously had a damn good clean too. But it's a funny thing, Mark. Blood will get into the nooks and crannies of furniture and is almost impossible to completely eradicate. If there's any blood to find, we'll find it."

Baines took over. "Let's move on to that freezer in your cellar," he said, "and what we found inside it. Some bondage gear, and some women's clothes, including a girl's school uniform."

"I told you. I had a girlfriend once who was into all that kinky stuff. Dressing up and a bit of mild S and M."

"Mild? Seriously?"

"It was all just a bit of a game for her."

"What, dressing as a schoolgirl?"

"She thought it would turn me on. It didn't."

"Of course not."

"It didn't."

Baines made a show of stroking his chin, then scratching his head, as if baffled.

"So why keep it? Why keep it in a freezer? Why padlock it?"

"Is this relevant, DI Ashby?" Adina Walker's cut-glass tones cut in. "I thought you brought my client in in connection with a traffic accident and the disappearance of two girls – not to ask about his sex life."

"I think it's a relevant line of questioning," Ashby said. "We're not in court now. Answer DS Baines's question, Mark."

The suspect stared at the table. "I don't know why I kept it. It was hers, not mine. Maybe I thought she'd want it back some time. I kept it there so my cleaner wouldn't stumble on it, and I kept it locked because the lid was dodgy. Back when the freezer worked and I kept food in it, I needed to keep the seal tight, and I guess it's become a habit."

"You have a cleaner?" Baines asked, and Archer felt a twist of doubt in her gut. Holding schoolgirls prisoner in a house that saw regular visits from a cleaning lady wasn't going to be easy.

"Not any more," Briscoe said. "I couldn't really afford her, so I knocked it on the head. Not literally," he added hastily.

Archer relaxed a little at the news.

"All right," Ashby said with a sigh. "For now. Let's move on from school uniforms to schoolgirls. We know Jade Sheldon phoned you at your school the day she disappeared."

"I had no such call."

"Do you deny you know Jade?"

"I…" He ran a hand through his hair, looking suddenly wary. "No. No, of course I don't deny it. I taught Jade. She was a pupil of mine before she moved on to secondary school."

"And she phoned you on Tuesday."

"No."

"DS Baines?"

Baines made a show of referring to his notes, running through the call from Jade's school to Briscoe's at the same time Jade was caught in the secretary's office; and Briscoe having been called to the phone at the same time.

"The call lasted three minutes and twelve seconds."

There was a long silence. Then, "Oh," Briscoe said. "*That* call?"

Baines's smile was thin. "Yes, *that* call. Slip your mind, did it?"

"Well, I didn't know who it was. I was told there was a call for me. A young woman. But when I came to the phone, she didn't say anything. I knew there was someone on the other end, but…" He held his hands out, palms turned upwards, and shrugged.

"You're saying it was a silent call?" Ashby said. "Why would Jade do that?"

"How would I even know it was Jade?"

"Even so," Ashby pressed, "why not speculate? Just to help us out."

"I…" Briscoe shrugged. "I always felt she might have had a bit of a little girl's crush on me. You know how it is. You have to be so careful…"

"So she's called you before?"

"Never."

"Yet more than a year after leaving your school, she suddenly calls you. A silent call? Again – why would she?"

"No idea."

"And why would you hang on for over three minutes?"

"Look, I didn't even know it was her."

"Oh, I think you did. I don't think she was silent at all. She'd seen you driving the car that mowed down Leanne Richards in Houghton, an incident we already suspect your Ford Focus was involved in. It's not hard to figure out why she called you, is it?"

"I told you," said Briscoe. "My car was stolen."

"No." Baines took over. "I think you were driving it the night Leanne died. I think you knocked her down, killed her, fled the scene. I think you've hidden the car somewhere and then you reported it missing to get yourself off the hook."

"No. It was stolen. I wasn't in Houghton. I didn't knock that girl over. You should be looking for whoever stole my car."

"Oh, you were in Houghton," Baines chipped in. "And Jade Sheldon, your former pupil, saw you. But for some reason, the silly girl decided to phone you instead of reporting you to the police."

"Maybe she *did* have a crush on you," said Ashby. "Maybe she couldn't bear to give you up, but she wanted you to know how loyal she'd been. So she rang you."

"And you saw her, not as a saviour, but as a threat," said Baines. "You did what you had to do. You abducted her. We think you probably killed her. The blood in the living room was hers. Or Becky Day's."

"No. This is all nonsense!"

"Or you have her hidden somewhere else. Either way, you made her tell you who was with her that night. And then you abducted Becky, too. Just to make sure your miserable hide was safe."

"No."

"The only thing we haven't figured out," Ashby added, "is why you didn't simply stop when you killed Leanne. Presumably it was an accident. Were you over the limit? Or something worse?"

From where she sat, Archer thought Briscoe would make a good poker player. Yes, he looked like a man under serious stress, which wasn't surprising. But she didn't think he looked like cracking, either.

All they had was the circumstantial evidence that Jade had almost certainly phoned him shortly before she disappeared. The CSIs were processing his hire car as well as his home for traces of either girl, but it would take time. Meanwhile, if the girls were still alive, they were alone. Possibly without access to water or food.

"I wasn't in Houghton," Briscoe was saying. "I don't know how many times I need to say it. I don't know any Becky Day. And, if that call was from Jade, I didn't know, because she didn't say anything."

"For three minutes?" Baines sounded sceptical, exaggeratedly so. "I still don't understand why you'd hold on so long."

Briscoe looked at the table. "I didn't know it was that long. I can't explain why I held on. Maybe I thought it was a dodgy line or something. I know I kept saying hello."

"Still…" Ashby's tone was almost conspiratorial, "all that stuff with school uniforms. And then you had a real schoolgirl so infatuated with you she'd keep quiet even when you ran down her friend."

"I don't like what you're insinuating."

"I'm insinuating nothing. Just laying out some facts."

"They're not facts."

"Where's your Focus?"

"It was stolen."

"Where did you go on Thursday night?"

"I told you. I was at home."

"Where's your car really?"

"Asked and answered," Adina Walker said. "Have you anything else for my client, beyond reaching a very long way to implicate him in every high-profile case on your books?"

"*We'll* decide when we're finished," Ashby snapped. He took a sip of water, then smiled. Insincerity was written all over his face. "That is, we're investigating some serious matters here, Ms Walker. You know we can hold your client for up to twenty-four hours without charge. If we suspect him of a serious offence, we can apply to extend that to thirty-six hours, or even ninety-six."

"Ninety-six?" squealed Briscoe. He looked panicked as he turned to his brief. "They can't do that! Can they?"

Since Archer had last seen the lawyer, she had taken to wearing a pair of designer glasses whose frames made her look even more severe. She took them off now, with slow deliberation, and placed them on the table in front of her.

"DI Ashby," she said sternly, "all I've heard so far is a lot of vague questions and innuendo, with no actual evidence to back it up. It seems to me you have three choices: ask some new questions; charge my client with something; or let him go." The glasses went back on. "As far as I can make out, all you have is a car that my client reported as stolen, which might or might not have been involved in an accident on Thursday evening. And a phone call he received at work that may or may not have been from a girl who is now missing."

The lawyer folded her arms.

The sense of frustration in the room was palpable. Everything Adina Walker had said was true. They had no solid case. Unless Phil Gordon and his team found something, anything, all the suspect had to do was brazen it out.

Archer thought that, if she were Ashby, she might decide that now was the time for a break. She wondered if, instead, he might lose his rag. She knew he had a low patience threshold.

There was a long silence in the interview room. Briscoe started to look twitchy. Walker looked as if she was itching to say something more. Ashby and Baines were still and silent. It reminded her of a Western she'd seen. Gunslingers before the shoot-out started.

Then Ashby flashed another obviously bogus smile. "Have you finished, Ms Walker? Good. Then we'll take it from the top."

20

They continued to question Briscoe until 11pm, with breaks for him to consult with his solicitor, and for food. In the meantime, uniforms had asked Jade's parents about who Jade had been friendly with in primary school, and all had been spoken to.

The story they all told was strikingly similar. Briscoe was remembered as a popular teacher – certainly, no one had particularly disliked him. But nobody had a standout memory of him doing anything inappropriate or disturbing, either with Jade or any other pupil.

"Surely she'd have said something to someone?" Archer had mused in one of the breaks. They were gathered in the briefing room. "If she had a crush on him, even if she wasn't especially worldly wise. Surely one of her friends at the time would have noticed, or she'd have confided in them."

"I don't know," Petrescu said. "He wouldn't be the first paedophile to persuade his victim that it was their little secret."

"And Jade had an image to keep up," Collins added. "Cool, popular girls don't have crushes on teachers. It would have dented her street cred."

Gillingham drummed his fingers on a chair arm. "So maybe she was the reason he was in Houghton on Thursday. What if something started when he was her teacher and it's still going on?"

"No," Archer said. "That doesn't make sense, with respect, boss. There wouldn't have been time for anything to happen between the end of youth club and her going home, and she and Becky always walked home together. I doubt any feelings she might have had for him would have gone anywhere."

"Still," Gillingham said, "say she recognised him, and it brought out some sort of misplaced loyalty. Maybe she rang to say she'd seen him, but he wasn't to worry. A chance to resurrect that crush?"

Baines nodded. "Doesn't sound implausible, does it?"

"Now he's got a problem," Ashby threw in. "He's hidden the car, reported it stolen, hopes he's home free. He knows from the news that two other girls saw his car, just before he ploughed into Leanne, but there's been no knock at his door. He thinks he's safe. Until he gets that call."

"He's already panicked once, after the accident," said Archer. "Fled the scene. Now, maybe he panics all over again. Because someone can identify him after all. And he's not satisfied with a child's assurances."

"So he persuaded her to meet him, so he could shut her up permanently," Ashby said bluntly.

"It wouldn't be the first time someone dug themselves a deeper hole to make the first one go away." Baines found himself agreeing with Ashby.

"What I don't get," Collins interjected, "is why he hasn't simply torched the car? It would be one less thing to worry about."

Jason Bell spoke up. "Too much TV? Exaggerated ideas about what's forensically possible? He might fear that CSIs can find trace evidence even in a burned-out car. Which is, to be fair, occasionally true."

"If that's so," rumbled Gillingham, "then his TV viewing may have done us a favour. We haven't found it burned out, it hasn't been spotted in a car park, or in a layby. He's got it stashed somewhere. We need to find it. He must have access to somewhere he can conceal a car. The CSIs have recovered all Briscoe's paperwork from his home. I want it gone through with a fine-tooth comb." He frowned. "And check out the CCTV footage from around where the girls went missing again. We need to look out for that hire car of his."

In the next session, they'd pushed Briscoe hard over the phone call. Jade's crush, which Briscoe had mentioned as a reason for her phone call. What might have happened between them when he was her teacher. Even what he knew of Becky – where she lived, her route to school.

His motivation for not stopping after hitting Leanne.

He'd stonewalled the lot, either denying everything or saying he didn't know what they were talking about.

Ashby had decided to suspend the interview and start again in the morning, after interviewers and interviewee had had some sleep. Ashby had startled everyone by announcing that questioning would recommence at 6am.

"Blimey, Steve," Archer had said afterwards, "I didn't know you knew what 6am looked like."

"Ha ha," he'd responded, an edge to his voice. "Maybe if he's not a morning person either, he'll make a mistake."

Baines finally got home, beyond exhausted, after midnight. Karen was already in bed, the sandwich she'd made for him in the fridge, wrapped in cling film. He consumed it with a glass of milk and then headed upstairs.

Karen stirred as he entered the bedroom, untying his tie as he walked.

"Sorry. Did I wake you?"

"Not really." She propped herself up on an elbow. "Big day?"

"Yes, and frustrating. Early start tomorrow. Steve Ashby is going for a 6am start."

"You're making it up."

"No, seriously. I think he's trying to impress Amy."

"I still can't imagine him smitten." She yawned. "How was the session with Tracey?"

"Well, she doesn't want to see me again for another three months. That's good, right?"

She searched his face. "Does that mean she thinks you're starting to move on?"

He sat down on the bed. "I suppose. I mean, yes." He paused for a beat. "That doesn't mean I've accepted that Jack's dead. I probably never will until I see a body."

She nodded, taking his hand and squeezing it. "That's probably how I feel, too."

He squeezed back, a surge of affection washing over him, refreshing him in the midst of a horrendous week. Things had been ticking at the back of his mind lately, thoughts about where his life was going. What the future could be like if he could finally shrug off the suffocating chains of his past. Maybe it was finally time to share those thoughts with this woman he loved.

"I'm wondering if we should really move on," he said.

"In what way?" She sat up properly.

"I've been thinking – how long are we going to go on living in this haunted house?"

Her eyes were searching his face. "I thought we agreed that the only ghosts here were people who loved us and probably approved of us being together."

"We did. I still think it. But this was my home with Louise. Maybe, as long as we're here, we'll never be able to stop looking back."

She bit her lip. "If I'm honest, this has never quite felt like my home. It's still Louise's home to me."

It felt a little like a slap, but he understood. "I had no idea you felt that way." But maybe he did. He thought she'd probably been holding this back for some time. He'd just put those issues in a box and shut the lid. Like he always did. He put his arms around her and she laid her head on his shoulder. "We both know why I've never moved from here. I mean, it has some horrendous memories for me. Sometimes I still see Louise lying there, just for an instant."

"But you stay because of Jack. Because this was his home when he was taken, and you want him to be able to come back here if you ever do find him."

He nodded, and she took another breath.

"You know I'd welcome Jack wherever we live," she said. "You're not the only one who hasn't given up hope he'll come back one day."

"I know. And I'm so lucky to have you on my side." He held her closer. "We may never be able to completely stop looking back, but that doesn't mean we have to keep on living in the past. What about our future?" he whispered. "I'm hoping we've got years ahead together, but what does that look like?"

She lifted her head to look at his face. "What do you want it to look like?"

"Do we carry on as we are? Maybe get married?" There.

He'd said it.

There was a long silence.

"Say something," he said finally.

"Do you..." Her voice faltered. "Do you want to?"

He knew theirs was more complicated than most relationships. Both their families were weird enough about it as it was. He knew it must seem as if he had replaced Louise with her clone. Louise had been known and loved in the village, and he suspected some locals had also found it awkward to start with. But Karen seemed to have won most of them over just by being herself. So similar to Louise, but with her own distinctive personality.

"Maybe," he said, his eyes never leaving her face. "Yes, I think I do."

Even as the words left his lips, he knew it wasn't the most ardent proposal.

"Since we're discussing this stuff," she said, "there's another question we might as well get out there."

"Which is?"

"We're not getting any younger. My biological clock is ticking."

He stared at her, his insides churning. He was stunned. "You want children?"

"Honestly?" She looked genuinely puzzled by the thought. "I don't know. But do you?"

For the first time he realised how frozen in time he'd allowed them both to become. He'd kept Jack's room just as it had been when he'd been abducted, even though he'd known how increasingly ridiculous this was: the toddler who'd disappeared – if he actually was still alive – would now be in his mid-teens. It was highly doubtful that he remembered anything of his old home.

That Jack would probably have forgotten his parents too was something Baines chose to blind himself to. But if Jack ever did come home, if he did remember anything of his old life, how would he react to his mother's place in his father's life being taken by an aunt who looked and talked just like his mother? It was something that had nagged at Baines.

How would he react if that same aunt had had a baby? Would Jack think the baby had replaced him?

"I'm sorry," he said. "I honestly haven't thought about that. Can I have some time to get my head around it?"

She laughed and hugged him. "It's not a deal-breaker, Dan. I'm not making demands or throwing down ultimatums. I don't even know what I want." She looked at him with teary eyes. "I didn't think it would ever come up." She blinked. "Did I sort of get proposed to there?"

He stifled a ferocious yawn. "I think maybe perhaps you did." He realised that, complicated though it might be, it really was what he wanted. Perhaps he'd wanted it for longer than he knew. He realised his heart was pounding. "Will you…" He almost faltered, but it was now or never. He gulped. "Will you marry me?"

"I need time to think about it," she said. "If you're serious."

"I'm serious." He really was.

"Okay," she said, breaking into a huge smile, tears welling in her eyes at the same moment. "I've thought, and the answer's yes."

He held her tighter, and then he kissed her. The kiss lasted for a long moment.

"I love you," he said. "So much."

"I love you, too."

"It'll be difficult with our families."

"I know. But if they can't suck it up, sod 'em." She giggled through her tears. "When can we get a ring?"

"An engagement ring?"

"No, a curtain ring. What do you think, you idiot?"

"Two rings," he said. "One each. I want everyone to know I'm spoken for."

21

Thursday morning

Becky Day had been missing for almost twenty-four hours, Jade Sheldon over thirty-six.

Ashby and Baines were poised to renew questioning Mark Briscoe, and Archer had also arrived early to watch on the remote screen again, as had Amy Petrescu, arriving just a few minutes behind Ashby. She wondered if he'd revert to type once the DS had returned to Oxfordshire. She found herself hoping not.

The recommencement of Mark Briscoe's questioning was delayed until 6.20am, however, when a grumpy Adina Walker finally arrived, complaining – as she had last night – that such an early start was unnecessary.

"Don't give us that crap, Adina," Gillingham retorted. "You'll be the first to remind us we need an extension when our twenty-four hours are up."

Archer soon began to find the questioning boring and repetitive. Yes, Briscoe had taken that call on Tuesday. No, the person on the line hadn't said anything. No, he hadn't abducted Jade. He'd been on his way home at the time in question. No, he certainly hadn't abducted Becky. He'd had no idea who she was until the police had started making wild accusations.

No, no one could corroborate any of his alibis. But that was because he lived alone.

All in all, Archer was grateful when, at around 10am, Collins slipped into the viewing room and touched her elbow.

"Guv, we might have got something."

She turned around. "Don't tell me the lab has processed those blood samples already?"

"Something else."

Archer nodded, asked Petrescu to keep watching and look out for any slips by Briscoe, or points that needed following up, then followed Collins back to the office, where Bell, Tyler and Ibrahim Iqbal all waited by her desk.

"I hope this is good," she said as she sat. "We really need a break."

"You go first, Ibrahim," Collins said.

The civilian nodded. "It might be nothing, Lizzie, but Jason and I have been examining the CCTV footage from around where Jade Sheldon was last seen and from Houghton, where we assume Becky Day was taken."

"Yes?"

"Nothing of use from Houghton. But then we know from the hit-and-run that the village has some serious CCTV black spots. But we did pick up Briscoe's rental car in Aylesbury around the time Jade must have got off the bus."

Archer sat up in her chair, giving him her full attention.

"First question," Iqbal continued. "Why was he not still at school? It's not as if teachers rush off as soon as the kids leave."

"It's interesting," Archer said. "A bit thin, though. He might have had a plausible reason for leaving early." She shrugged. "Speak to the school, though, and see what they say."

"Already done," Bell said. "He complained of having a migraine."

"We can't disprove that," she said, her heart already sinking. The team were doing their jobs, but coming up with nothing concrete.

"Hold on, though," Iqbal said. He woke up the laptop and flashed a street map up on the screen, then approached it with the pointer. "Look," he said. "Here's where Jade got off the bus. Here's where we've got his hired car, heading that way, around the same time. And this," he moved the pointer again, "is the school where he teaches."

"Okay," she said doubtfully. "But if he was on his way home with a migraine at that time, you'd expect his car to be in Aylesbury."

"True," agreed Iqbal, "but not there." He moved the pointer once more, inscribing a route on the map. "This is the obvious route from his school to Winslow. The opposite direction."

She allowed herself a smile, seeing his point. "I need more," she said, "but this is good work. If we get lucky, he'll over-elaborate on why he went that way, and we might be able to catch him out. Anything else?"

"Yes, guv," Collins said. "Will's been going through the paperwork from Briscoe's house, and he's found something interesting."

Archer turned to Tyler. "Speak to me, Will."

He nodded. "It seems our man has another property."

Archer's mouth went dry. "Seriously?"

"Seriously. I can show you all the documentation, but Briscoe's father died a couple of years ago, and his mum had already been diagnosed with early onset dementia. She's now in a home. Mark put her house on the market to pay for her care. There's an estate agent pack amongst his papers. But here's the thing. He took it off the market on Tuesday evening."

The day Jade Sheldon went missing.

She thought of the white Ford Focus. "Is there a garage?"

"Round the back." Tyler smiled. "There's more. The house is on the outskirts of Aylesbury, in a quiet cul-de-sac, so less risk of being observed. Of course, if he had the car there, or was holding the girls there, there's the risk of a viewing throwing a spanner in the works."

She turned to Collins. "Joan, slip DI Ashby a note, suggesting they take a break. And get DCI Gillingham."

Five minutes later, Ashby appeared in the briefing room, Baines in tow. Gillingham was already there. Archer let Iqbal and Tyler lay out what they'd told her earlier. As they spoke, she saw the other DI's eyes brighten.

"So the car could be at the other address? And so could the girls?"

"Taking the house off the market when he did can't just be a coincidence," Baines said. "Either he's got the bodies stashed there – or maybe they're alive, and he's holding them."

"He's off sick," Gillingham pointed out. "It gives him a chance to slip over there every so often and feed and water them. Why would he go off sick if they're dead?"

"Let's not get too optimistic," Archer said, determined to keep a lid on the growing euphoria. "It could be the stress of the situation that's making him ill."

"But why keep the bodies there?" Petrescu argued. "If I had a body on my hands, I'd rather just dump it in a river, or woodland, like Carly Eustace. Up to now, he's had no reason to think we'd suspect him for Jade's or Becky's abductions." She glanced from face to face. "If he took them – and I think he did, I reckon they're alive."

"I'm not sure we can take that for granted," Archer said, "but we need to get into that house, don't we?"

"Or should we wait and see if forensics can tie the hire car to the girls?" Ashby wondered.

"No," said Gillingham. "If they're at that house, I want them out now."

"Break the door down, then?"

"You could just confront him with this," Archer said. "He might crumble and admit everything."

"No," Gillingham said. "We've wasted enough time. Those girls could be dying, or dead, or anything. I'll take full responsibility." Gillingham had daughters of his own. Maybe this case was closer to home for him than Archer had realised. "Steve, Lizzie – we've got the address. Find a couple of uniforms and get over there with the Big Key. Suit up before you go in, though. It could well be a crime scene. We don't know what you'll find."

"What about the interview?" Baines asked.

"Suspend it. Stick him back in his cell to stew."

Archer could almost smell the testosterone in the room. Gillingham had picked her for the raid because, he'd said, the girls would welcome a woman's presence if they were found alive. Everyone else was getting pumped up to do macho things.

"One thought, before we go charging off," she offered.

"Quick, then." Gillingham was impatient.

"Well," she said, "didn't Briscoe empty his pockets when we brought him in here?"

"They always do. What's your point?"

She slipped her hands into her pockets. "Silly, really. I just wondered, before we break a perfectly good door, whether it was worth seeing if there were any keys on his ring that would fit his parents' old house."

The DCI looked at her. "Oh." He shrugged. "Fair point. Take the Big Key as our Plan B, though."

* * *

In the end, Ashby suggested they take Collins along with them.

"We might need an extra pair of hands, and an extra woman might come in handy if we find the girls alive."

Now the three of them, with a marked squad car behind them, drew up outside an unloved-looking house at the end of an unremarkable cul-de-sac. They got out of the car and Ashby strode up to the door, Briscoe's bunch of keys in his hand.

"We probably ought to knock," Archer said. "Just in case."

"In case his mum's broken out of her care home?" Ashby rolled his eyes.

Archer reached past him and pressed the bell. There was also a knocker, and she banged that a couple of times for good measure. Ashby folded his arms, but at least he waited a reasonable time before looking questioningly at her.

"Okay," she said. "Let's try the keys."

He had a Yale key at the ready and was about to put it in the lock when he paused.

"Hey, Joan," he said. "Make yourself useful. Nip round the back and see if you can see under the garage door. See if there's a car in there."

Collins nodded and followed the block-paved driveway down the side of the house. Meanwhile, Ashby tried the key in the lock. It went in, but wouldn't turn. He withdrew it and went through the other keys until he found a second Yale. This went in and turned, but the door still didn't budge.

Archer pointed at a keyhole lower down. "Deadlock?"

There were three possibles on the ring to choose from. The second Ashby tried turned, albeit a little stiffly, and then he tried the Yale again. This time the door swung inwards on creaking hinges.

"Christ," Ashby muttered. "It's like a fucking horror movie."

"Let's get those suits on," Archer suggested.

They walked back to the Audi. Ashby opened the boot and they all started to struggle into crime scene suits. Both were old hands at getting the paper coveralls on, so it didn't take long. They'd just about got their overshoes in place when Collins reappeared again.

"His white Focus is there all right. The garage has a side window. You can see a nasty dent at the front. Smashed headlight, too."

"We're going to get him for Leanne at the very least." Archer's satisfaction was muted. They still had two young girls to find. "Good work, Joan. Call Phil Gordon and get some CSIs here to check it out. Then grab a suit and follow us."

Ashby stepped over the threshold and Archer followed.

The house smelled stale and felt cold. Archer wasn't sure whether it felt chilly because it had stood empty for a while, or whether it was psychological.

"Anyone here?" she called. "Police!"

The silence seemed to mock her.

"They could be bound and gagged, drugged, or…"

"I suppose it's still possible that the call from Jade's school had nothing to do with her disappearance," Archer suggested.

"You know that's not true. My bet? They're dead and we won't find them here."

Archer grimaced, remembering the blood at Briscoe's home. "Ever the optimist. Shall I take the upstairs?"

"Be my guest."

She climbed the stairs, tired boards groaning under her feet. Five doors led off the first-floor landing, so she checked them all, starting from the first on the right, which proved to be a bathroom. The next three doors led to bedrooms. All were empty, with nothing under the beds but dust balls.

The final door turned out to be an airing cupboard, containing nothing but towels and bed linen. She returned to the bathroom and stood looking at the panel on the side of the bath. It wouldn't be the first time a corpse had been stashed behind one of those.

She could hear some banging about downstairs and hoped Ashby wasn't making life harder for the CSIs.

The bath panel was held in place by six screws. Archer stared at them, then opened the medicine cupboard above the wash basin, catching a glimpse of her pale face in the mirror on the door before it swung open.

On the shelf, she spotted what she was banking on: a nail file. She found, as she'd been hoping, that it made an adequate makeshift screwdriver. But it was awkward work, and she'd just removed the second screw when Collins joined her, her footfall on the protesting stairs announcing her.

"There's an under stairs cupboard down there," she said. "DI Ashby's turning it out."

"Is that what the noise is all about. Shit!" The nail file slipped, going through the latex glove on Archer's left hand and taking a bite out of her palm.

"Shall I?" Collins held out a hand for the file.

"You might as well earn your keep." Archer handed it over.

Naturally, the sixth and final screw gave her the most trouble. By now, Ashby had joined them, watching Collins struggle.

"Steve," Archer said, "I noticed a loft hatch above the landing, and there's one of those poles for opening it in the second bedroom."

He nodded. "I'll get it open."

"Come *on*," Collins was snarling at the stubborn screw. She jiggled the nail file again, trying to find an edge that would give her better purchase. "Aha!" she said. "About time too."

The screw turned slowly and finally gave up. Collins pressed down on the top of the panel, separating it from the lip of the bathtub. As she began to prise it back, Archer held her breath. In her mind's eye, she could already see the bodies of two twelve-year-old girls crammed into the space.

But when Collins removed the panel, she exhaled. There was nothing in there but pipework, bathtub and bits of debris from when the bath had been installed. She could hear some clunking from outside the door, and then the scrape of a loft ladder coming down. The two women joined Ashby on the landing.

"Anything?" he asked. Archer shook her head. Ashby shrugged and looked at Collins. "You're younger and fitter than me, Joan. Up you go."

Eager enough, she climbed the ladder until her head was poking through into the loft.

"It's like a junk shop up here," she called down. "I'd say Mr Briscoe's parents have never thrown anything away."

"Can you see any bodies?" Ashby wanted to know.

"No, but that doesn't mean they're not here."

Archer's patience was already straining. "Shall I come up?"

"Up to you, guv. There's not much room up here." She climbed right up and Archer heard her moving about.

"Most of the junk is in plain sight," she said, "and there are no bodies in view."

"Anything they could be in?"

"Not really. The boxes are all way too small. There's a couple of quite large suitcases. Hang on."

Her footsteps in the loft sounded unnaturally loud, amplified by the roof space. Archer could hear Collins shifting things around.

"They're dead," Ashby announced. "He's buried them somewhere."

"Give her a chance," she murmured.

"Guv," Collins called down. "The cases are empty. And there's nowhere else the girls could be."

Archer cursed to herself. Dead or alive, she wanted Jade and Becky found, and their families given some closure.

"Nothing at all?" she asked Collins. "You're sure?"

"Yes, guv."

"Damn."

"You might as well come down," Ashby told Collins. With Collins back on the landing and the loft ladder stowed, the three stood looking disconsolate.

"They'll turn up in shallow graves," Ashby opined. His gloom was getting on Archer's nerves, but she was beginning to agree with him.

"If they're dead, I hope they do turn up," said Archer, "and soon. At least their poor parents will know what happened."

Disappointed, she headed for the stairs and then stopped. "Hold on. There's still one place we haven't looked."

They found a garage key on the ring. Moments later they stood alongside Briscoe's damaged Ford Focus. Archer tried to pop the boot.

"Locked. We should have brought Jason Bell with us. He seems to have learned some dodgy tricks in Glasgow."

"Well," Ashby drawled, "as luck would have it, he's not the only one. Joan, I don't suppose you noticed a tool box in here?"

"We could just wait for the CSIs."

"We could. But the weather's been warm, it's stuffy in here, and the air in the boot won't be good. What if they're in there and still alive?"

"Surely they'd hear us and make a noise?" said Collins.

"Not if they're unconscious," said Ashby.

Archer saw that he was right. She let her gaze rove the garage, then pointed to some neatly arranged shelves. "Tool box."

Collins retrieved it and Ashby opened it. He selected a putty knife and a pair of wire cutters.

"We need a wire coat hanger," Ashby said. "There must be one in one of the wardrobes."

Collins disappeared and returned soon after with what Ashby wanted. The women watched Ashby cut through it and then carefully straighten it.

"A bit crude," he said, "but effective, with luck. Watch and learn."

He rammed the blade of the putty knife between the boot lid and surround and used some leverage to create a slim chink of space. Then he pushed the straightened wire in.

"Just need to locate the locking button." he said, wiggling it.

Just as Archer was beginning to think he was full of crap, there was a click. Ashby straightened and raised the boot lid.

Archer gasped. She couldn't help it. Jade Sheldon lay on her side in the boot, her wrists and ankles secured with cable ties, duct tape over her mouth. She lay very still, her skin marble-pale.

Archer felt tears welling in her eyes.

"Oh, the bastard," Ashby breathed.

But Collins reached in and placed two fingers on the girl's neck.

"There's a pulse," she said, "but it's thready. Can one of you call an ambulance?"

Her heart leaping Archer pulled out her phone.

"Can you help me get her out into the fresh air, sir?"

Neither of them argued with Collins taking charge. They knew she'd done advanced first aid training in her own time. So Ashby bent to take Jade's shoulders while Collins took her feet. By the time Archer came off the phone, they had her laid on the driveway with Collins' jacket under her head. Collins was pulling the tape away from the girl's mouth to help her breathe more easily.

"Ambulance on its way," Archer said, pocketing her phone. She watched Collins working, quickly checking the girl over. She imagined Jade trapped inside that steel coffin, the air inside turning staler by the minute. How long had she been in there? It was a miracle she hadn't already suffocated.

"We need to get some fluid into her," Collins said.

"I'll find some water," said Ashby. "Hopefully Briscoe hasn't had it turned off."

"Lizzie, can you go and get those wire cutters?"

Archer ran to the garage and returned with the cutters. In quick, efficient movements, Collins snipped the cable ties that bound the girl's wrists and ankles.

Ashby ran back with a glass of water, contents slopping over the side.

"We need to try and bring her round so she can drink it," Collins said, gently patting Jade's cheeks. There was no response. "She's out cold. The paramedics might have to put her on a drip."

"Of course," Ashby remarked, "there's still one unanswered question."

"I know," Archer said, suddenly very weary. "Where the hell is Becky Day?"

22

With Archer watching through the glass again, Ashby and Baines got back to work on Briscoe with renewed urgency. Briscoe's car – and both of his properties – still needed to be subjected to painstaking processing, which Phil Gordon had warned would take some time. Petrescu and Collins had been dispatched to Stoke Mandeville Hospital to take a statement from Jade Sheldon as soon as she was well enough to give one. But meanwhile, the team members weren't prepared to wait on any of that with Becky Day still missing.

"All right, Mark," Ashby said without preamble. "We've found your car, and we've found Jade Sheldon. Alive, if you're interested. So, basically, we know pretty well everything. It's time for you to stop pissing us around and tell us where Becky Day is."

Baines could have sworn that, just for a moment, a look of panic fleeted across Briscoe's face. But Adina Walker raised a manicured hand, forestalling any reply he might be about to make. "Indeed, Inspector? And what is this 'everything' you profess to know?"

Through gritted teeth, Ashby laid out today's events.

"Mark, please don't make it any worse for yourself than it already is," he concluded. "Jade's lucky to be alive. Maybe Leanne's death was an accident, and you panicked. Maybe things just got out of hand with Jade. We'll know more when we've spoken to her. But if you've got Becky somewhere, we need to find her. So just tell us where she is. Before it's too late."

Once again it was Briscoe's solicitor who stepped in to do the talking.

"Inspector, all this so-called evidence is news to us."

"So-called?" Baines burst out. Walker froze him with a

glance.

"Officers, you must know I need to speak to my client in private about this alleged new evidence before he makes any response."

"But," Ashby was barely containing his obvious frustration, "a young girl's life is in danger. You'll be doing your client no good if she dies and he finds himself facing a murder charge."

Baines thought the teacher winced at that, but Walker was adamant: they would have a private consultation before Briscoe would say any more.

* * *

As Baines led Walker and Briscoe back to the room they'd been using, Ashby rejoined Archer.

"Bloody woman," he grumbled. "Everything's by the book with her. They both know we've got him. And that if Becky dies…"

"I know," Archer agreed. "But she'll put her client first, come hell or high water."

He shook his head. "I won't forget finding Jade in a hurry. I thought she'd gone."

"Me too, for a moment."

"I don't want to go through that again."

She couldn't remember him really talking about his feelings before. "Shall I make us a drink while we're waiting?" she suggested, realising even as she spoke that the offer was another first.

He looked surprised, then nodded. "Great, thanks. Tea, two sugars. Not too heavy on the milk."

She returned with the drinks a few minutes later, plus a coffee for Baines, who had joined Ashby by the two-way glass.

"She'll make him see sense, surely," Baines said. "He's already going down. A little co-operation won't hurt him now. Better than the consequences if we find Becky dead."

"Unless he thinks we'll never find her," Ashby said, half-slipping a pack of cigarettes out of his pocket. Archer gave him a look, and he put them back.

"You think she's dead?" Baines looked grim.

He made a face. "Let's see what Briscoe says when he comes back."

* * *

They didn't have long to wait. Ten minutes later, Ashby and Baines were back in the interview room and Briscoe was ready to make a statement. Things had happened on Thursday night almost exactly as they had surmised.

"I was on my way to Aylesbury to check out where PC World was," he began.

"At that time of night?" Baines challenged. "What time do they close?"

"Oh, I wasn't going in. I was thinking of buying a new laptop, and I just thought it would be easier to check the route on a weekday evening, rather than attempt it at the weekend."

"Seriously?" Ashby arched an eyebrow. "No satnav?"

"Don't trust 'em."

"Isn't there a PC World at Milton Keynes?" Baines asked. "Surely that'd be closer."

"I hate MK."

"If you'd let my client make his statement," Walker interjected, "this might go faster. You were the ones suggesting the clock was ticking."

Baines looked furious, but refrained from any outburst. Ashby's jaw worked for a moment, and then he nodded curtly.

"All right, Mark," he said. "The floor's yours, but you'd better get to the point quickly."

Briscoe looked at Walker, whose nod was almost as brusque as Ashby's.

"I was on my way to PC World," he said again. "The main road goes straight through Houghton, as you probably know." He shrugged. "I suppose I might have been going a little over the limit, but it wasn't my fault. That girl—"

"Leanne," Ashby snarled.

"Leanne, right. Well, she simply came out of nowhere. I swear, she must have just stepped into the road without looking.

It was an accident. I never stood a chance."

"So you admit you knocked her down."

"It was an accident."

"Maybe," Baines said. "But you didn't stop, did you?"

"Well, I did…"

"Yes, but only for a matter of seconds, right?"

Archer saw Briscoe swallow.

"I'd had a couple of glasses of wine with my dinner, before I decided to check out that store. I couldn't be sure I wasn't over the limit, and it didn't look like there was much I could do for her. Besides, someone else would call an ambulance."

Baines was suddenly glad he wasn't in the room alone with him.

"So, what?" he pressed. "You decided to just… drive off? You've run over a kid, and your first thought is self-preservation?"

"I'm not proud of it. I thought I might go to jail. I'd definitely lose my licence. Lose my job, my career…"

"Boo hoo." Ashby dismissed his excuses. "Get on with it. Where's Becky?"

"All in good time, Inspector," said Walker.

"All right," Baines took the lead again. "So tell us about Jade Sheldon. You're not denying abducting and falsely imprisoning her, are you?"

"No," Ashby interrupted. "Ms Walker's quite right. One thing at a time. So what about the car, Mark? Why did you report it stolen?"

"Well, obviously, I wasn't thinking of PC World any more, but I had all these worries going through my head. I'd passed two girls moments before the accident. Could they identify me? The car? What about CCTV?" He covered his face with his hands. "I stopped further up the road and had a look at the car. The damage. There had to be broken glass in the road. I know what forensics can do now."

He had a glass of water in front of him and guzzled it. Baines thought of Becky Day, possibly dying somewhere, and wanted to shake him. Yell at him. But he remained in control of himself. Just.

"So you took it to your parents' house?" he suggested.

"That's right. I guess I was running on instinct and adrenalin. As you know, it's quiet around there. I stashed the Focus in the garage. Then I walked into town and got a bus back into Winslow. Next day, I took the house off the market to avoid the agent coming round for a viewing and seeing the vehicle, then I reported the Focus stolen."

"You did all that?" Ashby sounded beyond incredulous. "To cover your tracks?" He shook his head. "I suppose you realise that the car being reported stolen was what got us so interested in it in the first place?"

The teacher stared at him. He looked ready to cry. It gave Baines a savage pleasure.

"I... I was trying to buy some time, at least until I could get my head straight. Decide what to do next. And you appeared to believe me, even when you did take an interest in the Focus."

"It was all going so well, wasn't it?" Ashby said softly.

Briscoe nodded miserably.

"And then Jade called your school," Baines said. "Didn't she?"

"Suspect is nodding," Ashby said, for the benefit of the tape.

"Oh, Christ..." Briscoe moaned. "That damned call. Yes, all right. I remembered Jade, of course. How could I forget? Those spaniel eyes. Her eagerness to help with any silly job – putting things away, getting things out. Her hand up every time I asked a question. She scared me. You have to be so, so careful these days. Kids get these stupid ideas in their heads, say the wrong things to the wrong people, and next thing, you're branded a kiddie fiddler."

The phone call had totally unnerved Briscoe. Jade had told him she'd seen him on Thursday night, but he'd had enough self-control to tell her he didn't know what she was talking about.

Just before you ran over Leanne, Jade had said, and he'd almost thrown up, there and then. But then she'd added, *I only called because I didn't want you to worry. I'll never tell.*

The prospect of a twelve-year-old keeping something like that to herself had hardly reassured him, and he'd said the first thing that came into his head.

" I said I'd like to meet her that afternoon, in town. Buy her coffee or a milkshake, and cake, to say thank you."

"And she went for it?" Baines checked.

"Of course she went for it," Briscoe said. "I knew she would."

Just for a moment, he looked so full of himself that Baines was once again glad he and Briscoe weren't alone. It would have been touch and go whether he knocked his teeth out.

"After that, it was easy. I picked her up, round the corner from the bus stop."

"She got in your car?" Baines checked again.

"Poor kid trusted me, right up to when I drove her to a quiet alleyway I knew. I acted nasty, threatened her, forced her into the boot of my hire car, then tied her up with duct tape. After that, it was just a matter of getting her to my parents' house and transferring her to my own boot."

"And then you left her there."

"Yes."

"But first, you made her tell you who the other girl was who'd seen your car."

"No. She'd have said if the other girl had been able to identify me or the car. Besides, this Becky would have told you if that was the case."

"You wanted to make sure."

"Jade said no one else knew it was me. I had no reason to disbelieve her."

Baines sighed. "Were you ever going to go back?"

"I don't know." Briscoe hid his face again. "I just didn't know what to do. Leanne – that was an accident. I never wanted to hurt anyone." He looked from Ashby to Baines. "I had a car the police were interested in, and I had a girl who could give me away for knocking Leanne down – and now I'd made that worse by locking her in the boot. I just didn't know what to do next. So I threw a sickie and then I just sat at home, stewing over the mess I'd made for myself."

"You weren't even going to go back and check on Jade every now and then? Feed her? Give her something to drink?"

Ashby jabbed the questions at him, like a boxer's punches.

"I was afraid someone might see me. Get suspicious. I was in a hole, and it was like I couldn't stop digging..."

Even Adina Walker, his own lawyer, was looking at him with something like disgust.

"I'm sorry," he moaned. "I'm so, so sorry."

"So what about Becky Day? What have you done with her?"

"Nothing. I know nothing about her. You have to believe me."

"Why should we do that, Mark? You've lied from the start. You knew you had Jade hidden away, slowly dying, and you just left her there, denying all knowledge of her. Why should we believe the same doesn't apply to Becky?"

"I swear. I'd never even heard of her until she was on the news."

They kept at him, but he stuck to his story until they finally took a break so he could get some rest and food. Gillingham had ordered in some sandwiches, and they fell upon them in the briefing room.

"What do you reckon?" the DCI demanded after they brought him up to date.

"Honestly?" Ashby said. "I reckon she's dead."

"No," Archer protested. "He's just got another bolthole he's stashed her in."

"You think?" He shrugged. "Then why would he stick to his story? We know everything else. If we find her, and he's let her die, he can't keep playing the panic card. Not now. I think she's already dead. It's the only thing that makes sense."

"Steve's got a point," Baines said. "If Becky's alive and Briscoe tells us where she is, he can avoid a murder charge. But if she's dead already..." He put down his half-eaten sandwich, his appetite gone. "If she's already dead, then it's too late. His only hope is to brazen it out."

"He's right, Lizzie," Gillingham said. "I reckon we're looking for a body now."

23

Round about the time Ashby and Baines were resuming their interrogation of Mark Briscoe, a nurse told Petrescu and Collins that they could see Jade Sheldon for a few minutes. They found the girl in a visitor's room, wearing a hospital gown and a threadbare robe. Her parents were with her, her mother holding her hand. The parents had been tearfully thankful, especially when they learned that Collins was one of the officers who had found their daughter and probably saved her life.

The room had that antiseptic-and-burned-cabbage hospital smell, and looked as though it had seen better days. Every wall was festooned with posters carrying instructions for a healthier life.

"Mum's going to bring me some clothes," Jade said, not looking at them. "Your people have taken the ones I was wearing."

"They'll want to do some tests," Petrescu explained.

"You look better than the last time I saw you," Collins commented.

"I'm so sorry," she said. "For all the trouble I've caused. Am I in a lot of trouble?"

Petrescu supposed she might be. Jade had concealed what she knew about a fatal accident and arguably conspired to pervert the course of justice. But she was only twelve, and she'd already suffered a lot for her foolishness. Petrescu thought, if she were a betting woman, her money would be on no charges being pressed.

"Let's not worry about that now," she said. "Just tell us what happened. We'll take a formal statement later, but we need some quick answers, to help us. Is that okay? We've got a portable recorder here."

Collins held the device up, then set it down on the Jade's

tray table.

"I've messed everything up," Jade said. "Now I just want to help."

* * *

It was late afternoon when the full team had gathered in the briefing room for a recap. Briscoe was still insisting he knew nothing about Becky, even though he'd been assured that, if there was a trace of her in either of his houses or cars, the CSIs would find it.

"That blood on your living-room carpet, or your coffee table," Baines had thrown at him. "If they find out it's Becky's, that's game over for you. It's time you told the whole truth."

But even that hadn't thrown him. It was as if the break had reinvigorated him.

"I have nothing to add to my previous statement," he'd repeated, like a broken record.

Jade had at least confirmed to Petrescu and Collins that she hadn't given Becky's name or address to Briscoe. She said he hadn't even asked her about the other girl, which seemed strange.

"Maybe he scared her so badly she's wiped it from her memory," Petrescu speculated.

"Or maybe he didn't even think about the second girl until he'd walked away and left her locked in his car boot," Archer said. "He admitted he wasn't thinking straight. He's guilty of the hit-and-run, and he locked Jade in his car and left her there. But when he played the accident back in his mind, he realised, maybe for the first time, there was a second girl out there who saw him drive by. What if she remembers something? Is it all going to come back and bite him?"

"So why not go back and ask Jade?" Petrescu wondered.

"That's easy," Baines said. "He was bricking it. No way was he going back there in a hurry."

"So how did he know how to find Becky?"

"Well," Archer said. "Houghton has a village store and a pub, right?"

There was general nodding and muttered confirmation.

"What if there is?" Gillingham looked mystified.

"What if he hung out in the pub or visited the store, listening for gossip, maybe asking the odd innocent question? Someone gives him an innocent answer, so he thinks he'd better get Becky out of the picture?"

Ashby jabbed a finger at Tyler. "Will, get some pictures of Briscoe printed off and then, Jason, take some uniforms over to Houghton with them. See if anyone recalls seeing him, speaking to him, mentioning Becky to him."

"Meanwhile," Gillingham said, "I'm going to put a rocket up Phil Gordon. He's got to give us something to work with. Anything."

"With respect, boss," Archer said, "Phil and his team are already working all the hours God sends…"

"Yeah? Well, now they can work all the hours the devil sends, too, " he snapped.

Bell lifted a tentative hand. "Sir, just a thought…"

Gillingham swivelled Bell's way. "A thought, DC Bell? Well, I sincerely hope it's a good one."

Bell blushed just like the old days. Some things never changed. Archer found it oddly reassuring.

"Well, sir," he pressed on, "what if Mark Briscoe didn't take Becky? What if it's just a big coincidence?" He held up his hands. "What if we're focusing on Briscoe when we ought to be looking elsewhere?"

"Really?" The DCI massaged his temples. "I'm sorry, Jason, but we haven't anything like the manpower to divert down more rabbit warrens. Briscoe's our man, and we just need one more break. Either for Phil Gordon to come up with something, or someone in Houghton to confirm that Briscoe knew Becky Day was the other potential witness to the hit-and-run. Then he'll crack. We've got to keep hoping she's still alive. Although I've got a bad feeling that DI Ashby's right, and we're already too late."

His gaze traversed the room. "Right, then. Steve, Dan, I want Briscoe formally charged with what we've got on him so far, and then he's going nowhere. Then start questioning him again.

See if he slips up. Amy, get Jade's statement written up. Will, get those pictures for Jason and then make sure everything's logged."

Archer was reflecting that she hadn't been given a task, when Gillingham spoke again.

"DI Archer, a word in my office, please."

* * *

Gillingham sat back in his executive chair. He'd clearly been proud of it when he'd first wangled the fancy piece of furniture, but it hadn't been built to last. It was looking worn and shabby, and the swivel mechanism had a creak that Archer suspected would need more than a squirt of WD40.

Gillingham looked as worn as the chair: pasty-faced and haggard, his shoulders more slumped and rounded than usual.

"I'm being asked by our brass and Amy Petrescu's where we are on the Carly Eustace murder," he remarked in a way that Archer knew was going to precede a bollocking.

She wasn't in the mood. "Meaning?"

"Any progress?"

"Oh, yeah, tons." She did her best to make her tone light. "Paul, you know Joan and I have been working on finding those girls. You told us to drop everything."

"Still," he persisted, "a murder inquiry. I hoped you'd have pushed it along somehow."

His expression was sour. He was being unfair, she thought. He looked knackered, but they all were. She wasn't having that.

"It's down to teamwork – to all of us – that Jade was found and is still alive."

"I suppose. But Amy Petrescu's hardly touched the case she was attached to us to do. Her bosses want to know what we're doing with her."

"What should I do, then, Paul?" she demanded. "Take me and Joan out of the search for Becky? Take Amy out? She'll get recalled at some point, and so will Will. Then we'll be even more stretched for manpower."

She paused for breath. Because, even as the words tumbled

out, she felt a sharp twinge of guilt. Yes, all their emphasis had been on finding two girls who might be still alive. Because, important though it was to catch Carly Eustace's killer – especially as no one could be certain he wouldn't strike again – it was already too late for Carly. Jade's life had been saved, and Archer still prayed that Becky would be saved too, however unlikely that looked at the moment.

And yet.

She remembered the anger she'd felt when Carly's body had first been discovered: the signs of violence Carly had suffered before her death, her body dumped like rubbish in an obscure corner of Millett Wood.

And then, when Carly had been identified, she remembered hearing the news that Carly had probably been playing away the night she died, and how her death had devastated her husband, Harry Eustace, who had surely deserved better.

Archer's last relationship had ended when she found that the man she was sleeping with was still married.

Did she have some innate prejudice against people who were cheating that had caused her to not work Carly's case as hard as she should have? To be all too willing to back-pedal? Becky needed to be found, but Carly still needed justice.

Archer looked Gillingham in the eye. There was still a sullen hostility about his expression, but she thought she saw something else there too.

"Paul, this isn't like you. I know we don't always see eye to eye, but…"

He drew a hand across his face. "Maybe you're right. Maybe I'm taking it out on you…"

"Taking what out?"

He looked at his desk. "I had some bad news today."

Her annoyance evaporated. *Was he ill?*

"Tell me."

"This is in confidence."

"Of course." This was a first.

"The Super's taking his pension. He'll be gone in a month."

"Really?" She took it in. "But does that mean you might be moving up, boss?"

160

His face said it all. "No. So there won't be an immediate DCI vacancy for you here, if that's what you're thinking."

"I wasn't." The dig riled her, but she let it go.

"Well, you should."

She stifled a flash of irritation. She wanted to go home, not play at riddles. "Now you're losing me. And what do you mean, no *immediate* vacancy?"

He sighed. "A new Super's already been lined up. So I might not be here for long. I wouldn't be surprised if she wanted me out."

"Who is it?"

"Andrea Lambert. She's only thirty-nine."

"Wow! Younger than me." Archer felt a tug of jealousy alongside a dart of pleasure that another female officer was doing well. She'd heard of Lambert, but never met her.

"Oh, yes. Single-minded, is our Andie. She was one of my detective sergeants when I was a DI at Reading. Now she's going to be *my* boss. Well," he added, without a hint of irony, "she always acted like my boss, even then." He shrugged. "We never got on, and I don't reckon she thought much of me. So there it is. I'd polish up my CV if I were you."

She felt a flush of sympathy for her downcast boss. "Buy you a pint later?"

"No, I want to get home. Break the news to Mrs Gillingham. Thanks for offering, though."

She nodded. "Don't be too down. Maybe you'll find Andrea's changed."

"Yeah." He barked a laugh. "Maybe she's learned to breathe fire." He sighed. "Spend a couple of hours in the morning reviewing the Carly Eustace case, and then we'll talk again."

24

Baines walked through his front door, ready to drop. The rest of the day had been a waste of time. The theory that Mark Briscoe may have found out who was with Jade the night of Leanne's death through the Houghton gossip chain had thrown nothing up so far, and meanwhile Briscoe continued to insist that he had nothing to add to the statement he'd already made.

Even if someone could place him in the village, asking questions or eavesdropping, that was a long way from proving he had taken Becky too – or getting him to tell them where she was. Especially if he'd murdered her.

Time was running out. That had been one of Baines's recurring nightmares, after the Invisible Man's killing spree had ended with Louise's death and Jack's disappearance. The possibility that the serial killer had simply fled the country, or even died, and Jack was trapped somewhere, alone and terrified, slowly running out of air or starving to death.

At the time, he'd dwelt on the horrific case of Mark Dutroux, a Belgian serial killer in the 1990s who had buried two young girls alive and left two more to starve in a filthy, freezing cell under his house while he was in prison. He was a monster.

What kind of man was Mark Briscoe?

Or was it possible they had the wrong man for Becky's abduction?

He realised he was ravenous, a feeling reinforced by the delicious smells that assailed his nostrils. He had phoned ahead, and Karen had said she would heat up a beef casserole she'd made and frozen at the weekend. She'd left it defrosting in the fridge this morning and had had hers earlier when she'd got in from work.

"Hi," she called from the kitchen. "Wine?"

"I think so." He walked in, kissed her, and sat at the table while she poured.

"You're all over the news," she said as she handed him a well-filled glass. "Still nothing about Becky?"

"Still nothing," he said after his first couple of sips. "I'm really thinking it might not end well." He shrugged. "I think I'm going to try and take an hour off from thinking about it. How was your day?"

She talked about her day at work while she dished up his food and then sat with him as he ate. It felt good to hear about something that had nothing to do with the misery human beings can inflict on one another, and Karen's anecdotes about her colleagues and clients even made him laugh – something he found he badly needed. It felt good to laugh at something that was actually funny rather than the gallows humour that was a stock in trade of his profession.

He realised that he'd hardly given a moment's thought all day to the amazing thing that had happened last night. He'd woken this morning with a feeling of elation. He was, to all intents and purposes, engaged to the woman who was everything to him. And, now the decision was made, he couldn't wait to exchange engagement rings and make it official. He couldn't wait to set a wedding date, although he wasn't sure who would come. They weren't exactly flush for friends, and he wasn't holding his breath waiting for family support either.

Archer and Dominic would come, he was sure. He realised that he hadn't even told Archer his news yet. He needed to find a moment to do that tomorrow

"Dan?"

He started guiltily, realising he hadn't been listening to Karen. "What was that?" He tried to make out he hadn't quite heard the last thing she'd said.

"I said, what do you think I should do about it?"

It wasn't much of a clue. He sipped some more wine, hoping it looked as if he was thinking about Karen's dilemma, whatever it was.

But he'd told her too much about techniques for interviewing a suspect. She just sat there, leaving the ball in his court, letting the silence build, knowing he'd have to say something eventually.

"I'm sorry," he finally admitted. "I must have tuned out. What were you asking about?"

"My boss asked if I'd join him and his wife for a threesome."

He almost choked on his wine. "Seriously?"

"No. It doesn't matter."

"Tell me again."

"It doesn't matter."

She got up from the table and started to unload the dishwasher. Baines sat eating on autopilot, feeling guilty now, the food like ash in his mouth.

"I said we could be downsizing," she said, relenting. "I might be out of a job."

He looked at her. "Really?" Karen loved her job.

"It's just an option they're looking at right now. They need to cut costs. It mightn't even be me for the chop – if it happens." She turned and faced him. "Probably nothing to worry about."

"But you *are* worried?"

"We might be trying to crawl our way out of recession, Dan, but jobs aren't exactly growing on trees."

"We'd manage if we had to."

"I don't want to just manage." She looked at the floor. "And I don't want to be a kept woman."

He couldn't help laughing. "You make that sound a bit dirty, in a Victorian sort of way."

"Well, I don't think it's funny. I want to pay my way."

"Sorry," Baines said. It was just one other way she was like her sister. Louise had been determined to get back to work as soon as Jack was in nursery school.

"Hardly your fault." She sighed. "Nothing's going to be decided for a while. If I do get made redundant, maybe there'll be a retraining package as part of the deal." She turned back to her task.

He swallowed the last mouthful of his meal and swigged some more wine. "Yes? Was there something you had in mind?"

"No. Something creative, though."

"Well, if it happens, whatever you decide, I'm right behind you."

"No, you're not." But her laugh was good-humoured. "You'll be out all hours dealing with dead people."

He got up, came up behind her and rested his hands on her shoulders. "Do you mind that?"

"What, mind you going after the bad guys? The more the better."

He changed the subject. "Have you given any thought to what sort of ring you want?"

"I thought you might be planning on bidding for one on eBay."

"No way. I want to take you to a fancy jeweller and choose something really special."

She closed the dishwasher door and turned to face him. "A Christmas cracker ring would do for me."

He shook his head. "Not nearly good enough for my lady."

She kissed him lightly. "Well, then. If you really insist…"

* * *

Amy Petrescu lay in Ashby's bed, snuggled in the crook of his arm. This whole thing was crazy and totally unexpected.

Was she falling in love with him? She wasn't ready to call it that yet. But she did know that he made her feel like no one else had been able to in a very long time. He listened to her, seemed to understand her, and had opened up to her too.

She was actually quite surprised at the extent to which this seemingly tough guy had confided his insecurities to her: how he had never felt liked, or appreciated, by work colleagues in Aylesbury. How no one really understood his role, and assumed he was a lazy bugger who used what he did as a front for swanning off.

But she had seen some of his methods at first hand, and was impressed. He really did seem to know all the go-to people who might have intelligence or information with a bearing on the case.

"Even that's a double-edged sword," he'd told her, when she said as much. "Some people – especially in Lizzie Archer's team – think I'm more in with the bad guys than the good guys. They probably think I'm on the take."

"You should take some of them out with you, like you have me. Once they see—"

"No. It's taken me years to build trust, without turning up every time with another copper in tow – not all of who will give off the right vibes. You're different," he added, pleasing her.

"But," she persisted, "Gillingham must trust you, to give you carte blanche like that."

"Yeah, well, we go back a way."

She laughed. "There's even a joke that you must have some hold over him."

He didn't laugh back. "So you've heard that too? I won't ask who from."

"Well, good. Because I'd rather not say."

He shrugged. "You don't need to."

"But it's bollocks, right? I mean, you're good at what you do. Gillingham's been astute enough to recognise that. So what? Other people get jealous. I mean, what hold could you possibly have over him?"

For the first time since they'd met, he gave her a hard look. "Are you fishing?"

"What? No! I was just talking."

"Well, don't."

She looked away, a little hurt.

"I'm sorry," he said after a few moments. "It's just that I take all this crap from the others..."

"I get it. And crap is all it is, right?"

She dropped the subject then. This evening, he'd brought her to his place, the first time they'd not gone to her hotel room. It had felt like a step forward in their relationship. He'd even cooked for her – a passable risotto. The lovemaking had been nice, too.

"So," she said sleepily, "how are we going to work this?"

"Hmm? Work what?"

"Seeing each other. I might not be at the Vale much longer."

"Yeah. Yeah, I can see that'll be tricky."

She turned towards him, propping herself up on an elbow. "It needn't be. We're hardly going to be on opposite sides of the world."

"No, that's true." He sat up. "You really want to? Keep this going, I mean?"

Her stomach flipped over. "You mean you don't?"

He didn't answer for a moment. She berated herself for being such a fool. She'd been imagining weekends alternating between Ashby's home and her own: walks, pubs, taking turns at cooking. Nights of passion. He seemed to like her. But what if she was just a convenience to him? What if, just like her every other attempt at a relationship, it had gone hideously wrong?

But, when her eyes searched his face, they saw only vulnerability.

"Steve? What is it?"

He gave her a half-smile. "I wanted to ask you if we could keep on seeing each other, but I was scared. I thought maybe this was just a fling for you. A bit like a holiday romance. I thought, if I didn't ask, you wouldn't have to turn me down."

Her stomach gave another flip, but this was a good one.

"I didn't want this to be the night you let me down gently," he said. "I didn't want to spoil it."

She sighed and snuggled up to him. "It just shows we need to get to know each other better. I've made a lot of mistakes, especially with blokes."

He laughed humourlessly. "I've just made a lot of mistakes. There's a lot you don't know about me, Amy. But maybe I'd like you to."

"I think I'd like that a lot. So how are we going to work it?"

"Don't go home tomorrow evening. Stay here for the weekend."

"Yeah?" She was pleased.

"Yeah. I was seeing some mates, but I'll cancel. Unless you had plans."

"Just doing my washing. Which, actually, I do have to do."

He laughed. "I see you've got a practical side. But, like you said, we're not on opposite sides of the world. You can go home, grab some stuff for the weekend, and wash your smalls or whatever here. I mean," he added, "I might be a bit of a caveman, but I do actually possess a washing machine. What do you think?"

She kissed him. "Mister," she said, "I think you've got yourself a deal."

25

Friday morning

Archer was at her desk before 7am. Only the redoubtable Joan Collins had beaten her in. Archer had mentioned to her the previous evening that they needed to review the Carly Eustace murder, and the DC had already spent God knew how long this morning making sure they had all the paperwork and that the board in the briefing room was up to date.

Her guilty feelings returned afresh as she realised how badly they'd allowed the case to slide. Two days with negligible input, while the trail went ever colder. With hindsight, maybe the case and Amy Petrescu should have been handed back to Oxfordshire to lead on.

Not that there was a scrap of evidence to go on, however you looked at it. The case review took little time, and Archer could hear noises in the corridor, telling her others were starting to arrive, as she stared at Carly's picture.

"Who were you really?" she mused. "Not the person everyone thought you were. Where did you go that night? Who were you meeting?"

Carly's frozen smile seemed to mock her.

She turned to speak to Collins. Just then, the door opened and Phil Gordon walked in.

"Bright and early, Phil," she remarked.

"Yes, well, some of my guys have worked through the night, Lizzie – and we might have found something at Briscoe's home – not his parents' house, but his own. I think you'll want to scramble the team."

Her pulse quickened. "What is it?"

"Well, we've taken the cars apart and swept both houses. Some hairs and fibres – lots of them, all being analysed, of course, along with that blood. We started taking up floorboards. And then I put search teams in both gardens, working under lights, in case anything was buried there."

Oh, God. Becky.

"They found a body?"

His smile was unusually enigmatic.

"In Meeting Room One. Come and see for yourself."

She wished he'd just spit it out, but she had little choice but to follow him. She spotted Baines in the corridor and told him to come too.

"We swapped shifts about half five," Gordon said as he pushed open the meeting room door, "and they found it almost immediately. What are the chances?"

"For fuck's sake, Phil, just tell us!"

He led them to the table in the middle of the room, on which lay a full black bin liner, a few particles of soil still clinging to it. Archer had already surmised that, whatever had been found, it wasn't a body. Gordon was hardly going to lug that into the office.

The crime scene manager opened the bag and removed items in transparent evidence bags. Archer, Baines and Collins watched him. A chill was spreading through Archer's body. She could feel the hairs on the back of her neck standing up.

"Clothes and jewellery?" She could hear the puzzlement in Baines's voice. "And a handbag? But... these won't be Becky's. She was in school uniform."

"They're not Becky's," Archer said quietly, reaching out to touch the bag nearest her. "Green coat." She moved her hand to another, smaller, bag and held it up. "Green earrings."

"Oh, my God." Collins' eyes were wide. "Carly Eustace."

* * *

By the time Ashby arrived, Adina Walker had been summoned and told her client would be interviewed on a new matter, in light of fresh evidence. Gillingham arrived shortly before the grilling recommenced, and his demeanour as lightened visibly as he agreed that Archer should sit in.

Phil Gordon's evidence bags lay on the table in the interview room. Briscoe had, Archer thought, gone several shades paler.

"Have you got anything to say?" Ashby coaxed.

"We'll be showing these items to Harry Eustace," Archer said. "We both know he'll confirm that his wife, Carly, was wearing them when she left their home the night she died."

He looked at her, ashen, his mouth open. She hoped he wouldn't have a heart attack. Not yet, anyway.

She tapped the handbag through its plastic container. "We found Carly's purse in here, with her driving licence, credit cards and other forms of identification. We found two phones. One's a cheap pay-as-you-go, and the only number it's called is yours. Any comments so far?"

He stared at the table and mumbled something.

"Can you speak up, for the recording?" Archer said.

He looked up. "No comment."

"Oh, no," moaned Baines. "Not no comment. I blame the telly. They all see witnesses saying it, and they think it's like the States, where they claim the Fifth Amendment."

"Mark, there are bound to be traces of Carly in your Focus," Archer pressed. "Because she was in there, wasn't she? And that blood under the coffee table will be hers, too, won't it?"

"No comment."

"And any we find on the table itself," she went on relentlessly. "It's pretty obvious that, unlike Jade, Carly didn't go into that boot alive."

"No comment."

"Can you at least wait until we invite you to comment?" Ashby suggested. "This might go a little quicker."

"Look, Mark," Archer said. "Abducting Jade is going to get you put away for a very long time. You know we're going to be able to prove your car knocked down and killed Leanne. We know it wasn't stolen, as you've already admitted killing her. We know you abducted Jade and almost killed her too. Now we're going to prove that you also killed Carly Eustace on Thursday night."

"You might as well give it up, Mark," Ashby said. "Things look bad for you, but a bit of co-operation never goes amiss."

"We think you were driving through Houghton on the way from your home to Millett Wood." Archer fixed her eyes on Briscoe's pale face. "Not PC World. That never rang true. We suspect you weren't concentrating on your driving because you had something on your mind. A body in the boot, to be precise."

"A body you were planning to dump in the wood," Ashby added. "And, when you hit Leanne, you daren't stop in case the car was impounded and we saw what was in there."

"No," he said.

"Mark, all the evidence points to you," persisted Archer. "Unless you seriously imagine any jury would believe that somebody buried the evidence in your garden, just to frame you. Why not come clean? Was it some kinky sex game that got out of hand? You got too much into the violence?"

"No."

"What, then?" Archer persisted.

"Let it out, Mark," Ashby said. "You had an affair with Carly. Didn't you?"

"I never…"

"Mark, don't say any more," Walker said sharply. She looked at Archer. "I need a private word with my client."

"No," Ashby said, something of his old belligerence surfacing. "No more bloody private words."

But Briscoe was already shaking his head. "What's the use? It's over. I'll be glad to get it off my chest."

"Do you want to make a new statement?" Archer asked.

He nodded. "I never meant for any of this to happen. Carly… that poor girl, Leanne… Jade. It all just happened, and everything got out of control."

* * *

Briscoe admitted he had been having an affair with Carly Eustace. It had started almost by accident as a result of a work-related meeting: the possibility of Briscoe's school getting involved in Carly's project, to be precise.

He'd suggested coffee and they had exchanged numbers. Perhaps she'd been looking for a bit of excitement in her life.

Not the sort of excitement that involved bondage, though. Briscoe had been adamant that the subject had never come up, and she had never known what lay inside the locked freezer.

They'd met after work for sex at his house, Carly usually using her group of girlfriends as an alibi to her husband. Little by little, however, Briscoe had fallen in love with her, and had imagined she felt the same, even though neither of them had actually said it out loud.

He started applying gentle pressure for her to leave her husband. But instead, last Thursday, she'd met him as usual and let him drive her to his house. They made love, but when she'd got dressed, she told him it would be the last time.

"I can't do this any more," she said. "It's not fair on Harry. I'm never going to leave him."

Briscoe had been devastated at first, then angry, feeling somehow used. He started off trying to make Carly change her mind, but somewhere along the way he flew into a monumental rage. He swore he'd never lost it in that way before. Ever. In the living room, he lashed out, and she went down and striking her head on the edge of the coffee table. There was blood, she stopped breathing, and his attempts to revive her proved useless.

Horror-stricken, he'd sat on his living-room floor for an hour, staring at the body. Devastated that he'd killed the person he loved. Appalled at the personal consequences for himself.

Had he considered calling the police? Baines asked. Definitely. But Briscoe had been certain his life would be over if he did. Even if he got off on a lesser charge than murder, he'd go to prison. It would mean the end of his career. Chances were, he'd never work again in any worthwhile capacity.

Carly was dead, he'd reasoned with himself. Nothing could bring her back. But he was fairly sure no one else knew about their affair. Maybe he could still save his own skin.

Trying to get rid of the body, to cover up what he had done, carried big risks, he knew. He would be undermining any claims of mitigation – provocation – that he might later want to employ. But he persuaded himself that it was only a matter of degree: just how comprehensively his life would be destroyed. A chance of getting away with it altogether, when weighed in the balance, easily came out on top.

Afterwards, he had been amazed at how clear his mind had become. Disposing of the body was only part of the challenge. The longer it took for her to be found, surely the harder it would be for the police to connect her death back to him.

And then the idea had come to him. A wood he'd walked in a few times, when he'd been part of a rambling club. A corner off the beaten track, overgrown at this time of year. A fellow rambler had even joked that it would be a good place to hide a body.

He'd stripped her of all clothing and jewellery, figuring that if it took a while to identify her, the trail would go a little colder. He had a big enough suitcase with wheels, into which he'd managed to fold the body. Then he'd reversed his car up to his front door and managed to manhandle the case into the boot. He'd planned to give the house a damn good clean later, although he hoped the police would never come to his door.

He'd been incredibly lucky. Even if anything did come back to him, no one had seen him, and no one was about when he hefted the case out of the boot, wheeled it into the woods, and dumped its grim contents. He'd chucked the case in a skip at the local recycling centre at the weekend. He was hardly going to use it ever again.

All that had gone smoothly. It was the bit in the middle that had gone to hell in a handcart, when he had been driving through Houghton on the way to the wood.

As he sped away from the accident, he'd had to fight down hysterical laughter that threatened to bubble out of him. It was as if the gods of fate really had it in for him that night. He'd calmed down enough to dump the body, then gone home, looked at Carly's clothing and other effects and decided to shove them in a bin liner and bury it in his garden at night. At least it would be out of the house.

The rest, they knew. They knew everything – except what had happened to Becky.

26

It was mid-morning when the team reassembled. Members of the team had spent some time with the families of Leanne Richards and Carly Eustace, and the reactions had been markedly different.

For Leanne's family, there seemed some sense of relief. That a kind of justice for Leanne, some sort of closure might be possible. For Harry Eustace, it was obvious that everything would take a long time to really sink in. He would need some serious thought in the weeks and months ahead, Archer thought. She hoped he made sure he got it.

"All right, everyone," Gillingham said. "This has been a good day so far, and in many ways, a pretty good week. Three cases cracked. But we don't have time to sit around congratulating ourselves. Becky Day's still out there somewhere and, dead or alive, we're going to find her. Steve, Lizzie, Dan – you've spent a lot of time questioning Mark Briscoe now. What do you think?"

"He's killed her," Ashby said flatly. "That's why he's still denying all knowledge of her. Adina Walker, will have talked him through what he's confessed to so far. He'll be reasoning that we won't get more than involuntary manslaughter for Carly. Leanne was an accident, and Jade is alive. He's probably expecting some sentence reduction for admitting everything. Yeah, there are plenty of lesser charges too. But the whole lot won't add up to the sort of sentence he'll get if he's murdered Becky. If he's got her and she's alive, he'd tell us now, I think. But if there's the risk of a life sentence..." He left the point hanging.

"All right." Gillingham nodded. "Lizzie?"

She'd lain awake last night running through the permutations. Every time she thought she'd settled on a conclusion, she'd changed her mind.

"DI Ashby's probably right," she said, tentatively. "*If* Briscoe took Becky. But only if he killed her. Another accident, another rush of blood? It's possible, I suppose."

Gillingham frowned. "But you don't think so?"

She found herself hesitating again. If Becky was still alive, any time wasted chasing shadows could be disastrous. But she had to speak her mind.

"We can't entirely rule it out, sir, but how unlucky can one guy get? Even a fuckup like Briscoe? The alternative is that he's killed her in cold blood. I'm not sure he's capable of that."

"Desperate men are capable of a lot, in my experience," Ashby argued. "He made up a pretty good abduction plan for Jade on the hoof, remember."

"True. But then why not sneak back and kill Jade too? Tie up all loose ends? It doesn't smell right, that's all."

"Have you got a better theory?" Gillingham challenged.

"Not at the moment, no. I reckon we need to do some fresh thinking."

"There isn't time," Ashby protested. "Not if she's still alive."

"But you don't think she is, Steve."

He nodded. "Fair point. I'm not a hundred per cent sure, one way or the other."

"What do you think, Dan?" Gillingham asked.

All eyes were on Baines, who took a long time before he answered. "It's a tough one, but I think I'm with DI Archer. We've got Briscoe in custody, and we've charged him. He's not going anywhere. Maybe we should let him stew while we make sure we're not missing something."

"Let's get this straight." Gillingham looked uncomfortable. "We're saying Becky Day's disappearance might be unconnected with Jade's, after all?"

Archer thought that, after the news he'd shared with her last night, this was the last thing he needed to be breaking to his bosses.

"It's worth a shot," said Ashby. Archer shot him a grateful look. "Dan's got a fair point. Leave him sweating for a couple of hours and then, if we're no further forward, grill him all the harder."

The DCI looked undecided for a few seconds, then shifted his shoulders, as if adjusting a heavy weight. "All right. But we start again, then, with a clean sheet of paper, as if this is a completely new case. That means going back to basics. Talk to the family again, and to her friends. Could she have gone off of her own accord? Show her picture around. Do an appeal on TV. Check out known sex offenders – yes, I know we've done that once, but let's do it again. Have another look through what we got from the door-to-door yesterday, too." He paused. "I'm going to ask DI Archer to take the lead."

Archer glanced at Ashby. Saw the corners of his mouth turn down.

"Sorry, Steve," Gillingham said, evidently spotting it too. "You did a great job with Jade, but I need you to concentrate on working those networks of yours. Someone, somewhere, might know something. Use whoever you need to support you."

"I guess you'll be working alone on that, right, Steve?" Archer said. "I know how you like to keep your sources protected."

"Two heads are better than one," he said. "Maybe Amy could work with me."

"I don't know about that," Archer began, irritated that he was making off with a valuable resource again.

"Sort it out amongst yourselves," Gillingham interrupted. "I shall get very impatient if we waste time on a turf war when we should be finding this kid."

She decided Gillingham was right, even if she didn't like it.

"Okay, Steve," Archer conceded. "Take Amy for now, and I'll shout if I need her. Dan, you're with me on family and friends. Jason, Joan, I need you to check out those sex offender alibis and the door-to-door material. Will, everything goes through you. Log absolutely everything." She rose from her seat. "I'll dish out other jobs in a little while, so no one run off. Becky's been missing too long already."

* * *

Archer and Baines sat on Josh and Emma Day's sofa, cups of coffee neither of them really wanted going cold. A uniformed family liaison officer sat in the background. The last time Archer had been here, Becky had been here too, answering questions about Jade Sheldon's disappearance. Now Jade was safe and it was Becky who was missing.

She studied the family picture on the sideboard to her left. Becky and her parents, happy on holiday. You could see sand and sea behind them, the sky blue on a sunny day.

"I know this is hard," she said, "and I know it must feel like we're going over the same thing over and again, but as you know, we'd been thinking Becky's disappearance might have something to do with Jade's. We haven't closed that line of enquiry, but we're reviewing other angles, to be sure we haven't missed anything."

Emma Day's fair hair hung in lifeless strands. Her blue eyes were pinpricks in dark wells. Her skin was pasty. Josh Day didn't look much better.

"Ask us anything," Josh said. "Anything at all."

Archer mustered her thoughts. "What was Becky's mood on Wednesday morning?"

"A bit subdued. She was still upset about Leanne, and Jade was missing. And I made it worse by lecturing her on being careful."

"Have you noticed anyone hanging around lately, acting suspiciously? Had Becky?"

Josh shook his head, a flash of irritation unmistakable in his eyes. "If we'd noticed any dodgy-looking characters, don't you think we'd have said?"

"For Christ's sake, Josh," Emma moaned. "Why do you always..." She stuffed her fist into her mouth. Took a ragged breath. "I'm sorry."

Josh was rubbing his wife's shoulder. "No," he said to her, "I'm the one who should be sorry." He looked at Archer. "I apologise. Please ask your questions."

"Nothing to apologise for."

Archer had seen this before. The stress digging deep holes in relationships at the very time families needed to be there for each other. She hoped this wouldn't happen with the Days. Becky was their only child – probably the centre of their universe.

"Now," she continued, "I think you've said Becky has never had a boyfriend."

"Not so far," Josh answered. "She was in no hurry for that sort of thing."

"And can you think of any older men that she's friendly with that we maybe ought to take a look at? I'm not suggesting anything," she added hastily. "I just need to ask. Or older women, for that matter."

"Especially anyone new in her life?" Baines chipped in.

They shook their heads. "There's no one," Josh said.

"Emma?" Archer checked.

"No. She's got her friends, and she hangs out with them mostly. Goes to youth club."

"Your guys have her computer," Josh added. "We have parental controls on her computer. On her phone and tablet too, but she had those with her. And we monitor what she does online."

Archer saw despair in his eyes.

"The only thing she did that we didn't really like was use that footpath as a cut-through. But I made her late this morning. I bet she went that way. We're so scared that some random pervert has taken her."

But Archer had been reappraising the idea of this being a random snatch. Maybe Briscoe hadn't taken Becky, but the events in Houghton had to be either connected in some way, or to have been a catalyst.

Becky had made a fleeting, accidental TV appearance just under a week ago. It was obvious she lived in Houghton, and her address was probably easy enough to find out. If someone had targeted her, how hard would it be to monitor her routine for a couple of days and then wait for their chance?

She wasn't about to say that to the Days, though. Not yet. Their nerves were shredded enough already.

She took a sip of coffee, simply to buy her a moment to evaluate the couple, trying to cast her mind back to when she was Becky's age. She was fairly sure that by the time she'd changed schools at eleven, she'd no longer entirely seen boys as an embarrassing other species, but surely dating had come a little later? Her parents had been careful of her, but not stifling or controlling, and she saw nothing in Becky's parents that suggested any different. There was nothing wrong with being protective.

God knew, she'd come across her fair share of young girls whose parents had been too casual about their daughters and then been shocked when something bad had happened to them.

"I take it there's no question Becky would get into a car with a stranger?" she checked.

"We'd told her often enough when she was younger," Emma said. "She got it."

"Ever hear her mention a man called Mark Briscoe? A teacher at a primary school in Aylesbury?"

"Isn't he the one who had Jade?" Josh had turned even paler. "But... hasn't he just been charged with a murder? It was on the local news."

"Please don't worry," Archer urged, mentally cursing the efficiency of her PR department.

Baines interjected, "Look, there's no point in panicking. We don't know what's happened yet. I know Becky's a good girl, but she's at a funny age, too. Out of character though it might be, there could be dozens of reasons why she'd just go off somewhere, before we start looking at scary scenarios."

"You did really well there, Dan," Archer told Baines in the car afterwards. "I doubt they've completely calmed down, or have stopped torturing themselves with the worst thoughts, but you probably stopped them fixating on Briscoe."

"So where to next?"

"Becky's friends. Let's hope one of them has remembered something. Or has been keeping a secret for her."

He consulted a list of addresses. "One in Houghton. Two more in Aylesbury. Might as well do the local one first?"

She nodded and he started the engine. "Actually, I had a thought in there."

"Let's hear it."

180

"I'd like to go back to the end of the footpath we think Becky was probably cutting through when she disappeared."

"Okay. But can I ask why?" She trusted Baines' judgement, but the place had been overrun with CSIs already.. They'd found no sign of a struggle, nothing to suggest that Becky Day had even come that way this morning, let alone been abducted there. And the police had knocked at every door in the neighbourhood, but had drawn a blank there too.

Maybe she hadn't taken the shortcut at all.

"I'm not entirely sure. It's just that I haven't been there myself. I just wonder if something maybe got missed or misinterpreted."

"Nor have I," she admitted. "Okay, Sherlock. Why not?"

27

Baines drew his Mondeo up at the end of the footpath. The path itself was still closed off, crime scene tape stretched across the point where it emerged onto the road. If the CSIs wanted to come back for any reason, the tape might reduce the likelihood of locals trundling through and damaging the scene.

The path emerged from a gap in a hedgerow that was in need of cutting back. There were a couple of houses opposite, then a side road, the first houses on either side a little way down. The only other building that appeared to face the path's exit was a shop selling electrical goods. Baines crossed over, Archer following.

He examined the sign on the door. "It wouldn't have been anywhere near opening time when Becky came through."

He went back to the car and leaned against it, looking across at the houses.

"Will went through all the door-to-door reports," Archer said. "Every house in the area got a knock, and there was a response from each of them. No one saw anything untoward."

"Not even the nosey parker across there?"

She looked across. A net curtain twitched.

"Not even them. And they'd have seen anything there was to see."

"Hang on, though." He was pacing around now, as he sometimes did when he was thinking. It never failed to irritate her.

"I'm hanging on," she said.

He stopped pacing. "Okay. You said no one saw anything untoward. What if there was something toward?"

"Translate into English?"

"Sorry." He didn't look it. "I wonder if whatever happened looked normal. Didn't arouse any suspicion, so nobody noted it."

"Or it could just be that no one saw it."

She was growing impatient now, but then she saw the look on his face. She'd seen it a few times before, and it usually meant she should listen to him.

"All right," she said. "What's on your mind?"

"Let's start with the nosey parker. Can you remember what she said?"

"You're assuming it's a she." She smiled and shook her head. "It can't be a nosey male?"

"Could be. Whatever. Can you remember?" he repeated

She shook her head again. "Christ, no. There were dozens of notes."

"Well, humour me for a few minutes." He took out his phone.

"Who are you calling?"

"Will. I want to know exactly what we've got from Mr or Ms Nosey."

Baines sat in the car while he made the call, his notebook balanced on one knee. Archer stood by the car, her arms folded, looking across at the house Baines was so interested in. The nosey parker wasn't exactly subtle. Every few seconds the net curtain twitched.

Baines got out. "Well, it's a man. A Mr Roger Husband. But he said he saw nothing, apart from police activity. Which is odd."

"What's odd? We had a few cars in the village because of Jade that morning." She fell silent, puzzled, as she saw his point. "Except... what would we have been doing *here*? At this spot, I mean? At that time of the morning? It's not an obvious place for us to be. "

"That's what I thought. According to Mr Husband, though, there was a police car parked at the end of the lane. I made Will cross-check the door-to-door notes, and it doesn't make sense. None of our cars should have been parked here then."

She shrugged. "Well, perhaps one of our squad cars bought some grub from the village store and sat here for a while eating and drinking."

"But that would mean that Becky was taken from right under their noses."

"Or she didn't use the path after all. Still, we might as well knock on Mr Husband's door. Make sure we know exactly what he saw."

Roger Husband's front door was covered in stickers: no hawkers; no canvassers; neighbourhood watch; we neither buy nor sell at this door; no religious representatives. He opened the door with the chain on, eyed them suspiciously, and demanded ID.

Archer didn't blame him. The area had seen its fair share of distraction burglaries in recent years. "It looks genuine, I suppose," he said, "but then how could I tell if it was fake?"

"By all means, ring Aylesbury Police Station," Archer told him. "They can verify our warrant card numbers."

He considered this. "Well, I don't suppose you'd be suggesting it if you were frauds," he decided. "You'd best come in."

Inside, the house was immaculate. Nothing out of place, everything spotless.

"I suppose I ought to offer you a beverage," Husband said without enthusiasm.

"We're fine," Archer assured him.

"Yes? Well, take a seat, take a seat."

Feeling like she was about to crease or soil the sofa he indicated, Archer perched on the edge. She noticed Baines mirroring her.

She got straight to the point. "According to our records, you said you saw a police car parked opposite on Wednesday morning, around the time Becky Day disappeared."

"I did."

"A squad car?"

"What, white with those yellow and blue squares on the sides?"

"That's the one."

"No," he said decisively. "This was an unmarked car."

Archer nearly fell off the sofa. "Unmarked?"

"Oh, yes. A Merc."

"A Merc?" No one in Aylesbury nick drove anything like that. Ashby's Audi was possibly the flashiest thing in the car park.

"One of those big SUV jobs," Roger Husband was saying. "Silver. GLC, I'd say."

"That sounds very precise," Baines remarked.

"Well, I don't drive much, these days, but I'm still a bit of a petrol-head. I was a big *Top Gear* fan when Clarkson was on it." He curled his lip. "Mind you, you can see where my council tax is going if that's what coppers are driving these days."

Archer ignored the jibe. "If it was unmarked, what makes you think it was a police car?"

He looked at her pityingly. "There was a police officer in it."

"In uniform?"

"Yes. No. Well, they were wearing one of those fluorescent yellow things."

"A man or a woman?"

"You know, I'm not sure. They had short hair."

Archer was getting an increasingly queasy feeling.

"But you didn't see a young girl come down the path?"

"Well, I do like to keep an eye on things. But even the most vigilant man has to spend the occasional penny."

"And did you?" Baines pushed. "Spend a penny?"

"I might have."

"Did you see a girl or not?" Archer was trying not to shout. It was like drawing teeth. She wanted to shake this old codger.

"Look, it's not my job to watch that blessed path. I remember the car being there. Then I looked out and it had gone. It's not like I was watching it the whole time." He was getting worked up. "I mean, why on earth should I watch the police? I felt happy knowing they were there."

"Did you mention all this when our officers called on you before?"

"They didn't ask."

"Did you note the registration?"

He picked up the edge to her tone, and looked defensive. "Why would I note a police registration? Look." He held a hand up. "You're going to have to excuse me, I'm afraid. I need to spend a penny."

"Dear God," Archer said when she thought he was out of earshot.

"Don't knock it. We've got some useful stuff out of him."

"We ought to water-board him. No one fucking asked, indeed."

"Let it go." He grinned. "We need more nosey parkers. Silver Merc SUV? Could be a good lead."

"GLC, if you believe him. Whatever that is. Those Chelsea tractors all look the same to me. Still," she added, "it should at least be rarer than white bloody Focuses." She sighed. "I'll get Joan on it when we've finished here."

It was starting to rain, quite heavily, as they stepped out of Roger Husband's front door. It did nothing for Archer's humour. She phoned Collins and asked her to check with DVLA who owned a silver Mercedes SUV in the area.

"Any particular model?"

"Mr Observant here thinks maybe a GLC, but I'd rather check them all out, just to be sure. Maybe Audis and BMWs for good measure."

"On it, guv."

"Fingers crossed it's a short list."

* * *

The hastily assembled lunchtime briefing was, at best, inconclusive and, at worst, dispiriting. The silver SUV was the one possible lead they had, and Collins was still waiting for information from the DVLA database. For all they knew, the car had a legitimate reason for being there anyway, or possibly Roger Husband had been mistaken about the make. And, for all they knew, it could have come from anywhere in the country.

"One thing's for sure," Tyler said. "It wasn't one of ours. I double-checked. No copper in an unmarked silver Merc, or any other car, was there yesterday morning."

"Hardly surprising," Gillingham growled. "So, did someone pose as a cop and somehow persuade Becky to go with them?"

"Her parents swear she's too sensible to get in a car with a stranger voluntarily," Archer said. "But a police officer? She might feel she could trust them."

"She might even think she has to do what they say," Bell added.

"But why?" The DCI mused. "Why Becky? Why now?"

"It can't be random," Archer said.

"It must be like we said before. Some pervert saw her on TV – even if she was only on screen for a second – and got fixated on her?" Petrescu suggested.

"Maybe." Archer's face was pensive. "That still feels a bit random to me. And a tad unlikely. We've not heard of other girls vanishing after split-second TV appearances, so again – why now?"

Baines had been listening to the exchange, processing what was being said, and Archer's comment solidified a vague idea that had been forming in his mind.

"How about this?" he said. "It's not random at all, and it's really got nothing to do with the TV or anything else that's been going on. Well, almost nothing."

"Could you be a bit clearer, Dan?" snapped Gillingham. "Preferably today?"

Baines ignored the interruption. "So, say someone has a specific interest in Becky. I haven't got my head round a motive yet, but someone could have been stalking her. Or maybe, despite her 'good girl' appearance, she was into something illegal and someone was worried she was about to compromise them. Whatever. Then along comes Jade's disappearance."

"Yes!" Archer's head had been drooping, and now it came up as she grabbed Baines's idea and ran with it. "They figure that, if they move now, we'll do exactly what we did – assume the girls' disappearances are linked, and go off on completely the wrong track."

"Exactly. The abductor wouldn't even have to know she was a witness to the accident, like Jade. A second girl disappearing from Houghton was enough to force a connection."

"And we made it," said Gillingham bitterly. "And, as a result, we've wasted two days."

"Not entirely wasted," Archer said. "We strongly suspect

Becky was taken by someone posing as a cop. And we know to start looking for specific motives for going after her."

"That's the hard bit." The DCI didn't seem any cheerier. "What's the motive? If we had that…" He looked around the room. "Anyone got anything at all?"

No one had. Steve Ashby had nothing from his networks.

"Of course," Ashby pointed out, "that silver car could be a complete red herring. Just some guy in fluorescent yellow who happened to park up there for a while. We should lean on Briscoe again. Really hard this time."

"I think that might be flogging a dead horse," Gillingham opined, "but, on the off-chance that he did do anything to her, let's leave him to sweat for now."

28

Baines stood in a deserted briefing room, a mug of coffee in one hand and an unappetising vending machine sandwich in the other, staring at the case boards. The complexity of the cases they had been juggling for the past week or so, and the fact that more links between them might still be possible, meant that the boards for the closed cases hadn't been removed.

What a week it had been. It ought to be one to remember with pleasure and satisfaction: a murder, a hit-and-run, and a kidnapping, all solved. The team should be looking forward to big Friday night drinks.

And he and Karen were going to be married!

They were hoping to look at rings over the weekend. But, with Becky Day's fate still unknown, there was no time for celebration. The way things were going, weekend leave was likely to be cancelled. Some cases could wait the weekend to be solved. Not this one.

He'd had no inspiration when Archer entered with her own steaming mug and joined him, her gaze travelling over the notes and pictures on the boards.

"Cracked it?" she asked him, without a trace of humour.

He laughed hollowly. "I'm hoping to God that the answer is somewhere here."

"I know. I've got such a bad feeling about this, Dan. My suspicions are starting to drift back towards Briscoe. Maybe Ashby's hunch is right. Instead of stewing, maybe he's using this time to polish up his excuses for what we've already got him on. Trying to finesse them down to the minimum culpability."

"All mostly just poor judgement?"

"The last time he was questioned, he kept insisting that he would have let Jade out of that boot if we hadn't arrested him

189

first. But if he's murdered Becky, he'd struggle to mitigate that. If she's buried somewhere, his best hope is that we never find her. Or, if we do, that we can't pin it on him."

He took another bite out of the sandwich. It really wasn't worth the bother. He chucked the rest in a bin, chewed and swallowed, before turning to look Archer in the eye.

"So do we really like him for Becky's abduction?"

She raised her eyes to the ceiling, then looked back at him. "Honestly? No." She raised an eyebrow. "You?"

"No," he agreed. "He's not a stone-cold killer. At least, I don't think so. I certainly wouldn't stake Becky's life on it. If you see what I mean?"

She nodded and stared at Becky's board again. She had a way of peering at case boards through half-closed eyelids, as if that would somehow make things clearer.

She turned her head his way. "You know, there's something here that's been bothering me. Although I've only just realised."

"Go on."

"All right." She moved closer to the board. "It's about this." She tapped a family picture: Becky with her parents, Josh and Emma. Baines stepped forward to stand at her shoulder. "Notice anything?"

There was an anxiety in her voice, although whether she was seeking confirmation of what she was thinking, or dismissal of a daft idea, he couldn't quite tell.

"Not really," he admitted. "Just a happy family snap of people without a care in the world." He looked again. "Well, apart from the obvious, I suppose."

"Which is?"

"Becky's hair is dark, and both her parents are fair."

"Yes," she agreed. "It was under my nose and I've only just really thought about it."

"But so what?"

She nodded. "Exactly. So what? It's not unknown for a child's hair colouring not to match the parents. Red hair in particular."

"Regressive genes. But you're thinking something else?"

"I'm thinking, what if Becky was adopted? Or only one of

the parents is biological? Does that introduce a motive of some sort?"

"I suppose so." He looked at the holiday snap in a new light. Maybe it was clutching at straws, but they didn't have a great deal else right now. "Probably several, in fact. A father who discovers his daughter isn't his. A biological father who discovers he's got a twelve-year old daughter he didn't know about..."

"Or a birth mother who wants her child back?" she speculated.

"That's what you're thinking?"

"Honestly? I really don't know what I think. But let's talk to the Days again. Here, I think."

She took out her phone. "I'll give them a ring. Ask if they can drop in and help us with something. I'll pick them up myself."

"Will you tell Gillingham?"

She pondered for a moment. "Not yet. Let's see if it's a waste of time first."

He looked at the photograph again, then looked at Archer, knowing he was going to back her on this. "You know what you're doing, I guess."

And she normally did. He hoped this time wouldn't prove the exception.

* * *

Archer had chosen the least oppressive – not that this said much – interview room for talking to the Days, and she'd got Bell to nip out for some fancy biscuits, which sat on a plate in front of the couple, along with cups of decent coffee from her own stash.

Unlike Baines, she hadn't eaten, not even a crap sandwich, and the sight of the biscuits made her stomach growl. But the Days weren't touching them, and she felt it would look bad if she was the only one eating.

That, and her suspicion that Becky's parents hadn't told them everything they needed to know, made her irritable. She sincerely hoped Josh and Emma would satisfy her curiosity without any evasion.

She'd toyed with interviewing them separately. After all, one of the scenarios that had crossed her mind involved Josh not being Becky's natural father – and not knowing. But in the end she had rejected this approach. If there were any grounds at all for her suspicions about Becky's parentage, it was better to get everything out in the open. If that meant a hand grenade going off in these people's relationship, that was tough. They'd wasted enough time already.

"First of all, thank you both for coming in," she began when everyone had settled in and the tape had started. "I know this is a horrendous time for you."

"Is there any news?" Josh demanded. The strain they were both under was etched on their faces. Whatever they might be about to reveal in this room, Archer doubted if they would do anything to hinder the search for Becky.

"I'm afraid not yet," she replied. "Not at the moment. But there's a new line of inquiry I wanted to talk to you both about."

"New line?" Josh looked incredulous. "What new line? Christ, don't tell me you people have slipped up. This is our daughter we're talking about."

"Josh." Emma Day's tone was brittle. "Shut up." She turned to Archer, then to Baines. "Ask us anything. Please."

"Thank you." Archer slid the family holiday snap across the table to them. "I wanted to talk about this."

Josh frowned. "What about it?"

"Well," she said, "we couldn't help noticing that you both have very fair hair, and Becky's is dark. Quite a distinctive shade, actually."

"So?" There was a challenge in Josh's eyes, but something else too. She wasn't sure what it meant yet.

"You're not the first to notice that," Emma said. "We used to get all the milkman jokes…"

"Yes?" Baines leaned forward a little. "Anything in that?"

"What?" Emma's head snapped up. "No! God, no!"

Josh licked his lips. "I knew we should have told them, Em."

She blushed. "We agreed it wasn't relevant."

Baines slammed his palm down on the table. He and Archer had decided that he would appear to be the pushy one. "Enough. Becky's been missing for over forty-eight hours. We get to decide what's relevant – not you."

"Please," Archer added, her tone more soothing. "However awkward or embarrassing it might be, we need to know absolutely everything about Becky. It could be the key to finding her."

"But…" Josh looked at his wife. Looked at Archer. "I don't understand. I thought you'd arrested someone for Jade. This Briscoe. I thought he must have her somewhere."

"We said we were looking at other possibilities," Archer said. "Now, please. A simple question, to which I need a simple answer, Josh. Is Becky your daughter or not?"

"No," Emma said. "And she isn't mine either. She doesn't know it yet. We've been telling her she's a throwback to an earlier generation. The time's never been right…"

"So what's the story?" Baines pressed. "Come on, we haven't got all day."

"There's no need—" Josh began.

"With respect, there's every need," said Baines. "Was it adoption? Or what?"

"Adoption," Emma mumbled.

"Louder, for the tape," Archer said gently, playing the nice cop.

"Adoption. Becky was adopted."

"We always wanted kids." The belligerence had gone out of Josh like air from a punctured balloon. "It wasn't happening. We had all the tests, and it turned out to be a double whammy. I fire blanks and there's a problem with Emma's eggs."

Emma took up the story. "We were never going to have our own, so we applied to adopt. It wasn't easy getting accepted. Any monster can conceive, and then they move heaven and earth to keep the family together, but a decent couple looking to adopt has to jump through hoops—"

"Okay," Archer interrupted. "So Becky's adopted. And she doesn't know. Is there any way she could have found out?"

"I don't see how," Josh said. "I mean, she has an adoption certificate instead of a birth certificate."

"And there's a letter from her birth mother – the dad wasn't that interested, I don't think," Emma added. "And social services give you a life story book to share with the child when you're ready."

"But I keep all that in a box in my home office," Josh said. "She isn't one to go rooting around in there."

"You're sure?" Archer wanted to know.

The couple had turned several shades paler. "I'm not sure about anything any more," Josh admitted.

"And if she'd stumbled across this? How might she react? Might she run away?"

"I don't know," said Emma. "I don't think so."

"But with all she's been going through," added Josh. "First Leanne. Then the stuff with Jade. It's all very traumatic. A thing like this…"

"So why didn't you tell her?" asked Baines. "I thought the received wisdom was to tell them early."

"Between two and four, we were advised, yes. But it's just always seemed a lot for her to take in. You see, her parents were—"

"I said monsters get to have children," Emma said. "And that's what Becky's birth parents were. They were monsters."

"How do you know that?" Archer probed.

"They were completely open with us," Josh said. "The adoption people, I mean. Some people think the adoptive parents don't know anything about the birth parents and their circumstances, but they couldn't be more wrong. They told us exactly what we were taking on."

"We were getting virtually a newborn baby," Emma said. She was being forcibly adopted. She'd been taken from her mother at birth and put into foster care while the adoption was being sorted."

"Forcibly adopted?" And monsters? Something stirred at the back of Archer's mind.

"I told you," Emma persisted. "Both her parents were monsters."

"But what does that mean exactly?"

"They'd committed terrible crimes and were both in prison. Neither was considered safe to look after the child." Her eyes widened. "But this is all still irrelevant, surely. You really think Becky's found out and run away? Where could she have gone? You'd have found her, surely? Unless…"

Archer could see panic setting in as Emma started to imagine scenarios. Her girl being abducted from the street. Or out late at night, cold and hungry, and being offered somewhere to stay by the wrong sort of person.

But Archer didn't think Becky had run away.

"We need to keep calm," she said. "Is it possible Becky did find out she was adopted and then found out who her parents were?"

"No," Josh said firmly. "There was nothing in the paperwork that would have helped her. And surely she would have spoken to us about it? She'd have been curious."

"So what if one of the parents made contact with her?"

"What?" Confusion and panic mingled in both parents' eyes. "But how?"

"It's not unheard of for a persistent birth parent to piece information together," said Baines. "Make calls, scan local papers for clues. And then there's social media."

Archer recalled a case locally a few years ago where a birth mother had been reunited with her child in just that way. That had ended happily, with the mother becoming almost a part of the family. "Did you have any idea how long the parents would be inside?"

"More to the point," Baines said. "Were you actually told who the parents were?"

"Oh, Christ." Josh's eyes were wide. Emma looked about to faint. "The mother's out."

"Out? As in out of prison?"

Becky's father nodded. "She's been out about three years."

The thought that had been taking shape in Archer's mind assumed a more solid form.

"Who is she?"

But Emma was reaching across the table, grabbing Archer by

the wrist. "No," she whispered. "She can't have her. Not *her*."

"Whoa!" Archer gently withdrew her hand. "No need to panic. We've no idea what's happened right now, or whether it even has anything to do with Becky being adopted. Even if her birth mother *has* managed to find her, and they're together, she's not likely to be in any danger, is she? I mean, she'll have wanted to spend time with her child, not to hurt her."

"You don't know that."

"We don't even know that Becky's birth mother has her." Archer didn't want to make Emma feel even worse than she must feel already, but she was mightily annoyed. "But from what you've told us, we really do need to talk to her so we can eliminate her. I wish you'd mentioned this before."

"I told you." Josh was defensive again. "We talked about it. We thought it couldn't be relevant. We thought Becky must have been taken by whoever had Jade. And we thought, when we got her back, it wouldn't be the best time for her to find all this out."

"We'd have been careful how we used the information. We still will be." Archer sighed. "So tell us now. Becky's birth mother? Who is she?"

Becky's parents looked at one another. And then Josh said a name.

But by then, it wasn't a shock to Archer at all.

29

Archer stood in front of the board, the hastily called together team in their seats. Ashby sat in the front row, next to Petrescu as usual. Gillingham sat in his customary place at the back, his expression unreadable.

Her mouth was dry. Now it came to it, this had the potential to sound ridiculous – far-fetched, even. Even after her conversation with Becky's parents. Her adoptive parents, she mentally amended.

Well, crazy or not, she couldn't kick this theory into touch without at least seeing what the others made of it. All she had to lose was her pride, and there was much more at stake than that.

She half-turned to the images on the board behind her, and tapped Becky's photograph, still in the centre of the board, but with another now pinned beside it.

She cleared her throat. "We all know Becky Day's been missing since Wednesday morning, and we've been assuming all along that she was taken by the same person that abducted Jade Sheldon. But now we have Mark Briscoe in custody, he's admitted to everything except abducting Becky."

Gillingham folded his arms. Archer knew him well enough to know when he wanted her to come to the point. But she didn't want to just hit the team with her bombshell.

"It's still possible that Mark Briscoe took Becky, killed her, and dumped her body where we've yet to find it," she continued. "Phil Gordon's team are still working their arses off looking for anything that could connect her to him."

"Amy and I are still asking questions, everywhere I can think of," Ashby offered.

"I know you are, Steve, and we're all hoping you might shake the right tree. But Dan and I have been exploring another avenue, and some new information has come to light that I think we need to take seriously."

She recapped the interviews with Emma and Josh Day. The revelation that Becky had been adopted. That Becky didn't know. And that her birth parents had been jailed for horrendous crimes.

"And that's why we've got that new picture at the top?" Gillingham demanded. "You're joking."

"I wish I was, boss."

The picture showed two teenagers, side by side, smiling and apparently happy. Two nice, ordinary kids on the surface. Monsters underneath.

"Kieran Bardsley and Edina Maxwell – known as Eddie." She indicated the girl in the picture. "The press dubbed them the 'Angel' killers. Both jailed at sixteen for murder and sex crimes."

"And these are Becky's birth parents?"

"So they were told. I even remember thinking Becky reminded me of someone when I interviewed her after Jade disappeared. But I couldn't think who. Until now."

"Now you mention it," Ashby said. "I think I can see it myself. The eyes. Something about the nose and mouth, too. If someone said they were related, you'd have no reason to doubt it."

"Dear God," said Gillingham.

"I was only about fourteen when all that was going on," Collins piped up, "and I had a slightly sheltered upbringing, so I only had a sketchy idea of what they'd done. But I looked them up before I came in here. I can't believe either of them has been released."

"Nor can I," Archer said, "although I knew Eddie had been. About three years ago. She was given a new identity to give her a chance at a new life. And, as far as I know, she's kept her nose clean ever since."

"And the Days weren't apprehensive when they first heard she was out?"

"They didn't imagine she'd track Becky down."

"And Kieran Bardsley?" Petrescu wondered.

"He's done himself no favours at all in prison. I doubt he'll ever get out. He was given a much longer sentence in the first place, because he was reckoned to be the main instigator of all they did, and he's managed to add to his sentence since."

"In fairness," Baines said, "neither of them came from an ideal family background."

"That's true," Archer acknowledged. "My old boss at the Met, DCI Gibson, worked the case. It was a couple of years before I started working with him."

Bardsley and Maxwell had been two kids whose West London lives had already been hell when they met at the age of eight: both mothers drug addicts and prostitutes. Kieran Bardsley's father was a drinker and a junkie who knocked his wife and his young son about and, it later emerged, had also sexually abused his daughter, Kieran's older sister.

And then there were Eddie Maxwell's parents. A father who'd pimped his own wife to feed their habits, and who had prostituted his own child to raise drug money when she was just thirteen. Her mother had apparently been prepared to go along with it.

Psychologists talked about what the pair had done being a cry for help; an almost inevitable extension of what they saw as normal adult behaviour from their role models. Not that it cut much ice with the hangers and floggers, who would happily have locked them away and melted down the key.

Bardsley had been suspected of attacking and killing domestic animals even before he and Maxwell had met. Afterwards they had worked together. Nothing had been proved, but there had been a spate of horrific incidents: a cat maimed by fireworks tied to its stomach. Another cat nailed to its owner's back door like a crucifixion victim. A guide dog led away while its blind owner was distracted, and later found hanged from a tree.

Only in retrospect was the timing of these events traced back to the beginning of that unholy bond between the two children.

They'd moved on to human prey as they'd got older. Allegedly, they'd sexually assaulted two young girls when the pair were just twelve. One of the victims had come forward after their arrest, too scared to report them as long as they were at large. But her friend hadn't backed her up, perhaps too ashamed of what had happened, and that complaint had never been proven.

They had carried out their first rape when the pair were fourteen: they had abducted a slightly younger girl from the street at knife-point. It had been winter. She'd been walking home alone in the dark and had taken a shortcut down an alley. A sack had been shoved over her head and she'd been frogmarched to what was later believed to have been the derelict house the pair used as their den. Her ordeal had lasted about six hours, before she'd been taken back to the alley and released, unable to identify her attackers or the location of her assault.

At least three more attacks, but these on women older than themselves, had occurred over the following year. First, Charlotte Goodall, aged nineteen, was abducted, tortured, raped and left for dead in a skip. She had spent months in a coma. Then Jessica Winter disappeared, aged twenty. Her body was never found, but evidence – some jewellery kept as trophies, and traces of her blood and other DNA – indicated that she'd been at the den, and had probably met the same fate as Charlotte.

And finally, Gillian Harvey, a married woman of thirty-four. Her body had been dumped in an alley. The two killers were too young to legally drive, but that hadn't stopped them from stealing cars to transport their victims to their dump sites.

Archer had little doubt that their debauchery would have plumbed new depths – if it hadn't been for two lucky breaks. A nosey neighbour had noticed Bardsley and Maxwell following Gillian Harvey the night she disappeared. She'd been suspicious, and had recognised Maxwell. DNA found on the victims had matched both Maxwell and Bardsley, and that would probably have been enough to secure convictions. But then, in a second break, Charlotte Goodall had woken up and had been able to identify her attackers.

Sentencing, the judge had been more lenient with Maxwell because Bardsley was deemed to be the senior partner, allegedly exerting influence over his accomplice. DCI Nick Gibson had told Archer he believed they'd both continue to be a menace if they were ever released.

But Archer knew that what tormented him was his failure to find Jessica Winter's body. The two young killers had been convicted of her murder, but they had continued to protest their innocence, denying knowledge of how the evidence at their den had got there, and insisting they had no idea where she was now.

Gibson had grown close to Jessica's parents during the investigation. Archer had never been a parent herself, so she could only imagine how it must feel to lose a child and to have no idea what had happened to them. To have no body to bury. Gibson had sworn to the Winters that, as far as he was concerned, the case remained open, and Archer knew he still lay awake some nights, wondering where the girl's remains might be.

"I had a quick word with DCI Gibson today," Archer said. "Eddie was pregnant by Bardsley when they were convicted and sentenced. It raised massive child protection issues. Every attempt was made to keep the child within one or other parent's extended family but, in the end, it was just hopeless. It was simply too risky. Eddie's daughter was taken away at birth, fostered and then compulsorily adopted. Eddie never accepted it. Said her child had been stolen. DCI Gibson thinks that, apart from her poisonous attachment to Bardsley, that baby – who she named Annie – was the only human being she ever loved."

"So what are we thinking?" Ashby asked. "That Eddie – whatever name she's going by now – has tracked her daughter down and taken her? Why now?"

"I made another quick call," Archer said. "To Rachel Kidd, a psychological profiler I knew when I was with the Met. What she says is purely based on what I was able to tell her, but she suspects that the baby Eddie was forced to give up was probably all she could think of in prison. By all accounts, she was a model prisoner, and Rachel thought the incentive to get out as soon as possible and start searching might have been behind that."

"She thinks it was all an act?" Petrescu asked.

"Not necessarily. Motherhood might even have rehabilitated

her in some strange way. But she'd always have been motivated by the thought of being somehow reunited with her daughter."

"But that means she might have been plotting and planning for the nine years she spent inside," Collins said.

"But wanting to find her isn't the same as actually doing it," Ashby remarked. "I mean, I know parents do find their adopted children, but I've never understood how."

"I did quick web search on that, too," Collins said. "It seems the internet has made it a lot easier."

"In what way?"

"It's getting harder and harder to guarantee confidentiality to adoptive parents and their children. Official contact is supposed to be through a 'letterbox' system, where the adoptive parents send the birth family a letter and photos every year through a social worker or adoption agency. The birth parent has to use the same route if they want to respond."

"I don't suppose the Days kept channels open."

"The guv says not. But natural parents are finding ways of using Facebook and other social networking sites to track down their kids. And so much information is out there nowadays. The adoption agencies are getting huge numbers of calls from adoptive parents whose children have been contacted out of the blue."

"I'd imagine," Petrescu said, "that with social media, the smallest scrap of information – name, location date of birth – can provide clues to help birth parents track down their children."

"Yes," agreed Collins. "A lot of local authorities now advise adoptive parents not to include photographs with the annual letters, in case they're posted online in an attempt to trace the child."

"But if there were no letters, no photographs…" Gillingham looked bewildered. "What clues are out there? Would she look out for every single girl with the right birthday? That's a massive undertaking."

"It is," Archer said, "but I can't say where enough persistence might get you. I do know where she might have got some clues from, though. The case haunted my old boss, and he kept tabs on Eddie. It seems one of the social workers involved with the adoption developed a soft spot for her. Even visited her in prison a few times. She wouldn't have known who adopted Becky, nor exactly where they lived, but she might have let slip a few details she did know. Maybe even volunteered them."

"We need to talk to her urgently," Gillingham said.

"Good luck with that. She died of cancer a year before Eddie's release. The really worrying thing is that she apparently visited Eddie a few weeks before she died. She could have said anything. Especially if she had a misplaced fit of conscience."

"She could have even nosed around in official files and found out more than Eddie ever could," added Collins.

"If only we knew for sure," Bell commented. "That would clinch it."

"The social worker had a daughter," said Archer. "DCI Gibson's going to see if we can talk to her. If her mother told Eddie more than she should have, maybe she confided in her daughter."

"But even if we get lucky, how do we find Eddie Maxwell?" Baines voiced what everyone was probably thinking. "If she's got a new identity, that's the witness protection scheme, and they won't share any information easily."

"Dan's right," Gillingham said. "We could waste months getting the runaround. If Becky's with Eddie..."

"We need to remember that 'if' is the operative word," Archer reminded them. "We don't know for sure that Eddie has her."

"But how likely do you think it is?"

"Seriously?" Archer took a breath. "Pretty likely."

"Okay." Baines frowned. "If she wants the child back that much, she'd not likely to harm her, is she?"

"I don't know about that. She's probably imagined that reunion for over twelve years. What if, after all that time, Becky rejects her? Who knows what she might do?"

"But say Becky doesn't reject her. Maybe Becky's smart. She might realise that going with Eddie's flow is best for her safety."

"In that case, let's hope she's a good actor," Ashby

remarked. "If Maxwell sees through her…"

"There's no point worrying about what might be happening," said Gillingham. "That's out of our hands."

Ashby nodded, accepting the point.

"Bear me out," Baines persisted. "The point I'm making is that there's a good chance, if Eddie does have her, that she's in no immediate danger. Think about it. It could be better than some of the other possibilities."

There were a few nods and murmurs of agreement.

"And there's another thing. Wherever she's taken Becky, chances are they'll stay put for at least a while."

"She could already have taken her out of the country," argued Ashby. "Or she could be anywhere in this one."

"Not out of the country, surely," said Bell. "She'd need papers – forged ones. That all takes time, if she even knows how to get hold of them."

"We don't know how long she'd been planning this, Jason," Archer pointed out, "but it's a fair point. Especially as we posted an all ports warning the moment we knew Becky was missing. It would be risky, even if Eddie's desperate."

"By the same token, Becky's face is all over the news now," Will Tyler chipped in. "Isn't there a good chance Eddie's simply taken her to wherever she's living?"

"My money's on somewhere reasonably local, guv," Collins said.

Archer looked at the DC. "Why's that, Joan?"

"Well, we're sort of assuming that Eddie found out who and where her daughter is, maybe even before she came out of prison. We don't know how much she knew. Maybe she even caught that glimpse of her on that TV broadcast and somehow recognised her – unlikely, but it was on local news, so she'd have to be somewhere that received it. Or she knew Becky was in Buckinghamshire – maybe even more than that. If I wanted to watch my kid surreptitiously, maybe plan an abduction, I'd locate myself nearby."

Her logic was impeccable. Archer chided herself again for not making best use of Collins' talents.

"Makes sense to me," she said.

"I agree," said Baines. "She might well have been watching Becky for the three years she's been out of prison. But I'm less convinced this abduction was planned. Again, why now? Answer: because one girl from Houghton was already missing. We were bound to suspect that the same person had taken both of them. It was too good a chance to miss. She's been watching Becky, knows her routines, knows her route to school. Jade's disappearance seems like a sign."

"Pass yourself off as a police officer," Archer picked up his narrative. "Trick Becky into getting in your car…"

"Maybe drug her or something," Bell suggested. "Bundle her into the boot."

"Could be," Ashby said.

"No." Collins was shaking her head. "Not if she wants to win her confidence. Not a great start to get off to."

"She might not be thinking straight," argued Bell.

"Moving on." Archer cut the debate short. "Right now, our best guess is that, if the abductor is Eddie Maxwell, then she's holding Becky somewhere relatively local."

"A guess." Gillingham's tone was acid. "I hope this isn't a wild-bloody-goose chase."

"Me too, boss. Me too."

"So how do we find her? The Witness protection has more security around it than Fort Knox."

"There'll be flags," Archer said, "connecting Eddie and her new name to her dedicated handler. The local witness protection team might be in the know, but the trouble is, they're going to stonewall us with the old 'neither confirm nor deny' line."

"I know the DCI in that team," Petrescu said, "and I know how to push his buttons. Why don't I go and see him?"

"I'll come with you," Ashby volunteered.

She smiled at him. "Best not. And, before anyone asks, best you don't know."

Archer saw something like jealousy in Ashby's face, but he made a big show of shrugging.

"Okay, Amy," Archer said. "You'll need to explain the situation, and what we think we know, and then they'll have to make a decision about what they're prepared to disclose. And,

I'm afraid, how much we get to know will depend on what we *need* to know, in their opinion. In all probability our local witness protection team will be bypassed and it'll be a matter between the handler and one of us."

"One?" Gillingham queried.

"Need to know, boss. They'd have to blow her cover for the good of the operation to get Becky out. But if I'm wrong, all the time and money invested in her new identity will be down the toilet – unless they can restrict the number of people in the know. Right," she continued, eager to get on, "you're with me, Dan. We're going down to London to see my old boss and maybe that social worker's daughter. I'll ask him if he can pull her in for us."

She looked around the team's expectant faces. "Joan, Jason, Will. Sort out between you how you're going to do it, but I want that silver Merc narrowed down. Keep it within the Vale for now. Don't restrict it to women owners, but take an especially close look at them to start with. Cross-check them with driver information. Eddie Maxwell would be…" – she did the sum in her head – "about twenty-eight now. If Amy can't get anything, we'll have to do it the hard way."

Another thought crossed her mind. "Actually, get the driving licence pictures for any women on our shortlist. Obviously there are no recent photographs, but you're looking for a woman who resembles Maxwell. Joan, you take the lead."

She didn't know if that would piss off Bell or Tyler. She doubted it and, frankly, she didn't care.

"What can I do?" Ashby asked.

She looked at him. He was waiting for Archer, with whom he'd never got on, to allocate him a task, eager to contribute. It was a pity Petrescu wasn't sticking around indefinitely. Whether he was shagging her, or just would like to, she seemed to be having a good effect on him.

"Can you see how all the loose ends with Mark Briscoe are tying up, please, Steve? It's still all we have if this turns out to be a waste of everyone's time."

He actually smiled. "On it," he said. Then added with a twinkle in his eye, "guv."

30

Amy Petrescu and DI Ricky Dean had worked closely on a case a few years back. Working so closely together had led to a brief fling. It hadn't worked out and, a few months after they'd agreed to end it and parted on friendly terms, he'd met his future wife. These days he was a family man with a young child and another on the way.

She knew he was happy with his lot, but that didn't prevent him showing genuinely warm feelings towards Petrescu when their paths happened to cross. There was no suggestion that he still had the hots for her, but even if she'd thought that might be something she could exploit, she was sadly disappointed.

"The thing is," he said as they sat in his bijou office, "we create these identities for a reason, Amy."

"I do know that, Ricky."

"The protected person's legend is a whole new persona. It takes a team of police, prison and probation officers to create it. It includes a fake birth certificate and other documentation, and it's not a soft option for the subject. The whole point is for the subject to blend in. To disappear."

Petrescu did know this already. Most of the people living new lives under the witness protection scheme were, as the title suggested, courageous but frightened witnesses to serious crimes such as murder, organised crime or gun crime, who feared that their evidence could put themselves or their friends and family at risk.

But the scheme was not restricted to such witnesses, and more high-profile offenders were being given new identities to enable them to make a fresh start when they came out of prison. These occasionally included young offenders, such as Jon Venables and Robert Thompson, who killed two-year-old James Bulger in 1993 when they were aged ten, and Mary Bell, who was just eleven when she was convicted of the manslaughter of two boys in 1968. And, more recently, Eddie Maxwell.

"Giving up an entire life's not easy, Amy," Dean lectured. "It's a bureaucratic and costly business, and not everyone's mentally or emotionally equipped to handle it. They only have contact with a handful of police officers, including a designated local handler. And they're coached extensively to ensure they're word-perfect about their new identities. There are jobs to consider..."

"I get it," Petrescu protested.

"Do you, though? You think you've got Eddie Maxwell in your midst. She and Kieran Bardsley were the most hated teenagers in Britain. Wherever she is, whatever name she's going by, she's vulnerable to anything, from bricks through her window to being murdered, if her cover's blown. Even if she was anywhere near Thames Valley, we'd have to weigh up the damage that we could do to her against the evidence you have for investigating her. At best, we'd have to keep the additional people who knew her new ID to an absolute minimum."

"But you'd know if she was here? Hypothetically, of course?"

"Maybe, maybe not. I'd have to follow the flags through, speak to her handler, and explain the situation. The best option might be for the handler to visit her and have a word."

"Seriously?" Petrescu was aghast. "You'd be alerting her that we were on to her. Unless she was sitting in her living room with Becky tied to a chair next to her, the handler could go his merry way, fat, dumb and happy, and then God knows what she'd do." Her resolve to play nicely cracked. "Fuck's sake, Ricky. How's it going to look if Becky Day turns up dead, and we could have saved her, if only we weren't protecting a murderer?"

"Even a murderer deserves a second chance in life once they've served their sentence."

Petrescu felt like banging her head on his desk in frustration. That she'd do exactly what Dean was doing if she was in his position didn't help. Not when every wasted second could be increasing the danger to Becky.

If it wasn't already too late.

"Look," he said, his tone marginally more conciliatory, "I can make a few calls. For what it's worth. See if there's any way we can put your mind at rest."

"How long will that take?"

"No idea." He sighed. "I'll make it as quick as I can. But there may not be anything I'm able to tell you."

"I get it," she said again.

"I'll get back to you." He paused. "If you come back to me with something more than a theory, then it might change everything, of course."

* * *

Holborn Police Station was located in Lamb's Conduit Street, a short walk from London's vibrant Theatreland in one direction and the Royal Courts of Justice in another. It was the most convenient place to meet Lisa Brown, whose mother, Marion, had been the social worker who'd formed an attachment to Eddie Maxwell.

DCI Nick Gibson hadn't changed much in the few years since Archer had last seen him. Maybe he had a few more silver hairs around the temples, and a few more crags and crinkles around his eyes. He looked slightly tanned. His hair was, as ever, immaculately coiffured, and he was dapper in a suit that had plainly cost more than anything you could buy in M&S. The salmon-pink handkerchief in his breast pocket perfectly picked out the thin stripe in his silk tie.

Not that Gibson was vain. He just liked to look smart, and he had a taste for slightly higher-end clothes and grooming than the average copper. The contrast between him and Paul Gillingham was remarkable.

It was a comparison that didn't end with appearances, either. Gibson had spotted Archer as a rising star and had become something of a mentor to her, passing on knowledge and experience and stretching her at every opportunity. Gillingham was more aloof, and any advice he offered was generally as part of a bollocking.

Gibson greeted Archer with a peck on the cheek, shook hands with Baines, and then got down to business. "Lisa Brown should be here in about ten minutes. I wanted to make sure you were going to be here, or almost here, so she didn't have to hang around too long."

"Thanks for setting this up, Nick," Archer said.

"Yes, well, if Eddie Maxwell's done something that will get her back behind bars where she belongs, it'll be well worth it. Besides, you need to find this kid. You don't want another Jessica Winter. Missing without trace. Sometimes I wish this was the eighties and you could still beat information out of people."

"No, you don't," Archer said, laughing. It was no more Gibson's way than it was hers. "And I don't think it'll come to that. Not if we can confirm that Becky Day really is her daughter. The witness protection guys would have to give Eddie up to us then."

Lisa Brown was mousy in every sense of the word. Not just her hair colouring, but also her long, sharp nose and prominent front teeth. She seemed extremely nervous as she took a seat in the interview room, in spite of Gibson's smooth attempts to assure her she was in no trouble.

"Thanks for coming in," Gibson said, after the introductions.

"You said it was about my mother?" Brown's tones were clipped, her vowels flat. Her voice was high.

"I'll let DI Archer ask the questions. She's conducting an investigation in Buckinghamshire."

"Buckinghamshire?" There was a wariness in Lisa's voice. It would have been natural enough to ask what a case in Buckinghamshire could have to do with her mother. But she didn't.

"Lisa," Archer began, "did you know your mum had dealings with a woman named Edina – Eddie – Maxwell?"

"Rings a bell. Wasn't she some sort of child serial killer?"

Archer didn't have time for this. "Please don't play games with us, Lisa. A child's life may be at stake. You know damn well who Eddie Maxwell is, and pretending otherwise just makes us suspicious."

The mousy woman flinched. "Sorry. Yes, of course I know who she is. And yes, my mum knew her."

"So you knew she was involved in the adoption of Eddie's daughter?"

Brown nodded.

"And she continued to visit her in prison until she died?"

"On and off, yes. Quite a bit at the start, I think, then it got down to maybe once a year. What's this all about?"

"Would she have known who adopted Eddie's child?"

"No. That's done through the adoption agencies."

"But would she have known anything?" Archer persisted.

"I don't know. She had dealings with the agencies. I don't know what they spoke about."

"All right." Archer still thought Lisa was being evasive. "Say the agency let something slip. Maybe not a name or address, nothing too specific, but a general location. Would your mother have passed that on to Eddie Maxwell?"

"That's supposed to be confidential, isn't it?" Lisa was still avoiding eye contact.

"And you're making a rubbish job of evading questions," Baines put in. "Obviously it's confidential. But, at the risk of being insensitive, your mother last visited Eddie shortly before her death. If she felt sorry for Eddie, maybe she told her more than she should have. Getting something she felt bad about off her conscience. Would she have seen it that way?"

"Lisa," Archer picked up the reins. "We're looking for a twelve-year-old girl who's been missing for over forty-eight hours. She's Eddie's daughter, and we think Eddie might know that. If we're wrong, then we need to stop wasting time on that avenue of enquiry. But, if we're right, a young girl could be in the hands of a killer. If you know of anything that might help us, you need to stop being coy."

"Have you got kids?" Baines asked softly.

"Two."

"Well, then."

She drew a ragged breath and squared her shoulders. "Yes, all right. Mum always felt sorry for Eddie. She was always a collector of waifs, strays and sad cases. She thought Eddie had been used by Kieran Bardsley, knew she'd had a ghastly home life before that, and pitied her for having her child taken away almost as soon as she gave birth to her. Honestly? I don't know if Mum knew anything. I do remember her saying she wished she could do something to help her. And, after she saw Eddie for the last time, I asked her how it had gone, and she said something that bothered me at the time. Now it worries me even more, if I'm honest."

"What did she say?" Gibson couldn't resist stepping in.

"She said she felt much easier in her mind. I asked her why, and she wouldn't say. I didn't push it, because Mum didn't have long to live, and I didn't want to fall out with her. But, to tell the truth, when Eddie was released, I did worry that Mum had told her something she shouldn't have. About her child. I can imagine her thinking she'd made peace with herself."

"And hang the consequences for the child and her adopted family?" Baines looked angry. Disbelieving.

"You have to understand how disillusioned with the system Mum had become. She thought that, all too often, people lost their children due to their circumstances, not because they were evil. She thought the real criminals in Eddie's case were her parents, and that they should have been in the dock with her."

"Didn't she feel the same sympathy for Jessica Winter's parents?" Gibson sounded like he was chewing metal. "Getting on for thirteen years, and still unable to grieve properly because they don't know where their daughter is?"

Defensive anger flared in Lisa Brown's eyes then. "These are all questions you might ask my mother. But she's dead. Yes, I pushed it to the back of my mind when nothing came of it. Yes, I suppose I was always afraid something like this might happen. But I'm not going to answer for her actions. Or be pilloried on her behalf."

"Sorry," Gibson said. Archer thought he meant it. "You're quite right. You've been very helpful. DI Archer, DS Baines – any more questions?"

"Just one," Baines said. "Did your mother ever say anything at all to *you* to give you a clue as to where Eddie's daughter was? What her new name was?"

"No. Except..." Lisa Brown looked troubled again.

"Anything that might help?"

"I remember having Mum over one evening. We'd watched *Strictly Come Dancing* and a few other programmes on the telly, and then the news came on. There was an item about a school in Buckinghamshire, and we had to keep quiet for it. It was just a snippet. I couldn't see why Mum was so interested. I suppose it's possible she did know where Eddie's daughter was, and wondered if she was at that school. I can't even remember what the school was, now."

"Well," Archer said after Lisa gone, "that's enough to keep us digging, I think."

"Damn it," added Gibson. "I know it's joining the dots, but I suspect that's exactly what happened. Misplaced sympathy for a damaged young woman, leading to a misguided wish to help her. Eddie's had three years to fill in the blanks and find out exactly where, and under what name, her daughter's living."

"At least we can put real pressure on witness protection to help us now," Archer said.

"I just hope you don't have to jump through too many hoops to get anywhere," Gibson said. "For what it's worth, I'll see if we can dig up any of Eddie's old contacts, in case she's been in touch. I think it's unlikely, though."

"Me too, really. But great if we can tick that box."

"What now?" Baines asked.

"Back to the Vale, Dan. I hope the others have got somewhere. We have no idea what Eddie Maxwell's capable of now. But we know what she was capable of twelve years ago."

31

As the morning wore on, Becky felt a jumble of emotions.
Today was Friday and, if Eddie kept her promise, she would be
going home today.

Assuming she could believe a word this woman said.

And Eddie had told her lie after lie, right from the start.

Right from the moment Becky had emerged from that
footpath on her way to school, in fact. She knew her parents
disliked her going that way, but also knew she'd have missed
the bus otherwise. She never left herself enough time, and Dad's
fussing had made her later.

Was that really just two days ago? It felt like a lot longer.

What had happened to her since that moment kept running
through her mind in a series of flashbacks.

First, a woman in a yellow high-vis jacket, brandishing ID
that said *Police*.

"Are you Becky Day? Oh, thank heavens I've caught you.
I'm PC Short, and my boss – Inspector Archer – has sent me to
find you."

Becky's stomach had churned. The police wanted her?
"Why? What's wrong?"

"Now please don't be scared. But we think we know what's
happened to Jade Sheldon and, well, we think you're the next
target."

"Me?"

"There's nothing to worry about. We've got you now, and
I'm going to take you to a safe house. Inspector Archer's with
your mum and dad. They're getting some stuff together and then
they'll be joining us. You're quite safe, I promise, Becky."

Even though her dad's warnings to never get in a car with a
stranger had rung in her ears, this was the police. PC Short had
even mentioned DI Archer, whom Becky had met. So Becky

had gone with her. She seemed nice.

"Oh," PC Short said on the way, "you need to switch off your phone and give me the SIM card. We can't risk it being traced."

Becky did as she was told and the SIM disappeared into the pocket of the woman's yellow jacket.

She remembered little of the journey – had probably been too worried and frightened to notice much, despite PC Short's reassurances. Her next clear memory was of the car turning into a long, winding driveway that ended outside an isolated farmhouse where the only nosey neighbours were some grazing sheep. A good place to hide from the bad people, whoever they were, she supposed.

Then there'd been that big ginger cat, squeezing in through the cat flap while the PC was sorting drinks, and rubbing himself against Becky's leg. It was the first sign that something wasn't right.

"Why is there a cat? You said this place is only used from time."

"That's Barney. He's sort of adopted the place."

"He's got a name?"

PC Short didn't turn round. "Yeah, the people who come in to clean named him. They feed him, too. He's got his own bowl and everything. Silly, really."

Much later, when her parents still hadn't arrived, she'd looked at the policewoman's uniform more closely. And suddenly nothing about this person who'd brought her here, locked the door, and now had the key in her pocket, rang true.

"Excuse me." Her mouth was dry, her heart thumping. "Shouldn't your shirt have those black bits on the shoulders? With a number on?"

PC Short looked amused. "Shoulder flashes, you mean?"

"Is that what they're called? And your yellow jacket. Shouldn't it say *POLICE* on the back?"

Something was wrong about the tie, too.

PC Short smiled more broadly. "You're a clever girl."

And then her story changed for the first time.

"I've not been telling you the truth, Becky. I'm sorry. I was waiting for the right moment to tell you."

"Tell me what?"

"I'm not a police officer. You'll understand when I explain it to you, why I had to lie. To get you here." The woman smiled again, more shyly now. "My name is Hannah Josephs, Becky. This is my home. And I'm your real mum."

If that wasn't enough of a bombshell, she'd gone on to imply that Becky's parents had stolen her when she was a newborn.

All Becky's feelings played out again in her mind. She had gone crazy – still grieving for Leanne, shocked at Jade's disappearance, and then terrified at being abducted herself.

Her memory of rattling the door, demanding to be let out, panic rising, was especially vivid, as was the image of her captor, sitting calmly in her chair and speaking soothingly to her.

"I'm sorry to have to do it this way. All this must come as such a shock."

A shock?

Her parents? Baby abductors?

That was one lie Becky had never swallowed. The parents she loved? Stealing someone else's child? Surely she'd have known, somehow, if she didn't belong to them?

Yet, from the moment Hannah had claimed to be her mother, Becky hadn't been entirely able to deny the resemblance between them. They had identical blue-black hair and brown eyes with gold flecks. Similar features. A resemblance she'd never been able to claim with her parents.

Somehow Hannah had finally calmed Becky, promising she wasn't going to hurt her.

"All I want is for us to get to know each other. That's not asking much, is it, after I've spent so long looking for you?"

Becky had been trying to stay calm, not to annoy this person, but now she started to sob.

"Please don't cry," Hannah said, coming to stand beside her and putting out a hand towards her – but not quite touching her.

"I just want to go home."

"And I don't want to keep you here against your will. But look. Stay here with me just a couple of days – until Friday –

and then you can decide what you want to do."

"What do you mean?"

"Just get to know your real mum, eh? If you want to go home on Friday, I'll take you home, I promise. But if you decide you'd like to stay with me, then I'll find a way for us to get away together – perhaps abroad."

The whole thing sounded bonkers, but Becky felt she had little choice but to go along with it. Her parents would be frantic with worry once they realised she hadn't made it to school – just like Jade hadn't come home the night before. But she knew she had to somehow keep herself together. For all she knew, this woman was a maniac, whose kindly demeanour would vanish if Becky upset her.

She also had to admit to some curiosity mingled with the fear and upset. That resemblance. Her parents had always said she didn't look like them because she was a 'throwback'. She'd believed it – why shouldn't she? – but now part of her was a little less certain. What made this woman think *Becky* was her child, as opposed to any other? Or was that just another lie?

And if it was all lies or fantasy, who was this woman? Was Becky in terrible danger?

So, in spite of everything she was feeling, Becky had done her very best to join in what amounted to a strange game of mother and daughter. Becky had her own room, with an en suite and a selection of clothes she might have chosen for herself.

"I had to guess your sizes. I hope they're okay."

Hannah seemed to have got them spot-on.

Meanwhile, Becky couldn't figure Hannah out. Every time she went to her room, she was locked in, 'just in case', yet her jailer seemed to trust her in the kitchen, where there were plenty of knives. As if she knew Becky would never attack her with one. Which was true.

Then last night, Hannah's story had changed again. She'd made Becky sit down on the sofa and she'd sat next to her, all nerves and tension.

"I'm going to tell you the whole truth," Hannah said. "It's time I did."

She admitted that Becky's parents hadn't actually stolen her from the hospital. But they *had* adopted her almost at birth, against her real mother's will – and in Hannah's book, that was the same as stealing.

Becky wasn't so sure. Something didn't make sense to her.

"But why? Why was I adopted against your will?"

Hannah was silent for a long time, before giving a heavy sigh.

"Because of who I am, Becky. Hannah Joseph is my name now, but that's not who I always was."

The kitchen clock ticked. Silence stretched out between them.

"So who did you used to be?" Becky asked finally.

And the woman who had abducted her told Becky her real name.

Eddie Maxwell.

Murderer.

32

While the more senior members of the team were out rattling cages, the three DCs had been trying to pin down the identity of the person who had abducted Becky Day – and, in particular, to find the woman once known as Eddie Maxwell.

The pressure had increased when Petrescu had phoned from Oxford, frustrated.

"I must be losing my touch," she confided to Collins. "I thought I could wheedle something out of DCI Dean, but the best I could get was a promise to make some calls. He wasn't even saying Eddie Maxwell's definitely in Bucks, although I wonder who he'd have been making calls to if he didn't know *something*. He wants something concrete before he'll give us anything tangible at all. Have you guys got anything?"

"Masses of stuff," Collins told her. "We're sifting through it, cross-checking with each other, and looking to narrow it down. But you know what it's like, Sarge. "

"Amy."

"Amy." It wasn't the first time she'd been told to use the DS's first name. She kept forgetting. "You know what it's like. Even silver Mercedes SUVs are more common round here than I'd imagined. But I reckon, if she's in there, we'll find her." She hoped.

It was getting on for noon when Collins suggested they take a break from their intensive work and see what progress they had made.

Being asked to lead this little team that was doing so much vital grunt work had surprised and pleased Collins. So much about this week had boosted her self-esteem. And she knew, from the best bosses she'd had, that the trick of leadership was showing people their contributions were valued, and focusing on teamwork – not just dishing out orders.

"Okay," she said, when they'd assembled in the briefing room. "Will, you were looking for silver Mercs in the area."

Tyler nodded. "I've found quite a few, but I've singled out the GLCs. And I've got four with woman owners who are in the right ballpark age and are white."

"That's brilliant. Have you got driving licence photos?"

Collins and Bell had pulled their chairs round to form a loose circle with Tyler's wheelchair. He opened a folder and handed out copies of licences. Collins took them over to the board, holding each of them in turn beside the picture of sixteen-year-old Eddie Maxwell. None leaped out at them as the younger girl's older self, but they were only able to definitely rule out one of the four.

That left three. Two brunettes and a blonde.

"I'm not that interested in hair colour," Collins said. "She may easily have dyed it as part of her legend." She turned to Bell. "So we've got three drivers we think might be of interest, and we've got their registration numbers. Jason, how have you got on with CCTV?"

He cleared his throat, colouring. "Well, I've got a number of silver Merc SUVs that were somewhere in the Houghton area on Wednesday morning, an hour or so either side of Becky's disappearance. Like Will, I've filtered it down to the GLCs to start with. We were about to compare lists when you called this meeting."

There was no reproach in his voice, but Collins mentally kicked herself for not asking if it was a good time to do this. She could easily have waited.

"Shall we do it now?" she suggested.

"Sure," Bell agreed. "Will, if you call out your three registrations, I'll check them against my list."

Tyler did so. He'd only reached the second licence plate number when Bell held up a hand and asked him to repeat it.

Collins' stomach flipped. She found herself holding her breath as Tyler slowly called out each character of the plate number, and then she fastened her gaze on Bell.

"Well?" she demanded.

Bell smiled broadly, no hint of blushing now.

"Bingo," he said.

* * *

Archer and Baines were on the M25 when Archer's phone rang. Getting out of London had been tedious at times, especially around the North Circular Road, and Baines had sensed Archer's frustration.

It had been interesting to meet her old boss and catch a glimpse of her old life at the Met, before her injury and its consequences had driven her to the Vale in search of a new start. There was obviously a strong mutual respect there, and a friendship too. She'd told Baines on the way there that she'd had little contact with the old team since her move – a couple of phone calls, the odd Christmas card, promised meet-ups that never happened. But, seeing her back in her old environment, he'd found himself wondering what her life might be like now if she hadn't suffered that injury.

He cared about Archer. He knew that working with her had made him a better copper and, when he'd finally shared the news of his engagement with her, on the way down to London, he'd been rewarded with one of the broadest smiles he'd ever seen on her face.

"Oh, Dan! That's wonderful." She reached across and touched his arm. "I'd hug you, if you weren't driving."

"You're the first person I've told. We haven't decided when would be best to break it to our families. If there is a good time. Karen thinks her family might disown her. Mine will probably accept it and then be even more awkward around her than they are already."

"Well, sod 'em," Archer said. "If they can't be happy for you, that's their problem. You're so right for each other."

He laughed out loud. "That's exactly what Karen said."

He wondered if asking her to be his best man would be too weird. Well, it was no weirder than marrying his dead wife's twin.

She ended the call. "That was Joan. We've got a name."

"Really?" He forced himself to maintain his attention to the road ahead, despite the surge of excitement.

"A Hannah Josephs. She lives north of Aylesbury, in the direction of Bierton. By all accounts, she lives in a farmhouse with a lot of land around it. Pretty isolated. Ideal for holding a prisoner and no one knowing, don't you think?"

This could be the break they'd been praying for. "I do. So what's the story?"

"Right age, right make and colour of car, in the right place at the right time. Joan's even claiming her driving licence bears a faint resemblance to Eddie Maxwell's sixteen-year-old self, but that could be wishful thinking, I suppose."

If it was a breakthrough, it would have been produced by old-fashioned police work – with a bit of help from technology.

"How do you want to play it?"

"You probably heard me tell Joan to get hold of Amy and get her to put the name to her tame witness protection guy?"

Baines said nothing, not wishing to admit he'd been wool-gathering as she made the call.

"Well, let's see what comes of that," Archer said. "I don't want to waste too much time if this woman's not Eddie."

"We'd still check her out, surely?"

"Of course, but we'd probably take a different approach. They're doing a bit more digging into this Hannah Josephs meanwhile. Even the best of legends can only take so much scrutiny before the cracks show."

"But once we're sure it's her? Assuming we are."

"Proceed with caution and backup. We'll need her handler, a hostage negotiator and, frankly, an armed response team. Christ," she added, "what if it's an actual farm?"

"You think she might have firearms?"

"We'd probably be stupid to assume not."

He left the M25 to pick up the A41 to Aylesbury. "You can say that again."

* * *

Becky put the last piece of cake into her mouth. A late afternoon snack. She was eating as much to please Eddie as for any sustenance she might think she needed. She had no real appetite.

The extent to which Eddie was acting out whatever vision of family life she might have in her head was increasingly creepy. It was almost as though she imagined it had always been like this. As if Eddie had not only given birth to Becky, but had raised her too.

Cosy mother–daughter stuff, amusing themselves with jigsaws and card games, and simple food. Maybe Eddie just wanted to make it last – to have this for as long as she could, before she took Becky home.

The truth about the woman's real identity should have had Becky sick with panic. She'd heard of Eddie Maxwell. Bardsley and Maxwell were occasionally mentioned on the news, and once she'd asked her dad about Maxwell. He'd given her the facts – she supposed he'd thought a kid of her age could handle them. But it had sounded bad enough.

They'd been monsters. They'd killed people, including a kid not much older than Becky was now. She'd had a vague recollection of Eddie Maxwell's release a few years ago. A lot of fuss had been made about it. Hadn't her parents been a bit funny at the time? A lot funny, in fact. Her dad as angry as she'd ever seen him, had kept going on about how they should have thrown away the key.

Maybe Eddie had finally told her the truth. Maybe it was a truth her parents had always known and shielded her from.

But *was* it true? She found it hard to see the woman she was with now as a murdering psycho. Sure, she'd lured Becky here with lies, but she seemed desperate for Becky to like her, and was really affectionate – she'd even hugged Becky once when she'd got really upset, and to Becky it had felt sort of nice. Maybe not quite right, but not a bit scary either.

Eddie had tried to explain how she and Kieran Bardsley had both had really horrible home lives as kids, where awful things had been done to them. She said that was to blame for the bad things they'd done.

When they'd been caught, Eddie was already pregnant by Kieran, but the authorities had insisted she couldn't keep the baby.

But, she had said, prison and childbirth had changed her. Not only had she left jail with a new identity but, she insisted, she really wasn't that person any more. All she wanted now was her child back – a child she'd only got to hold once, but in that moment, she'd felt a love she'd never felt before. Not even for Kieran.

After prison, she'd searched for her child. Through persistence, luck and a little help, she'd finally found her. Soon after her release she'd met, and married, a man she'd never really loved, but had liked, and who'd left her with this house and plenty of money when he'd died in a car crash a year into the marriage.

At first, she'd been happy to watch Becky from afar. But, when things had kicked off in Houghton, she'd hoped the police would link Becky's disappearance with Jade's. It was the perfect cover, and Eddie had been unable to help herself.

Two days on, Becky thought she believed at least some of the story Eddie was now sticking to. But what she really wanted to do was go home and talk to her parents about it. To ask them outright if she really was adopted, and why they'd never told her. She didn't think it would have made any difference to how she felt about them, even though she supposed she'd have wondered about who her real parents were.

But if she started asking about that, it would drop Eddie in it. She'd surely go back to prison for kidnapping Becky? Becky didn't think she wanted that to happen. Despite the horrible things she was supposed to have done, Becky found she felt sorry for Eddie. And yes, she liked her, in a funny way. A big part of her *wanted* to protect Eddie.

And Becky couldn't deny she felt some sort of bond between them, a bond that had grown as the days had passed, in a way that she couldn't explain – unless they really were of the same flesh and blood, and that sameness was calling to her.

She supposed she could lie. Maybe come out with some rubbish about having needed to get away for some space after Leanne's death, like characters in films sometimes said. Would anyone believe her? And, anyway, could she just settle back into her old life without even asking her parents for the truth about her birth?

An hour ago, they'd been sitting at the kitchen table, doing a jigsaw, of all things. She liked jigsaws, and so did Eddie. One more thing they had in common.

Becky took a breath. "Today's Friday," she said. "You said I could go home today, if I wanted."

Eddie didn't look up. She just kept her head down, sorting through pieces.

"Have you got any more sky over your side?"

And Becky had instinctively known that Eddie had been dreading this conversation every bit as much as she had, although perhaps not for the same reasons.

She stared across at the woman. "Well, I've been thinking, and I really think I'd like to go home."

There was more she wanted to say, but she saw Eddie flinch, as if she'd been struck. Slowly, her head came up. When Becky could see her face clearly, there was a look there – just for a moment – that wasn't pretty. Not exactly anger, not exactly disappointment. But the niceness had slipped for an instant: it was the first time Becky had had a reason to fear her.. Then she smiled, reached across the table, and squeezed Becky's hand.

"Let's talk about it later," Eddie said, with a finality that brooked no argument. "Now, then, have you got any sky?"

"You said I could go home." Becky knew she needed to stand her ground, but she was also scared to do so. Her own voice sounded like a squeak to her.

"And now I've said we'll talk about it later." There was petulance in Eddie's voice. "There's plenty of today left. Don't spoil it."

She said it in just the way Becky's mother would say it, if something was happening to upset a nice family day. This wasn't a normal family situation. But now wasn't the time to annoy Eddie, she'd decided.

"Here's some sky." She passed a few blue pieces across.

"Thanks, sweetheart."

She swallowed. "When will we talk?"

There was another flash in those eyes.

"I just want to know," she mumbled.

"Later. Christ!" Eddie flared up in a way Becky hadn't seen her do before. "Do we have to put it in our diaries? We're a family. We don't need all that – all that formality."

This wasn't the moment to suggest that they weren't a family. That they'd just been playing at it. It wasn't real.

"Sorry," Becky said. "I just wondered, that's all."

"Don't you trust me?"

"Of course."

And she almost did, in spite of everything. Almost. She trusted Eddie not to hurt her – or at least she thought she did. Yet she wasn't sure she could read her or her moods, and it was always at the back of her mind that she was effectively trapped with a killer.

Don't push your luck, she told herself. *Don't push her.*

Now, as Eddie cleared away the cake plates, she remarked, "You're quiet."

"Just thinking about going home," Becky said, half-fearful of an explosion. "I know there's no hurry…"

"There isn't." She attempted a smile. "Maybe half an hour or so? Get the school run out of the way and get in before the worst of the rush hour?"

"Sounds great." Something told her that it would be a mistake to sound too enthusiastic.

"That's a plan, then. If you still want to go home?"

"I think I do. I've got a lot of questions to ask them."

"Yes, you have." Eddie brought two mugs of tea over and set one in front of Becky and one on her own coaster.

"Mind you don't let it go cold," she said.

33

Petrescu arrived at the station just as Collins was finishing up her call to Archer. She listened while the DC told her what she, Bell and Tyler had found out, and what Archer wanted her to do with it. Then she phoned Ricky Dean's number. It was engaged, so she made a couple more calls, each insisting Dean call her urgently.

He returned the call within a few minutes, and she updated him on developments.

"Come on, Ricky," she coaxed. "Is Hannah Josephs Eddie Maxwell, or isn't she? We can't waste days going through the 'usual channels'."

"Christ," he said. "I can't get decisions that quickly. I told you—"

"Yeah, yeah." She thought fast. "Look, is there any way you can confirm this without putting yourself on the line? Maybe if I ask you again if it's Hannah Josephs and you say nothing if it's affirmative?"

"I'm sorry. It's above my pay grade, and that sort of stunt is no different to me saying yes or no."

"All right. Well, then, you'd better get some answers damn quick, because we won't wait around. I'm going there myself now," she decided, "to have a covert look around."

There was a silence on the line.

"Ricky?"

"I'm here. Look, I can't stop you doing that, but for heaven's sake be careful. If this is our lady, you don't want to start forcing her hand. If she thinks this girl is her kid and she's snatched her, she could be pretty desperate."

"I'll be discreet," she promised. "Just have a little look."

"I'll push a little harder this end. I'll call you as soon as I know anything."

They hung up, and Petrescu thought about what she had just proposed to Dean. He'd made a fair point about not pushing the suspect, and it caused her to re-evaluate the idea that Becky wouldn't be in any real danger if their suspicions were right and she was with Eddie.

They couldn't be sure, Petrescu thought. Eddie Maxwell had almost certainly fantasised about this reunion for a long time. Years, most likely. Suppose she had hopes and expectations of how it would play out – maybe Becky accepting Eddie as her mother and then starting to love her the way a daughter should? What could happen if it didn't turn out that way?

Petrescu returned to Collins and told her of her plan.

"Want me to come with you?"

She gave it a moment's thought. "No, you're all right. The more of us there are, the more likely we are to be spotted. It's just a recce, Joan."

"All the same. You ought to have backup."

"I'll be fine."

"At least let the guv know," Collins urged.

Petrescu had a lot of time for Collins, but baulked at being told what to do by her. Maybe part of it was that she knew the younger woman was right.

"Tell you what," she said. "I'm popping over there right now. Why don't you call the guv and update her?"

She collected her coat and bag and headed for the door. On her way out, she made a quick stop at the ladies'. As she washed her hands, she looked at herself in the mirror above the wash basin. Since when had she been the sort of maverick who took off alone for a spot of surveillance, knowing she could be blundering into a dangerous and volatile situation? Maybe something of Steve Ashby had rubbed off on her. She grinned at the thought, and seeing that grin reflected back at her didn't displease her.

* * *

Becky was feeling drowsy, and she couldn't understand why. She was tired, and she knew that was because – not surprisingly

– she hadn't slept properly for over a week. First there had been Leanne's death, then Jade's disappearance, and then two nights here as a prisoner, her world turned upside down by Eddie's revelations. Even so, surely there was something unnatural about her drowsiness.

She was by the sink, drying dishes as Eddie washed. Neither was saying much. Even as she washed, Eddie seemed to be watching her with a curious, concerned expression on her face.

"What?" Becky tried to stifle a yawn. Failed. Her limbs felt heavy, her fingers clumsy.

"Just looking, while I can. It's been so lovely, finally having you to myself." There was s sadness about her tone and her expression. As if she had accepted that this was the end of something.

Becky wondered how Eddie would handle it. Would she take her home, hand her over to Mum and Dad, maybe turn herself in to the police? Or simply drop her in the middle of Houghton?

Or would she change her mind?

Eddie could try to keep her a prisoner forever, she realised. But she was going stir crazy now. She couldn't do this for the rest of her life.

"We'll see each other again," Becky assured her before giving another gigantic yawn.

"Of course we will." But the woman's smile went nowhere near her eyes. She handed Becky a plate.

Becky reached out for the crockery, but her fingers felt fat and numb. She didn't get a proper grip on it, and it crashed to the floor, shattering on the flagstones.

"I'm sorry." Her own voice seemed to come from far away. She swayed. "Oh. I think I need a lie down."

"Let me help you." Eddie swiftly dried her hands and came to lend support. Becky leaned heavily on her as they went upstairs. Eddie helped her onto her bed.

"There you go. You have a little snooze, love."

Eddie's face swam before her. Becky felt as if she was in some sort of warm soup, her brain barely functioning.

"I… don't know what's… wrong with…" Her lips felt fat, her tongue stuck to the roof of her mouth.

Eddie pulled the covers over her. "Shh. Don't talk any more. You sleep." She smoothed Becky's hair, leaned forward and kissed her on the forehead. "I'm so sorry," she whispered.

Becky wanted to ask her what she was sorry for, but her eyes had already closed. She felt suspended in thick liquid, her limbs too weighty to move.

The last thing she heard before darkness claimed her was the key turning in the lock.

* * *

"She's done what?" Archer snapped.

"DS Petrescu's gone to the suspect's house." Collins sounded uncomfortable.

They'd just passed the Chesham turnoff from the A41. In ten minutes or so, the dual carriageway would peter out and they'd be into the perpetually slow-moving urban traffic of Aylesbury. In the rush hour it was often at a virtual standstill. At other times, a slow crawl was likely. There were roadworks in the town this week, which didn't help.

"On her own? No backup?"

"Yes, guv."

"Yes, she's got backup? Or yes, she's gone alone?"

"Alone, guv."

"Terrific. We get ourselves a credible suspect, and now we risk spooking her. One of you should at least have gone with her."

"Yes, guv." Something in Collins' tone told her that Collins had made the suggestion and it had been rejected.

Archer rubbed her tired eyes. From not getting a break, things were suddenly moving too fast for comfort.

"Fuck," she muttered, trying to decide what to do for the best. She ought to bring Gillingham up to speed, but she was concerned about what Petrescu was doing, too. She felt her shoulders sag. Whichever option she chose was going to bite her on the backside, she just knew it. But maybe there was a middle way.

"Okay," she said. "Give me the address. Dan and I had better get over there. I'll brief the boss on the way."

34

Petrescu's phone rang just as she was parking her car at the bottom of the track leading to Hannah Joseph's house. The woman they were fairly sure was the killer Eddie Maxwell.

She didn't think anything as conspicuous as driving up to the front door was a terribly good idea.

"How's it going?" Ashby sounded cheery. "I've just been over to see Phil Gordon. They've got absolutely nothing to connect Becky to Mark Briscoe, while the pile of evidence tying him to Carly Eustace, Jade Sheldon and even Leanne Richards just keeps growing. I hope this notion of Archer's is amounting to something. Otherwise—"

"I might be about to find out." She quickly brought him up to date.

"And you're there now?"

"There's an unmade track to the house. I'm leaving the car and sneaking up on foot."

"Who's with you?"

"It's just me."

"Whoa!" he said sharply. "You should have backup."

"That's what Joan said."

"Always listen to Joan. Tell you what. I'll be passing that way in about five minutes, if you hang around. You don't know what that woman's capable of."

His concern touched her. "All right. But I can look after myself, you know."

"I'm sure you can, but let's not take risks. Give me the postcode and I'll be there soon."

She waited, thinking – not for the first time – about how good things could be found in the most unexpected places. When she'd come here at the beginning of the week, she had to admit that a small part of her had hoped that what she and Dan

Baines had once had might be rekindled. Baines hadn't been interested, but maybe she had something better now.

She thought it sweet that Ashby was dashing over here to support her. That he'd felt the need to call her in the first place. Maybe she was ever the optimist, but maybe – just maybe – she'd got it right this time and found someone to give her what she needed.

In rather less than the promised five minutes, his Audi pulled up behind her car and he got out.

"I thought these might come in handy." He brandished a pair of binoculars.

They trudged up the muddy track, splashing their shoes and trouser legs. As the large house came into view, Ashby pulled Petrescu almost into the hedgerow lining the trackside.

"Let's see what we can see before we go any further."

He put the binoculars to his eyes.

"We're going to have to get closer to see anything. The silver Merc's there, though." He hesitated. "Hang on, someone's coming out of the house."

"Is it Eddie Maxwell?"

"No idea, Amy. It's a woman, though. Shortish, dark hair. She's going into the garage."

"Maybe Becky's inside. If we're quick, we can get there and get her out while Eddie's in the garage."

"We've no idea where in the house she is." He was still squinting through the binoculars. "For all we know, she's in the garage herself. Or somewhere else entirely. We were lucky with Jade. I don't fancy another scene like that. I thought the kid was a goner."

"So?"

"So we know the car's there and the woman we think's Maxwell is there. We wait until she goes back in the house and then creep up and have a peek through the windows."

"And if we don't see Becky?"

"I dunno. Maybe we knock on the door and say we're Jehovah's witnesses. I'll think of something. Hang on," he said again. "She's coming out." Then, "Oh, that doesn't look good."

"What's happening?"

"She's heading back into the house. And she's carrying what looks like a can of petrol."

* * *

By the time Archer had given Gillingham the news and persuaded him that assembling a team with marksmen and hostage negotiators, and then going in with all guns blazing, would take too long and could get Becky killed, Baines was in a queue waiting to leave the roundabout and join the slow-moving Aylesbury traffic.

Archer tried Petrescu's number from Baines's car, but got no response. It was only a couple of miles to the house Petrescu had taken off for, but it took Baines forever to get there. Not only was Petrescu's car there, at the bottom of the track, but Ashby's was there too.

"Oh, no," she moaned. "This just gets better and better."

"I guess they walked up, so as not to alarm Eddie. If it's her."

"I guess. What do you think? Do the same?" She was impatient to get to the house, get to Petrescu and get a grip on whatever was going on, but she saw the sense in taking a cautious approach.

So they followed the track almost to the top, where Petrescu stood alone, tucked in behind a tree.

"Where's Steve?" Archer demanded.

"We saw his car," Baines added, stating the obvious.

"He's slipped around the back," Petrescu said. "We saw the woman carrying a large can of what looked like petrol into the house—"

"Petrol?"

"Yeah, I know. Christ knows what she's up to."

"Shit, Amy, you should have waited. Or called."

"I tried. There's no mobile signal here. But she'd still be in the house with a couple of gallons of petrol, signal or no."

Archer tried to think. "And Ashby? What's his plan?"

"He told me to wait here in case it is Maxwell and she comes out with Becky. Steve was going to see if he could get in at the back. He took a screwdriver with him. Sort of smiled and said there's always a way in."

"Oh, sweet Jesus," groaned Archer. "Save me from macho heroes. All right. You stay here. If they do come out, yell. Come on, Dan. If this is a mess, maybe we can still save the day."

* * *

Baines and Archer approached the house with caution. Baines whispered to Archer to wait and then scuttled up to the front window, keeping low. Carefully, he raised his head and peered in.

He was looking into a large open-plan space. A dark-haired woman stood with her back to him, her stance stiff, a jerry can dangling from one hand. Just inside a doorway opposite her stood Ashby, his hands raised in a placatory gesture as his lips moved. For an instant, his eyes met Baines's, but he broke contact immediately. The last thing they needed was for the woman to turn round and see Baines looking in. He backed away and returned to Archer.

"No sign of Becky, but Ashby's in there, talking to a woman with a can of petrol. At least, I assume it's petrol."

"Jesus. I don't suppose she's got matches, too? Maybe a lighter?"

"I couldn't see her other hand, but Ashby looked like he was being ultra-cautious with her."

"If she means to torch the place, she might have already splashed it around."

"Why now, I wonder?" he puzzled.

"We can find that out later. If Becky's in there, we need to get her out." She grimaced. "What do we do for the best? If we go round there and spook her, she might light it up. But do we trust Ashby not to do or say anything stupid?"

"Especially if he's playing the hero for Amy."

"Meaning?"

"Ask me later."

She looked less decisive than he'd ever seen her. Finally, she said, "There's nothing else for it. We're going to have to go in.

But very, very gently."

They made their way round to the back of the house and found a back door open. It looked as if Ashby had forced it, which he was entitled to do if he felt life was at risk.

"Carefully, carefully," Archer whispered as she stepped over the threshold. They were entering a utility area with washing machine, tumble drier and a big freezer, plus a vacuum cleaner, ironing board, and other assorted household stuff.

Baines felt wound as tightly as a spring. After all they'd been through together, he and Karen were planning to marry. Did the gods have some sick plan to snatch everything away and for him to die a fiery death?

He could smell the petrol fumes from here, and he knew that often the fumes ignited before the fluid. And it would only need a spark. He and Archer should have turned off their mobiles. He wondered if Ashby had. If one of them rang now…

A door from the utility area into the house was open, and he could hear a woman's voice.

"It's all I've ever wanted," she was saying. "A family. A proper one. Not people who hurt me, or used me, or manipulated me."

Archer motioned him to move – quietly – closer to the door.

"I got to hold Annie – Becky – just one time," the woman was saying. "I've never known love like it. I thought I loved Kieran, and he loved me. But now I think we were just… kindred spirits. We were both in the same boat and, when we found each other, we clung on."

She was crying. "The woman who did those things… Eddie Maxwell… she feels like a different person sometimes. But she's also the person who gave Becky life. We belong together. We're blood, and nothing binds like blood. Right?"

She started as Archer's movement, just ahead of Baines, caught her eye. She raised the lighter in the hand Baines hadn't been able to see before. She'd set the petrol can down at some point. Baines could see the fuel pooled around Eddie's and Ashby's feet. Baines and Archer were standing in it themselves. God, if she flicked it now…

"Don't come any closer," Eddie warned. Then, to Ashby,

"Who are they? You promised you were alone."

"I was," he assured her, turning towards Baines and Archer. "They must have come looking for me. Back off," he instructed them. "Please."

Archer held up her hands. "Sure." She took a backwards step and Baines was obliged to follow suit.

"I've got this, Lizzie," Ashby said, returning his gaze to Eddie Maxwell, the woman who held all their lives in her hand. "Eddie, think about this. You're putting Becky in danger. Where is she, by the way?"

A fond little smile. "Up in her room. She'll be sleeping. I slipped a couple of my sleeping pills in her tea. She'll not feel a thing – she'll just not wake up." She laughed mirthlessly. "I even let the cat out. I love that moggie. And to think, the first time I met Kieran, I helped him torture a cat."

Baines saw Archer open her mouth to intervene. He touched her arm and shook his head. Ashby had established a dialogue here. Someone else trying to hijack it could be a disaster. She met his eyes and nodded.

"Come on, Eddie," Ashby coaxed. "You say you love your daughter. Then don't do this. Give her a chance to live. She's only twelve. She's got her whole life ahead of her. The kind of life you never had – a loving family. Maybe marriage, kids. A career. If you set this place alight, with her inside it, you'll steal all that from her. Just like your childhood was stolen. Do you really want to do that to Becky? To your Annie," he amended.

"But those people who stole her from me…" She swallowed. "Who adopted her. They've been lying to her all her life. They're not who she thought they were. *She's* not who she thought she was. I did a memory book." Tears were streaming down her face. "She's never seen it. Knew nothing of me, apart from what she's heard on the news. We should have been together. Or she should at least have had a chance to know me."

She was rambling. And Baines knew how dangerous that could be. She could ramble herself into lighting them all up. "And Kieran's turned out to be nothing. A fuckup. He made a killer out of me, and now he's probably never coming out. Not that I want him." She held the lighter higher in an aggressive gesture, and Baines's heart jumped into his mouth. "Why shouldn't I do it? Eh? Maybe this way's better for Becky and me."

"Dying's never better," Ashby said. "And doesn't Becky deserve a choice? To decide whether she wants to live? Your parents took your choices from you. Maybe Kieran Bardsley did, too. Becky's parents denied her a choice about you. But aren't you better than that?" Baines saw that Ashby was maintaining eye contact with Eddie. He had barely blinked since Baines and Archer had arrived.

"I don't know. I don't know." Eddie's shoulders slumped in defeat.

"Why don't you give me the lighter?" Ashby held out a hand.

Her eyes blazed instantly. "Take one step towards me and we all burn."

"It's okay," soothed Ashby. The uncouth, sarcastic creep was nowhere to be seen. "It's okay. I'm staying right here. You're the one in charge. But you say you're not the monster any more. You don't have to be her, ever again."

She raised her free hand to her temple, massaging it. The silence was pregnant with dread.

"All right," she finally said. "You can get Becky out of here."

"Where is she?"

"Upstairs, second door on the right. The key's in the lock. She'll be out cold, though."

"Can my colleagues get her?"

"Okay. But any funny business…"

"No funny business." He didn't turn his head towards Baines or Archer, but addressed them anyway. "Dan, Lizzie? Will you get Becky, please? I'll keep Eddie company."

35

Upstairs, Archer turned the key in the lock and pushed the door inwards. Becky Day was tucked up in bed. She didn't stir as they walked in. Archer stepped over and checked her pulse. Her breathing was steady.

"I think she's fine," she told Baines. "Do you think you'll be able to carry her downstairs?"

"I'm about to find out." There was no humour in his tone. He pulled back the covers and lifted the girl in his arms. Her head lolled.

"Careful with her," Archer said. "The sooner she's out of here, the better." She remembered a series of nasty arson attacks from her Met days. One family had been burned alive by the arsonist, who had thought they would be out for the evening. A sick child and a change of plan had cost them all their lives.

But it had been a subsequent fire – one that had started just as she and her partner, DS Sam Strong, had arrived on the scene, hoping to be in time to prevent it – that preyed on her mind now. The *whump!* as the fuel had ignited. The heat. And, relatively soon afterwards, the windows exploding.

And all Eddie had to do was flick the wheel on her lighter.

They moved back to the stairs, Archer helping to ensure that Becky's head didn't hit anything. Downstairs, the fumes seemed even stronger. Eddie Maxwell and Steve Ashby were frozen in a tableau. Whatever Ashby was feeling, he was giving nothing away.

"Can we take her out the front?" Archer asked Eddie.

"No. The front door's locked and it stays locked. You can go out the way you came. And be careful with her."

They manoeuvred the girl past Ashby.

"You, too," Eddie said. "Steve, wasn't it? Go now."

"No way," Ashby said. "We walk out of here together,

Eddie, or not at all."

Archer turned back. They were getting Becky to safety. If Eddie was intent on suicide, it was madness for Ashby to risk her taking him with her.

"Steve—" she began.

For the first time, he looked her way. "I told you, Lizzie. I've got this." His smile was sad. His eyes were a little frightened. But there was a determination about him too. "Now you and Dan get Becky the hell out of here. For once in your life, trust me."

She hesitated for a second more, trying to think of something to say. Then she just gave him a nod and turned back to Baines.

"Dan?" Ashby's voice had the slightest tremor in it. "Just in case? Tell Amy..." He shrugged. "Just tell her, will you?"

"Sure, Steve." He turned away with his burden, and Archer saw no alternative but to follow.

Outside, they walked round to the front of the house, where Petrescu stood chewing her lip.

"Amy," Archer said, "go with Dan and help him get her in his car."

She looked at them wide-eyed. "But... Steve?"

"Still inside. Says he's not coming out without Eddie."

"Oh, God." Petrescu moved towards the house.

"He's got it under control, Amy." Not strictly true. Only one person was in control, and she had a lighter. "The last thing he needs is a distraction."

"Can we go?" Baines asked. "She's getting heavy."

Petrescu looked about to argue, then gave a tight nod and headed off down the track with the now puffing Baines.

Archer was left waiting outside the house. What remained of this case was in Ashby's hands now. His coolness and his appeal to whatever voice of reason still resided inside Eddie Maxwell's head had saved Becky Day's life. Should he have called it quits, removed himself from danger, and left Eddie to do whatever she decided to do?

Would Archer?

Almost as soon as she had asked herself the question, she knew the answer. Apart from being surrounded by the contents of a large jerry can of petrol, and having the means to ignite it in her hand, Eddie was not so different from the guy Archer had once talked down from a narrow ledge outside an office block. She didn't have the best head for heights, but she'd gone outside to join him anyway, talked to him calmly, persuaded him to come back inside.

There had been a moment when she'd nearly lost her footing, but she tried not to dwell on that. She knew that, if she were in that house, instead of Ashby, she'd try to talk Eddie down, whatever the risk.

What if Eddie decided to do it? Would she give Ashby any warning? Urge him to get out? If she did, would he do so? Or would she give him no warning at all, thinking he'd made his decision?

All Archer could do was wait. Wait for the sound of petrol igniting, or the tell-tale orange flare in the window. How long was it since she and Baines had come out with Becky? How long would the stand-off continue before it ended one way or the other?

She thought about calling the fire brigade in case the worst happened, but fire appliances arriving with lights and sirens going could precipitate action. She had never felt so useless.

And she loathed Ashby. On the odd occasion, she'd even had to restrain herself from striking him. Now she was praying to a god she only half-believed in that he'd make it.

Maybe she could go back in after all. Ashby was surely out of practice in empathy. Maybe she could do better, woman to woman.

Or maybe she'd make matters worse.

She was still debating what to do when the front door opened.

Ashby stepped outside and then held out his hand to Eddie, standing behind him, framed in the doorway. There was no sign of the lighter, thank God. Maybe Archer's prayers had been answered.

After a long moment, Eddie took the DI's hand and came out of the house. Her knees buckled then, but Ashby was there with support.

"Call the lot, Lizzie," he said. "Police, ambulance, fire. But keep your distance with that phone. We reek of petrol. We're probably human torches. So no sparks, okay?"

36

Baines's Mondeo drew up outside the Days' house. Petrescu, in the passenger seat, turned around to address Becky, who was seated in the back.

"Are you ready for this?"

The girl nodded. She'd been checked out by doctors, who'd declared her to be fine, but in need of rest. Baines thought that, physically, it was probably a reasonable opinion. Assessing her mental condition was a tougher call, and he knew from experience that counselling –

which was being put in place for her – and careful monitoring would be crucial. He'd put off seeking help for too many years, and the results had almost been catastrophic.

Right now, Becky looked somehow smaller and younger than her twelve years. She'd said she was eager to come home to her parents, but there had been a troubled look in her eyes that was still there. Hardly surprising, under the circumstances.

"Come on, then," Petrescu said, getting out of the car. "Let's get you home."

She walked around to the rear and opened the door for the girl. For a moment, Becky seemed to shrink into the upholstery. Then she appeared to take a grip on herself, and slid towards the door.

By the time she had climbed out, the front door of the house had opened. Josh and Emma stood on the step.

Emma was clutching her husband. He had his hand to his mouth. As Becky took her first few slow steps away from the car, her parents came running towards her, Emma screaming her daughter's name.

Becky reached the bottom of the drive, and Emma swept her into her arms. Josh joined them, hugging them both at the same time.

But Baines thought there was a stiffness about Becky. Her parents seemed to sense it too, because they soon stepped away, Emma's hand still on her daughter's shoulder, as if she feared that Becky would disappear before her eyes.

All three were crying, but the girl's obvious misery contrasted with her parents' initial joy.

"Oh, love," Emma said. "I know it's been awful, but you're home now. You're safe." She mouthed 'Thank you,' to the detectives.

But Josh looked worried. "What's up, Becks?"

"Why didn't you tell me?" Becky demanded. "That Eddie woman – she says I'm adopted. Is it true?"

Emma and Josh exchanged a glance.

"It is true," Josh admitted. "But—"

"You never told me. *She* told me."

"I know." Emma tried for another hug, but Becky stepped away. "I know," Emma repeated. "We should have. It just never seemed like the right time."

"You were never going to tell me, were you?"

"We're sorry," Josh said. "So sorry. I promise we would have, eventually."

"When?"

Emma's face crumpled. "Don't you… don't you love us, now you know we're not your real parents?"

"Don't be stupid," Becky snapped. "Of course I love you. You *are* my real parents. But you should have said – not treated me like a baby."

"You're right," Emma said. "We've messed up. Can you forgive us?"

"I don't know."

Baines saw Becky for what she was then: an intelligent twelve-year-old whose life had been turned upside down. Perhaps things would never be quite the same for the family again. Becky had been kept in the dark about her parentage for way too long.

There was nothing Baines or Petrescu could do for them. He felt like an intruder.

"We'll leave you to it," he said. "You've all got a lot to catch up on. We'll need Becky to make a statement later, though."

Josh looked at him and nodded. "Thank you so much for finding her. And for bringing her home."

Baines returned the nod then turned towards the car.

"Wait, Mr Baines!" cried Becky. He turned back to see her hurrying towards him.

"Yes, Becky?"

She looked suddenly shy. "Can you get a message to my other mum, please? To Eddie?"

* * *

Archer and Ashby were preparing to formally interview Eddie Maxwell. She'd been charged with kidnap and false imprisonment, although it was possible that those charges could be amended or added to. Her solicitor was on his way.

She had asked to be referred to by her original name, since her Hannah Josephs cover had effectively been blown anyway. She didn't seem to care too much.

It was the first opportunity Archer and Ashby had had for any conversation since the events at Eddie's farmhouse. Not that, in the past, they'd had much desire to converse anyway. But Archer had a burning question she'd been gagging to ask.

"What did you say to her? To change her mind about torching the house with you and her inside it?"

He gave her a twisted grin. "Maybe I played on her emotions about her kid, turned them round on me. Told her if we both burned, my wife would be a widow and my children would be left fatherless."

"But you're divorced."

He winked. "She didn't know that."

"You lied to her." Well, she'd never doubted he was a good liar.

But he looked down. "I said, *maybe* I said that. But I didn't."

"So?"

"All right." He met her eyes now, challenging. "I told her it wasn't a good time for me to die. Because I thought I might have found someone I could be happy with. But there was no way I was walking out of the house without her."

"And that got to her?"

"She said everyone deserved a chance to be happy." He looked and sounded awkward. Embarrassed. It was another side to Steve Ashby she'd never seen before. This was turning into a week of revelations, and no mistake.

She'd thought the notion of a man saved by the love of a good woman only existed in the lyrics of country songs. Now realised she really wanted to believe it could happen – even to a man like this.

"This someone you told her you'd found?" She knew she was grinning at him. She couldn't help it. "It wouldn't be a certain Detective Sergeant, perchance?"

He looked annoyed. Maybe even disappointed. "So Dan Baines has been flapping his mouth?" He shrugged. "I should have known he'd tell you."

"Dan said nothing. Just using my amazing deductive powers. I suspected as much before you said what you did to Dan when we were taking Becky out of Eddie's house."

He frowned. "So Dan kept my confidence?"

"Yes. He didn't say anything to me."

"Do you think the whole station suspects?"

"Probably. Does it matter?"

He shrugged. "Probably not."

"Besides, I think it's great. Like Eddie said, everyone deserves a shot at happiness. I hope it works out for you."

He nodded. "Thanks."

She hesitated. A lot could be about to change. Gillingham thought he could be ousted. Where would that leave Ashby? And would it even matter, if the change Petrescu had brought out in him continued? *In for a penny*, she thought. "Maybe you and I could make a new start, too?"

She held out her hand to him. He regarded it, allowed a smile to cross his face, then shook it. "Maybe."

* * *

Eddie Maxwell, seated across the interview room table from

Archer and Ashby, was very pale, her features pinched, her eyes red-rimmed and fearful.

Most of what she had to say tallied with the team's own surmises about the events of the past few days and why she'd done what she'd done, and her story wasn't so very far removed from Becky's.

She'd also confirmed that the social worker, Marion Brown, had told her that her daughter was somewhere in Buckinghamshire.

"I don't think she imagined I'd find her. I think she was trying to comfort me. Let me know my child had a good life. She didn't understand how much I wanted to get her back."

She gave Archer the ghost of a smile. "After my husband died, I put everything I had into finding her. I already knew I was living in the same county, and there's just so much on the internet now. I was pretty sure I'd found her about a year ago. You can apply for a copy of an adoption certificate if you have enough information, and I thought I'd pieced enough together. Even her middle name."

"Annie," Archer said. "The name on her birth certificate."

"Adoptive parents are encouraged to keep the child's original name. Even though Becky was only a baby, the Days must have decided to include it. Much as I've hated them for having her when I couldn't, I was grateful for that, at least."

"Rebecca Annie Day. She told us she'd been teased that Becky Annie Day gave her the initials BAD."

Eddie's smile was broader at that. "Well, it was one of the things that convinced me I'd found my daughter. Once I had that adoption certificate, I knew for sure. I had an adopted girl in the right place, of the right age. The resemblance. That middle name. It had to be her." Her eyes searched Archer's. "And she's really okay?"

"She's safe and reunited with her parents," Archer said. "We'll be taking a formal statement from her later. She asked DS Baines to let you know she sort of understands."

Eddie swiped tears from her eyes. "I wanted to be part of her life. I wasn't thinking straight. That was what I really wanted, though. I suppose that's never going to happen now?"

"I can't answer that. It's going to be something only Becky can decide, and she's got a lot to work through." Archer smiled. "I wouldn't give up hope altogether, though. She did say she'd write a letter for you, if it helps with court."

Eddie's eyes widened. "Really? And would it? Help?"

"Who knows? It might. Let's not worry about that now. I have to take a statement from you, if you're up to it."

"All right. But, before we start, can I ask you a favour?"

"Try me."

"My cat. Barney. He'll need feeding, and I guess he'll be needing a new home, if I'm going... away. Would you...?"

"I'll sort something," Archer said. "Don't worry about it."

* * *

There had been too much tying up of loose ends to be done for the team to make its customary visit to the pub to celebrate its successes. Baines had managed a quick farewell coffee with Amy Petrescu, who'd told him what she thought of his earlier advice about Ashby.

"What can I say?" he defended himself. "I can only speak as I find people, as my dad always says."

She sipped her coffee and shook her head. "Good thing I didn't listen to you, Danny Boy."

Baines wondered if Petrescu would ever be party to some of the secrets Ashby guarded so jealously. Baines and Archer had always joked that there was something in Gillingham's and Ashby's past – some bond between them, something Ashby held over his boss. Eddie Maxwell, Hannah Josephs, whatever you called her, had done what she'd done because of imagined bonds of blood. But there were other kinds of ties. The kind that had connected Eddie to Kieran Bardsley, for example.

What might it be with Gillingham and Ashby?

Baines had told Petrescu his own news – that he and Karen were to be married. He'd left out the complicated details of their relationship. She'd seemed genuinely pleased for him.

She'd given him a chaste peck on the cheek before heading for home, but it was enough for the place she'd brushed with her lips to burn afterwards. Maybe it was as well that she was going.

He arrived home, glad that some sort of balance had been restored.

Well, almost. There were his new dreams still to contend with. He'd have to figure out what they meant.

But meanwhile, he had a free weekend ahead – and engagement rings to shop for.

He realised that, for the first time in very many years, he was looking to the future with something like optimism.

* * *

It was really way too late to be ringing Dominic's doorbell, but his lights were on and it *was* Friday night. That meant no work for Dominic tomorrow, so maybe he was sitting up watching a movie or reading a book.

Archer felt that she'd neglected her friend and neighbour this week. It wasn't as if she had so many friends that she could afford such a luxury, and he'd probably still be a bit down after Monty's untimely death. Maybe she could cheer him up a little.

He opened the door a crack, looking cautious, then threw it open, a grin splitting his face.

"Hi, Lizzie. Everything okay?"

"Fine." She stifled a yawn.

"I heard that Becky Day was safe. You must be relieved."

"To say nothing of the family. Obviously I can't say too much…"

"Of course not." He shifted from one foot to the other. "Um. I've got a bottle of red on the go, if you're interested? I was just thinking, it's either put the cap on or drink the lot."

"Sure. Better save you from yourself." She bent down and picked up the case at her feet. "Actually, there's something I need your opinion on."

She followed him into his living room, carrying the case carefully. The TV was on – he *had* been watching a film – but he picked up the remote control and zapped it off.

"You didn't have to do that," Archer said.

"It was rubbish. Let me get you a glass."

He disappeared into the kitchen, and returned with a generous-sized wine glass. He poured one for Archer and topped off his own glass before raising it in salute.

"To solved cases. And to Monty, wherever he may be." He took a sip. "You wanted to ask me about something." For the first time, he looked properly at the case she'd put down by her chair. "Is it to do with that? And is it what I think it is?"

"Tell me if I'm being presumptuous," she said, handing over the cat carrier. "It's just he needs a new home and, you know…" She tailed off. This had been a dreadful idea.

Dominic opened the case and lifted out the fat ginger tom.

"His name's Barney," she said hopefully. Then, "If you'd rather not, then I guess I'll take him in."

But he was smiling and stroking the cat. He put Barney down and he slunk off, exploring his surroundings with a clear air of entitlement.

"Tell you what," Dominic said. "Let's share him. You said when we first met you'd been thinking about a cat. He can live here, as you work such crazy hours, but we can share him. I dunno. You can get his food sometimes…"

"I barely remember to get food for me." But she liked the idea.

"We'll work it out. Everyone should have at least a half-share in a cat."

"He's not meant as a replacement for Monty. Well, not exactly."

"No cat could replace Monty. But I like the look of this guy." Barney had returned and was rubbing himself against Dominic's legs. He bent down and scratched between his ears.

"Actually," she said. "I've no idea when he was last fed."

"Good thing I haven't chucked out Monty's stuff then. Don't know why I haven't. I've still got his bowls, too. Silly, sentimental sod. Right," he continued, "I'll open a tin and you can put it in the bowl. We'll do him some water, too."

A few minutes later, they watched as Barney tucked in to the food.

"He seems to like that," Archer said.

"I hope it doesn't give him a complex," Dominic remarked. "Living in an unusual family unit."

Thoughts of Becky Day briefly jumbled through Archer's mind: the only parents she'd ever known weren't her parents at all. And that was nothing compared to the hideous childhoods that had shaped Eddie Maxwell and Kieran Bardsley. In spite of everything, Archer sensed that Eddie was a different person from the young killer who'd been jailed twelve years ago. There was hope for her yet.

Archer smiled, her eyes still on Barney, their shared pet.

"I think he'll do just fine," she said.

37

One week later

North-west London's Gladstone Park, formerly Dollis Hill Park, had become a public park at the turn of the twentieth century, and was named after the former Liberal Prime Minister, Sir William Gladstone. Many of its features dated from that time, including its fine tree-lined avenues.

Archer only knew this stuff because this part of London had once been on her patch, and they had gone on about it somewhere around 2003 – or was it 2004? – when the park was being renovated using Lottery money. It must have worried Kieran Bardsley and Eddie Maxwell at the time, but the works had never come near this neglected, scrubby area to the south-east. It was somehow cut off from the main park, a short walk from the car park, and screened by a bunch of old trees so rotten that they looked like they might fall down at any moment.

It had turned a little chilly, and Archer and DCI Nick Gibson had their hands in the pockets of their warm coats as they watched the search teams at work.

"You're sure this isn't a wild-goose chase?" Gibson asked for at least the twelfth time. "All this on the word of Eddie Maxwell?"

"We got to her, Nick," Archer insisted. "Or, I think, Becky did in a way. Eddie understands how Jessica's family must have felt all these years. She wants to make some sort of amends."

That, and the letter Becky Day was determined to write to the judge, would do Eddie no harm when she came to trial. That she would go back to prison was not in any doubt, but the judge would consider these facts in her sentencing.

A shout went up where two men were digging. A few minutes later, a figure in overalls approached them. It was an

Asian woman in her thirties.

"We've found remains, sir," she said to Gibson. "Pretty much where we were told they'd be."

"You think it could be Jessica Winter?"

"Obviously we'll have to confirm that, after all this time, but what's left of the clothes are the right colours."

Gibson looked as if he'd seen a ghost. In a way, maybe he had. "Jewellery?"

"A crystal pendant. Turquoise."

Jessica's birthstone – topaz for December. A birthday gift.

Gibson released a breath. "It's her. It must be. But I'll wait to be sure before I tell her parents." He looked at Archer. "I'd almost given up hope, Lizzie. I made a foolish promise that I'd find her for them, and it's sat on my shoulder ever since." His voice almost cracked. Nick Gibson was not a man given to shows of emotion.

Archer squeezed his arm. "You'll be sure soon. Then you can tell them. But we both know already, don't we? Their girl's coming home."

THE END

ACKNOWLEDGEMENTS

An idea for this book came from an item in a newspaper I picked up on a train home from London. Many people have helped me to turn that idea into the book you have in your hands.

Huge thanks are again due to Debbie Porteous and Chris Sivers, who read the manuscript more than once and provided comments and suggestions that improved the story immeasurably. I'm also deeply grateful to Keri Michael, Clare Heron and Rosie Claverton for their input and guidance on adoption procedures, CSI techniques and psychology, respectively. As ever, all mistakes are my own.

Praise is also due again to my brilliant, lovely and highly professional cover designer, Jessica Bell, who has produced another gorgeous wrapper for my product; to my eagle-eyed and insightful copy-editor, Jane Hammett; and to Chris 'the Guru' Longmuir, who gives so generously of her time and experience to help me out with the technical aspects of publication.

Thanks too to the real Karen Smart, Lara Mosely, Tracey Walsh and Kim Frank for lending their names to some of my characters.

I'm indebted to my amazing network of writing mates, including the members of Chiltern Writers, the Alliance of Independent Authors, and very many more online. They are always there to support and encourage, and to offer an understanding ear when the going gets tough

Most of all, thanks to my family: to my lovely wife Chris, for her patience, love and endless support; and to my dad, who never, ever misses an opportunity to plug my books. And finally, thanks to all the readers. Lizzie Archer and Dan Baines only truly come to life when you open the book.

Dave Sivers
www.davesivers.co.uk
Buckinghamshire
2017

Also by Dave Sivers

Archer and Baines
The Scars Beneath the Soul
Dead in Deep Water
Evil Unseen

The Lowmar Dashiel Mysteries
A Sorcerer Slain
Inquisitor Royal

Short Stories
Dark and Deep: Ten Coffee Break Crime Stories

Printed in Great Britain
by Amazon

40830240R00148